MIG MASSACRE

"Fox one and two, we've got more company. Second bandit at eight o'clock . . . moving to seven."

Vic had temporarily ignored the approach of the Mig leader's wingman who was now back in the fight and maneuvering for firing position.

"Keep your eye on him. Let me know when the rice-ball starts to pull his nose into us. I'm still working on his boss."

"Rog."

"Fox two . . . how's it look? Can you get this guy off my back?"

"Negative, he's outside minimum range of my missiles."

"Fox Flight! Fox Flight!" the radio suddenly roared. "Radar contact, four more bandits!"

SWEET VIETNAM

BY RICHARD PARQUE

ZEBRA BOOKS
KENSINGTON PUBLISHING CORP.

ZEBRA BOOKS

are published by

Kensington Publishing Corp.
475 Park Avenue South
New York, N.Y. 10016

First printing: August, 1984

Printed in the United States of America

Prologue

His experienced eye caught a hint of a reflection at 11 o'clock. He continued to pierce the blue, straining to pick up the glint again. There it was! A momentary shimmer of light once more. Then two almost imperceptible dots appeared, growing in his windshield, moving to 12 o'clock. He continued flying toward China, his heart pounding in his chest, daring to hope that after these long weeks . . .

The dots continued to grow and he could now discern the faint outline of airplanes. They couldn't be F-4s, no smoke, he thought to himself. The F-105s were all behind him, beginning their run on the target.

"I've got two bogies," Balinger said.

"I see them, Dick," he quickly replied.

"Two bogies. Roger," Pellegrini acknowledged.

Just a few more moments and he would have them identified. The seconds became eternities.

They flew on. Was it too much to hope for? He wondered if they had seen him yet. Friendly or enemy? He checked his fuel. Not critical. Above joker.

"They're Migs!" barked Pellegrini.

"What?"

How could Pellegrini have identified them at this range. They were still no more than specks on the plexiglass. His eyes stretched again, probing the space ahead.

"They punched off their tanks, Flamingo lead. Do you have them?"

Tanks, where? Good grief that Pellegrini has good eyes. He became nervous.

"They're rolling in on us, Vic!" yelled Pellegrini.

A sudden surge of adrenaline shot through him. Fear and confusion clawed at his gut. Lord, what was happening? Was he dreaming?

"Get ready to break!" screamed Pellegrini.

In a flash it all came clear. How could he have been so stupid? Already it was probably too late. He had waited too long. He instinctively shrank in his cockpit trying to make himself smaller, waiting for the hits that were about to come.

The scent of harvested rice was heavy in the air and the girl drank deeply of its sweet fragrance. A light ocean breeze washed across the fertile valley, toying with the ends of her long, raven black hair. From her sitting position on the paddy dike, she dropped her bare legs into the water and wiggled her toes in the cooling mud. A flight of F-4

6

Phantoms swept overhead, banking into their landing pattern.

"*Thieu-ta Benedetti den nha,*" Major Benedetti has come home, grandmother said, looking up at the U.S. jets.

"*Khong,*" no, the girl answered. "*Con son lam,*" it is too early.

She pulled the conical, peasant basket hat lower, shielding her long Asian eyes from the brilliant tropical sun. She followed the Phantoms until they disappeared below the tree line in the distance.

Suddenly she was on her feet. She stood rigidly staring north, out of the valley, beyond the hills. North. Something was wrong. She sensed danger out there. A cold shiver passed through her small body and she began to tremble.

"*Toi ro so anh ay . . . toi ro so anh ay,*" he's in trouble, I can feel his fear . . . I can feel his fear, she whispered to herself, still looking north. "God help him. Please God, help him."

I

RICE, MIGS, AND LOTUS BLOSSOMS

"Major, I Love You Forever . . ."

Somewhere she waits to make you win, your soul in
her firm, white hands —
Somewhere God has made for you, the woman who
understands!

As the tide went out she found him
    Lashed to a spar of Despair,
The wreck of his Ship around him —
    The wreck of his Dreams in the air;
Found him and loved him and gathered
    The soul of him close to her heart —
The soul that had sailed an uncharted sea,
The soul that had sought to win and be free —
    The soul of which she was part!
And there in the dusk she cried to the man,
    "Win your battle — you can, you can!"

Broken by Fate, unrelenting,
    Scarred by the lashings of Chance;
Bitter his heart — unrepenting —
    Hardened by Circumstance;
Shadowed by Failure ever,
    Cursing, he would have died,
But the touch of her hand, her strong warm
hand,
And her love of his soul, took full command
    Just at the turn of the tide!
Standing beside him, filled with trust,
    "Win! she whispered, "you must, you
must!"

Helping and loving and guiding,
    Urging when that were best,
Holding her fears in hiding

Deep in her quiet breast;
This is the woman who kept him
    True to his standards lost,
When tossed in the storm and stress of strife,
He thought himself through with the game of
life
    And ready to pay the cost.
Watching and guarding, whispering still,
    "Win you can—and you will, you will!"

This is the story of ages
    This is the Woman's way;
Wiser than seers or sages,
    Lifting us day by day;
Facing all things with a courage
    Nothing can daunt or dim,
Treading Life's path, wherever it leads—
Lined with flowers or choked with weeds,
    But ever with him—with him!
Guidon—comrade—golden spur—
    The men who win are helped by her!

Somewhere she waits, strong in belief, your
    Soul in her firm, white hands:
Thank well God when she comes to you,
    The woman who understands!

                    —Everard Jack Appleton

CHAPTER ONE

In the dim light of dawn two shark-nosed Phantoms pulled out of their revetments and taxied to the end of the runway. Silhouetted low against the surrounding dark hills, they appeared as prehistoric reptilians rising from the rice paddies. Hungry. Going hunting. The major looked left at his wingman coming into position alongside. A thumbs up signal and the two jets simultaneously exploded into a deafening roar as the masked fliers pushed their throttles forward and the ships began their takeoff rolls. The moment of transformation had arrived once again. He could not recall a time that compared with the exhilaration that accompanied these seconds preceding a mission. His blood coursed. It was a combination of the thunderous power and energy generated by the aircraft, the confidence silently felt between the two crews, and the thrill of flight itself. He lusted in it. This is why he had

13

come. He belonged here. The F-4s lifted off the runway in close formation and banked into the rising sun over the South China Sea as the South Vietnamese countryside slipped below them. North. They pushed north — toward the guns.

The weather was clear. Maximum visibility. He slid the helmet visor up. Spreading before him was an endless stretch of pearly sea sparkling over a panorama of diamonds that danced in the pure Co-China sunlight. Like a spectator viewing a picture being exhibited a part at a time he watched the spectacle of stainless beauty unfold before him. For a brief moment he was totally overwhelmed by this pageant of oriental water-lights, transfixed by the splendor of natural creation. Good morning, Southeast Asia!

He leaned forward pulling against the inertia reel, stretching the protective harness — a ritual he always went through to help relieve the terrible growing tension. He settled back into the armored seat and pressed the mike button.

"Bring it up, Fox two."

"Roger, boss."

He watched over his right shoulder. His wingman eased the throttle forward with his left hand and pulled the control stick back with his right. The shark-nosed Phantom instantly responded — slipping into position — tucked in tightly behind its leader's right wing. They pushed on. North. Always north. The guns.

Inside the confined cockpit the major's amplified, rhythmic breathing created a dreamy, surrealistic undertone with the pneumatic sounds of the

F-4's life support systems. From around the tight-fitting earphones built into the helmet liner he could faintly hear the pulsing oxygen regulator and the steady throbbing surge of jet engines. Violently displaced air rushed past the aircraft's canopy. A maze of lights, instruments, gauges, switches, handles, and circuit breakers stared back at him. His world for the next few hours of intense activity and furious human conflict.

Under him resting on launch rails and settled in wells within the fuselage were the death-dealing air-to-air, radar-guided Sparrow and heat-seeking Sidewinder missiles—a violent contrast with the spangled loveliness of life-supporting open sea stretching ageless and without end before him. The counterpoint to the joy and beauty of the Asian morning that saturated his senses. He continued north—toward the waiting guns.

"Two—one."

"Go."

"Switching to strike frequency."

"Roger."

"Tattoo, this is Fox leader on station with two Phantoms. Do you read?"

Static and crackle. The major waited a few seconds. He pushed the mike button again.

"Strike force Tattoo. This is Fox Flight. Two F-4s standing by for MigCap."

"Uhh, Roger, Fox. This is Tattoo striker leader. What is your altitude?"

"Angels twenty."

"Roger, Fox leader. Estimate rendezvous . . . three minutes."

The Phantoms circled over the Gulf of Tonkin, draining precious fuel from their tanks. Waiting, watching. The seconds ticked off. The major leaned forward in the seat harness, scratching his nerves. Circle some more. The guns.

"One — two."

"Go."

"Strikers two o'clock, level."

"Roger, two. I've got 'em."

Four needle-nosed F-105 Thunderchiefs dressed in brown and green battle colors, full racks of bombs juggling under short wings, swept into view.

"Okay, let's take it around," the major said.

The horizon tilted and the shimmering sea slid across the front of his canopy and dropped off his right wing. For a moment he continued to watch the glittering tinsel play against the deep blue water, then — sadly — it was gone.

He took off his glove and wiped the sweat from his hand on his suit. He pulled forward on the inertia reel again. Scared? No. Piece of cake. He pressed the mike button.

"Tattoo — Fox. Have you in sight."

"Roger. Those Phantoms hot?"

Smart guy. "Sidewinders and Sparrows full-up. Why?"

"Just checking. You'll need them. Migs are up! Better call Red Crown. Big fight developing over Phuc Yen."

He felt his stomach muscles tighten. The dance of the butterflies began. Forward in the seat harness. Okay, settle down. He wiped the perspiration from his eyes and put the glove back on. Zip-up the survival vest. Check the fuel readout. Centerline running dry. Where are we? He glanced at the map on his kneepad. What do you mean, where are we? You're right where you were yesterday at this time.

"Fox leader—Tattoo."

"Go."

"Let's get this over with. You ready?"

"Roger."

"Okay, let's do what we're paid for."

The two fighters joined up with the bombers and the strike force wheeled around, turning west, and streaked for North Vietnam. Behind them, like an afterglow, the brilliant, flashing luminosity from the ocean slowly faded from view and finally sank into the deeps of the Gulf of Tonkin. The major strained against the seat belts. The guns.

What am I doing here? What? What did you say? What kind of talk is that?—You know what you're doing here. It's what you wanted, isn't it? Yes, of course. It's what I wanted. What's the matter—scared? No. not at all. Sure? Well, I don't know. Maybe. No one said it was going to be easy. Right? Right—not going to be easy. Isn't that how you wanted it? Isn't that why you came? Right. That's why I came.

His heart was beating wildly. Would he ever get used to this? Like clockwork, his adrenal glands went into action just as they passed over the coastline and slipped into North Vietnam.

"Tally-ho! Migs—twelve o'clock high and attacking!"

"Damn, they're pretty, Buz."

Who's Buz?

"Okay, Fox — They're all your'n."

Fire control panel. Check. Switches. Check. Radar. Check.

"Dump the tanks, two."

"Roger, lead."

"Let's take em. Going to afterburner."

Full throttle. Stick into the belly. Right pedal. The Phantom leaped into the vertical, breaking hard into the attacking Migs. His g suit automatically inflated, squeezing his tissues, preventing blood from draining into feet, legs, and stomach . . . stopping blackout.

"Too much angle off."

"Good grief! We missed it."

"Bring it around. Keep thundering."

"Roger."

"Tattoo's breaking right."

"Am I clear, Fox two?"

"Clear."

Boom! Boom! Boom! Boom! Just then the four Mig 21s went supersonic, crashing through the sound barrier as they dove past the major, ripping into the strike force. Shock waves buffeted the F-4s. He broke left and looked back over his shoulder. Two of the Migs had scissored the Thuds and were insidiously rolling into firing position from six o'clock.

"Tattoo — Fox leader. You've got two twenty-ones at your six. Break left, *NOW!*"

He watched in amazement as the strikers continued on course, being bore-sighted by the communist pilots. Break! Why don't they break? He could feel the Mig pilots' fingers settling on their firing

18

buttons. Rivulets of sweat poured down his legs.

"Tattoo . . ." He was cut off by his WSO in the backseat.

"Major, I've got a launch light at two o'clock."

"Okay, SAM is up. Two o'clock."

"June time! June time!"

"SAM launch — two o'clock."

He rolled his ship ninety degrees and watched the long, white telephone pole rising from its dust cloud far below. Undaunted, the 105s thundered on without taking evasive action.

"Tattoo leader this is Fox leader," he said slowly and deliberately into the RT, a hint of exasperation in his voice. "SAM launch, strong signal, rising directly below you. Migs closing within ATOL limit at your blind six. You have about five seconds to stay alive," he said with icy detachment.

This time Tattoo reacted. The four strikers instantly broke left and lit their afterburners. The rapidly closing Migs pulled hard to stay with them but Tattoo's fast break caused them to swing wide and overshoot. The SAM went ballistic, harmlessly falling off in a long trajectory back to earth. Tattoo thundered on toward the target.

"Fox — Tattoo. How's it look now?"

"You're clear for the time being," the major said.

"Okay, start your music, guys. Bring it up and let's keep thundering."

"Got a light at one o'clock . . . fading . . . okay, no threat," someone said.

The F-4s climbed to altitude and began a weaving pattern over the slower Thud formation. The strike leader called for a course correction and together the force turned north again, passing over the heavy guns at Bac Ninh. They searched for Migs.

The major pushed his sun visor up again and rubbed his eyes with a gloved hand. He wiped the heavy sweat from his face. The jet rocked in the turbulent air. He looked around. Flak began to dot the formation. The guns. Fear clawed inside his stomach trying to get out. The guns. Why did he fear the guns more each mission? He should be getting used to them by now. The SAMs and Migs didn't strike fear in him. But the guns. He could see the SAMs and Migs. But the guns were hidden. And they shot invisible stuff at him.

The hot steel sizzled and crackled around his canopy. The air snapped and popped. His body involuntarily contracted and he sank deeper into the armored seat.

In his mind's eye, through the gun sight and directly in front of him over the aircraft's nose, he saw a field of beautiful blue and gold wildflowers spread across the green veldt of a hillside meadow back home. Suddenly, the flowers and grass wilted horribly before him as the hot breath of napalm passed over the meadow.

The guns.

Now he is strolling carefree along a white sand beach, the South China Sea happily lapping at his bare feet. From nowhere the sand begins to trickle blood, running between his toes and staining his feet red.

The 105s swung into their bomb run on the radar station at Phuc Yen. The flak intensified. SAMs rose for them. The major and his wingman continued their weave above the strikers.

"Are you still with us, Fox?"

"Roger, Tattoo."

"Starting run on target. Keep us clear coming off."

"Rog, Tattoo."

"My indicator light is going ape," someone said.

"It's at three-o'clock. One at two."

"Junetime, Baby-cakes. Let's get it on!"

"One."

"Two."

"Three."

"Four."

"Here we go!"

He watched with great respect mingled with reverence, dread, and wonder as the strikers pitched off, rolling over in a long, hurtling power dive. The lead Thud flier toggled his five-hundred pounders and the laser guided ordnance homed in on the target. At the same time, the major's radio frequency crackled a distant warning from the Gulf of Tonkin—a U.S. cruiser equipped with sophisticated radar systems stood off the coast of Vietnam.

"Fox leader this is Red Crown. We have radar contact—two bandits bearing two seven zero. Bullseye ten and closing."

He pulled twice in the seat belts. He could feel the shot of adrenaline racing through his body, bringing his nerves to the surface. Every fiber was stretched. More Migs! Fear etched with excitement and high adventure. Oh, the intensity of it all!

Today he was blessed. Not once but twice he would be allowed to engage the enemy on the battlefield — pitting his skill against theirs. Warrior-knights flung into battle, mounted on their aerial steeds of steel, jousting with supersonic lances. A grand tournament in the clouds. Oh, those wonderful Migs! If you had one you were everything. If you didn't, you were nothing.

And now his opponents, two incensed oriental knight-errants, were speeding toward him to exercise their sovereign feudal rights on the ethereal plains of Shen-si and the Three Kingdoms. Black knights encased in gleaming silver. Wild riding Tartar Huns preceding the Teutonic invasion of the Empire, the blood of Genghis Khan and his Mongol hordes coursing through their veins. And he, a descendant of the Roman Caesars, a knight-templar defending the fiefdom of his allies, answering the bugle-call in the tournament lists above Hanoi. The spectators and combatants were already moving toward the tournament grounds. The lists were open. The marshals and heralds were already on the field, making preparation for the day's contest, enrolling the names of the knights who wanted to fight.

He thundered on in his metal charger, the war stallion's hoofbeats resounding across the sea of air, across the crystalline pure splendor of the early Asian morning.

The sun gleamed on the polished armor. Lances were poised. The first trumpet sounded and the knights entered the lists at either end.

"Fox — Red Crown. Bandits Bullseye fifteen. Turning to two eight zero and attacking."

"Red Crown — Fox leader. Altitude of bandits?"

"In the dark."

"Roger, Red Crown."

"Tattoo one—Fox one. You copy Red Crown?"

"Uhh, Roger. Fox. Egressing target. Keep us covered."

And now to battle—into the fray. The second trumpet sounded and at full gallop the steel horses plunged toward each other, breathing smoke and fire from their entrails, eagerly responding to their pilot barons' lusty shouts of encouragement. Today a new champion would be crowned.

The major vectored for intercept and pushed over into the haze below, gaining energy for the first break. He came through at 12,000 feet. Red Crown now positioned the bandits at five miles and bearing down on the formation in a right to left pass. He went to his own radar, picked up the two blips, and turned into their heading. He was bathed in sweat. Now he would prove himself. It was time for the testing.

After about thirty seconds on the new heading his wingman called "contact."

"Fox leader, we have two Migs at our three o'clock."

Two silver streaks with red stars painted on their wings and fuselages flashed under the F-4s.

"Wahoo! Take it around—it's Mig time. Keep me clear."

"Rog, boss."

The pipper burned a bright red, casting an incandescent glow over the plexiglass, almost alive, seeming to pulsate, waiting hungrily to be filled with Mig. In the backseat the major's WSO waited nervously for the points to slide onto his screen.

Instead of breaking into the Migs as they would expect, the major dug in the Phantom's stabilator and "unloaded," accelerating into a dive. The crew went weightless. Now in burner and rapidly gaining combat velocity, the U.S. aircraft broke hard and fast into the communists. The 7 g turn quickly reduced the distance between the jets, and the Migs sensing their predicament, broke right. The major capitalized on the error.

"Reverse it!" he shouted to his wingman, and the two F-4s rolled through the Migs' axis in a well executed high speed scissors, climbing into the enemy's rear quadrant.

"The iceman cometh," the WSO whispered to himself and shaking his head in wonder.

Pulling through the roll, the major gave the ship some right rudder, cutting off the Migs' turn even further. Unexpectedly, his mind flashed home again and he glanced at the small card his father had sent him, taped to the fire control panel:

"And it shall come to pass, if thou shalt hearken diligently unto the voice of the Lord thy God, to observe and to do all his commandments which I command thee this day, that the Lord thy God will set thee on high above all nations of the earth. And all these blessings shall come on thee and overtake thee, if thou shalt hearken unto the voice of the Lord thy God.

"The Lord shall cause thine enemies that rise up against thee to be smitten before thy face. They shall come out against thee one way, and flee before thee seven ways.

"And the Lord shall make thee the head, and not the tail; and thou shalt be above only, and thou shalt not be beneath; if that thou hearken unto the commandments of the Lord thy God."

Abruptly, the Mig wingman broke away from his leader in a climbing turn to the left. Pressing the attack, the major continued to maneuver with the lead aircraft in an attempt to get radar lock-on. The g forces tugged at his head, neck, and shoulders. He fought the grayout. The anti-gravity suit pressed hard against his stomach and lower extremities. He tried to lift his head. No good. His chin was cemented to his chest. Got to get the advantage. The cockpit faded to gray again. He cranked harder. Through the blur he could still see the Mig high on the nose. Just a little more. Pull. Pull. Pull.

Back and forth, twisting high over the gleaming Indo-China sky, the two adversaries fought for an advantage. They made crushing vertical climbs to 40,000 feet, slowed to a chilling 60 knots as they went over the top inverted, and then boiled down the reverse side of the hook with the airspeed indicator bouncing off Mach 1.5. Hard breaks pushed their stress limits, placing heavy g loads on human bodies, aircraft skins, and structural members.

Up again, over the top, hanging in the straps, slowly turning horizon; then the crashing, jerking, wild roller coaster ride down, setting up for another screaming break.

"Fox one and two, we've got more company. Sec-

ond bandit at eight o'clock . . . moving to seven."
It was his backseater.

The major had temporarily ignored the approach
of the Mig leader's wingman who was now back in
the fight and maneuvering for firing position, trying to force a break.

"Keep your eye on him. Let me know when the
rice-ball starts to pull his nose into us. I'm still
working on his boss."

"Rog."

"Fox two—how's it look. Can you get this guy off
my back."

"Negative, he's within minimum range of my
missiles."

"Okay, keep it moving. Where's Tattoo?"

"Streaking for home."

"Fuel check."

"Forty-five hundred pounds," his wingman answered.

"Fox flight, this is Red Crown. Radar contact,
four more bandits, two sixty, bullseye twenty and
closing."

"Copy two sixty at twenty."

Good grief! When it rains it pours.

"Say altitude, Red Crown."

"Nineteen thousand . . . now turning to two
fifty . . . speed point nine."

"Copy that."

"We've got a SAM launch at four o'clock," the
backseater warned.

"Rog. I've got it."

"Fox—Red Crown. Bandits two fifty, Bullseye
thirty."

"Got it, Red Crown."

Not much time left. Got to make a decision.

"He's starting in, Major! The Mig's committing," the backseater shouted.

"I'm reheating."

Sensing this new threat, he waited until the last moment then broke off the engagement without firing. The dogfight had already exceeded the two to three minutes of modern jet aerial combat and the thirsty Phantom was approaching "bingo" fuel.

The U.S. aircraft, bristling with its Sidewinders and Sparrows resting eagerly on launch rails under stubby wings and in wells within the fuselage, rolled off over Hanði with the determined second Mig-17 holding tight to its 8 o'clock. The Lake of the Sacred Sword was visible directly below them in the center of the city.

The Mig pilot, anticipating a quick victory, began turning his aircraft's nose into the F-4 in an attempt to get off a missile shot, but the major instinctively tightened his turn putting the Mig out of position once again.

"Am I clear?" he asked his wingman. "Where are those four Migs?"

"You're clean. Red Crown puts them about twenty miles out, speed Mach one, twenty-one thousand."

Suddenly, he dropped the Phantom's airspeed, losing energy in a high speed yo-yo. The communist, unable to compensate, overshot. The F-4 coming over the top of its maneuver rapidly regained energy. The major reversed and quickly tightened onto the Mig's 6 o'clock. The Phantom's Sidewinders growled in anticipation of release, sending a good tone signal to the instrument panel. He gave a little right rudder then pulled the trigger. A plume of smoke, a moment's hesitation, and a missile came off the rail perfectly tracking the Mig's exhaust heat.

The Mig, its role having rapidly changed from the hunter to the hunted, was now flying for its life. The communist broke hard left and the evasive tactic threw the Sidewinder off momentarily as it strained to turn with the Mig. The "17" tightened its turn but the heat seeker stayed with it. The Sidewinder made a final corrective move as the Mig came over on its back and dove for the ground. The missile flew straight up the Mig's tailpipe and disappeared in a fireball as the North Vietnamese jet exploded.

Two helmeted and masked figures slowly turned their heads dispassionately to observe the cruel wreckage as their aircraft blew through the debris. From somewhere across the cloudless plains the major heard the grand flourish of trumpets and for a fleeting moment he caught the distant image of Sir Cedric the Saxon, Prince John, and Lady Rowena cheering from their place of honor above the lists. His eyes crinkled behind the helmet visor and a contented smile, hidden by the black oxygen mask, stole across his face. He raised a gloved hand toward them in salute.

Then ever so slowly, twisting like a tiny, fragile water bubble searching for the surface, came the haunting, tacit, terrible, pristine clean question. The one he must always ask, drilling deep into his ethos, penetrating the life-core of his personal Eucharist. Did God approve?

Ah, so simple, so pure—a spot in time without blemish—beyond the reach of situation ethics and humanism. The question, emblazoned across the interior of the Phantom's windscreen, screamed for an answer, echoing into eternity—*Did God approve?*

The front seater kicked hard left rudder, quickly glanced at his fuel readout, and set course for South Vietnam. On the way home they rendezvoused with a waiting aerial tanker, topped off their fuel supply, and forty minutes later let down on the sprawling U.S. base at Da Nang.

The Phantom rolled into its parking position and its two whining General Electric J79 jet engines slowly shut down. The canopy lifted and the major and his weapons system operator disengaged themselves from the aircraft, bringing the man-machine cybernetic relationship to an end for another mission.

Major Vic Benedetti, F-4 aircraft commander, USAF, pressure suit wringing wet from perspiration forced out of his pores by the high g aerial combat, dropped to the tarmac and made his way from the flight line to operations for debriefing. A warm glow of satisfaction spread through him. It was only his tenth mission and he had shot down his first Mig.

CHAPTER TWO

Vic stepped out of the Operations office and lit a cigarette. He took a long drag and slowly exhaled. He flicked the weed away.

I can learn to do without these, he said to himself.

He looked back toward the flight line where returning F-4s were taxiing into parking positions near his own Phantom. Ground crews were moving to receive the aircraft as waves of heat from the apron visibly rose to engulf men and machines. He watched his wingman, Capt. Bob "Drill" Davis, a married man with two children, emerge from his weapon and begin examining a 23mm cannon hole in the wing. A devoted husband and parent, "Drill" talked often of his family and was eagerly looking forward to returning home to them when his tour was over.

"You envy him don't you?" Vic's WSO asked.

"Envy him? He's satisfied with his life. He has a

wife and children who love him—someone to share his future with. Yeh, I guess I envy him."

"Do you ever feel restless, Major? I mean for a woman. Someone you can love without reservation."

"No. Not so much. Not any more, Dick. Why?"

"Just wondered."

"You have something on your mind? That girl in Tucson maybe? You plan to marry her?"

"I think she has the sensibility and maturity to accept me as I am. Sure, I think I'd marry her. Do you ever think about marrying again?"

"Me? You've got to be kidding." He pulled another cigarette from the pack and lit up. "I've got very uncomfortable feelings about developing a relationship with any woman."

"Why's that?"

Vic inhaled then threw the cigarette down. He stomped it in disgust.

"Do you really want to know?"

"Why not?"

"All right, I'll tell you. My survival depends upon the ability to make split-second decisions free from emotion. Do you notice that the unattached pilots are more aggressive with their machines? They have a finer edge when a fight develops. A flier who loses his concentration for even a moment quickly finds himself in trouble."

He felt like picking up the mashed cigarette and smoking it again.

"How about Drill? Don't you think he's aggressive enough?"

"Lieutenant, Davis is a good pilot. But his place

is on a wing — not leading. Want to know why?"

"Yeh."

"Because when he gets bounced his first thought is his wife and kids and what's going to happen to them if he gets flamed."

He pulled out another cigarette. Well, it was a good answer anyway.

"So you think it's better not to be married while flying?"

"That's how I feel about it," Vic said.

"What do you think of these Nam girls?"

"Wouldn't waste my time."

"Some of them are pretty cute," Dick's eyes widened.

"They don't show me much," Vic said.

"I wouldn't mind cuddling up to one."

"You're liable to get your throat cut. Watch yourself."

Vic threw the whole pack of cigarettes into the trash can.

"I prefer American women," he said resolutely.

"Women are women."

"Not to me. Besides, I'm not ready to worry about anyone special — except the guy who's climbing into my six o'clock."

He recalled with some pain how there had been someone special he had worried about. Maybe he hadn't loved her enough. Who knows. He had been young, fresh out of grad school, his whole life and a promising career in the aerospace business ahead of him when they had decided to call it quits. He had had ambitious plans for Betty, Vic Jr. and himself, placed a lot of hope in their future together. He had come apart emotionally when it became apparent that the marriage was irreparable and Betty had walked out with their young son. He had vowed never again to allow feelings to control his life.

It had been late Indian Summer when he climbed the Sierra Nevada crest seeking confirmation of who he was. He had come to those bastions searching for his permanence in the midst of his chaotic world of anxiety and confusion. He had wanted time to think. And he needed quiet. He had looked to the mountains for a refreshening.

Cleaving to the cold granite face, a crisp alpine breeze had caressed his city worn face, bringing fresh blood to the surface and rosying his cheeks. A long forgotten sensation, reminiscent of earlier days on the Rock. He had buttoned his down vest against the chilly bite of pre-winter.

The air had been crackling clear. No smog. The bright sunlight, unrestricted in the thin, uncontaminated atmosphere, clearly illuminated every crevice in the glacier polished granite, and cast long, jagged shadows along the high ridges overhead.

A pair of glistening black ravens sat tucked away in a horizontal crack extending across the rock face, guarding the entrance to their roost. A stone dislodged by a foraging golden mantled ground squirrel echoed off the bare canyon walls as it clattered down from its resting place a thousand feet above the twisted tamaracks.

The wind played a symphony through the swaying tops of a few unsubdued, weathered pines huddled together on a talus slope. Holdouts against the harsh elements of timberline; refusing to submit as had less hardy members of their species. The music rose in a gradual crescendo from double soft piano, moved through mezzo forte, into roaring double forte, and then quickly softened to piano again.

Black bibbed chickadees flitted happily among the low lying boughs of gnarled lodgepole pine, and nuthatches circled the furrowed trunks in joyful nasal beeping.

The Sierra timberline. Stark, barren, noiseless. Desolately beautiful. Rugged grandeur. Incomparable. His eyes had met slabs of white granite in every direction. A chubby marmot studied him from the top of a rocky monument. Everywhere was a great silence; so quiet that his pounding heart was clearly audible and he could hear his lungs inflating in the rarefied October air.

No traffic noise. No stereos. The absence of people sounds. Deafening. The quiet broken only by the occasional caw of a Clark's nutcracker. Nature. Unplundered wilderness.

He had unshouldered his pack on the shore of a little, pristine shelf lake and sat down in the middle of a pile of decomposing granite. He scooped up a handful of the rock and let it drain through his spread fingers. Over a period of a few hundred years it would be transformed into rich soil for supporting a new stand of tamaracks, continuing the unspoiled cycle. The web of life.

His mind had raced backward through thousands of years. He stopped. Peeked out. The granite basin in which he had been sitting had disappeared, replaced by an icy blue glacier covering everything in view. It rose to the tops of the ridges and peaks, reached for hundreds of miles along the Sierra crest, cutting and grinding, carving out the present day sculptures at the rate of a foot a day.

He hitched up his pack again and began exploring the igneous rock columns for a way to work himself out of the basin. Two hours' climb brought him to the crown of an imposing Pleistocene battlement from which he could see the sweep of the glacier's massive work. Magnificence spread before him. He was surrounded by rising ramparts of solid stone masses stretching in the distance, devoid of any vegetation. A spiritual silence crept across the ridges and flowed through the walled passes down into the canyons below.

To the east, icy cols, protecting snowfields left over from the previous winter, defiantly thrust their barbed peaks skyward in a grand display of united independence. To the north, colonnades of towering escarpments. To the west, more battlements. And to the south stood a superstructure of commanding, cloud dressed massifs running the width of the Sierra slab. He was standing in the center of an immense redoubt, an ancient stronghold valiantly holding out against the increasing encroachment of men and their gnawing appetites to compromise this last great California wilderness. A golden eagle circled in a canyon below him.

All over the earth, people at that moment were going to the movies, having conversations, eating together, enjoying each other, sharing. But here, on the sprawling giant granite rocks of the Sierra crest, stood only one human. One human, exclusive of anyone or anything else, solitary . . . alone. Glorying in the calm of his isolation, yet longing for companionship, someone with whom to share his experience. Feeling separation from his origins, but uniquely fascinated by the thought of his oneness with creation. The immensity of the beauty, power, and desolation. United with the quietness, the wind, and with the void.

He had watched as great waves of loneliness rolled across the reaches of white pinnacles and domes, and vanished into the green valleys far below. He listened to his hyperventilated breathing in the oxygen depleted air. It was becoming colder and he longed for the comfort and warmth of a fire. No wood above timberline. But he continued to watch, and to listen to the silence, sensing a unity with the moment. Feeling the rhythm and harmony of the universe.

He stood there in the soft brush of twilight, looking out over the Sierra Nevada, feeling its magnificence and indomitability. He watched the day begin to die, giving birth to night. The stillness. He had never known such complete silence. Peace. It filled the great pondering emptiness with wonder. Its source was beyond discovery or explanation. There was an order here, cemented in the vast reaches of time. He was standing in a master's workshop, experiencing his precise and functional universe. Rhythm. Harmony. Order. It was all so overwhelming. He had become a part of it, engulfed by the solitude, beauty, and power. For a moment he was one with creation, with the universe. A speck to be sure, but in oneness.

Standing among the great forces of nature and

her imponderable processes, he had sensed the perfect harmony of the universe. He was a part of it just as much as were the sentinels and spires that surrounded him, as was the orderly swing of the planets across the heavens.

The sun had changed from white, to yellow, to orange, and was now a deep red, resting on the back of a giant 14,000 foot monolith guarding the western reaches of the crest. Darkness began to fall from the wings of night. A deep chill stole across the ridge. He had unrolled his bag, climbed in, and resting his back against a boulder, continued to watch the ancient spectacle of night chasing day from the land.

Remembering Dad's Bible stuffed in the rucksack, he had pulled it from a buried corner and read:

"The heavens desire the glory of God; and the firmament showeth his handiwork."

A hush settled over the ridge. The silhouetted summits slowly began to dim into total darkness. Winking stars appeared and night came on. The cycle was completed. A human fell peacefully asleep; above timberline. He was not alone.

Davis finished inspecting his ship's battle damage and was now engaged in avid conversation with his crew chief and WSO. His flight suit pockets bulged with survival gear and a blue and white helmet with oxygen mask dangled from one hand while the other hand rested on a holstered sidearm. An assortment of pens and pencils were clipped securely in sleeve pockets on either arm and a bandoleer of gleaming .38 caliber ammunition was slung around his waist. The usual harnesses, belts, zippers, and equipment attached to his g suit completed the picture of the modern jet jockey returning from a mission.

He saw Vic and gave a brief wave, gesturing for Vic to wait for him. He began slowly walking away from the aircraft, glancing over his shoulder several times. He stopped again and turned squarely around with hands on hips staring at the F-4, shaking his head as if in disbelief. He pivoted and began jogging toward Vic.

He trotted up to Vic looking something like an unkempt spaceman in his bulky gear. Deep impressions were still visible under his eyes where the oxygen mask had bitten into his skin.

"Nice splash," he said to Vic.

"Thanks, Drill. You called the break just right. You take a hit?"

"Yeh. Didn't realize it until I just landed."

"Any trouble on the way home?" Vic asked.

"No. Smooth. Chief says he'll have it checked out though."

"Good. The Ops guys inside want you to confirm the kill."

"Roger. Good mission Vic. See you tonight?"

"Sure. Tonight. Got to celebrate. Right?" Vic said.

"Right. See ya. Congratulations again."

Davis disappeared inside and a crowd of pilots

39

coming off the parking area descended on Vic.

"Nice going, major," Pellegrini said.

"Yeh, congratulations," Moreno shouted over the others.

"It didn't take long, did it Vic?" Colonel Johnson the burly wing commander asked.

"No sir."

"How many missions?" Johnson asked.

"My tenth."

"That's just great, Vic. I remember when I got my first. Great feeling, eh boy?" Johnson was acting cavalier as usual.

"Roger that," Vic said.

"You should have been here when the Dragon Man was running wild," Johnson continued, in his typical macho style.

"The Dragon Man?" Vic asked.

"Yeh, Colonel Tan. Thirteen American kills! Their hottest stick."

Yes, he had heard talk of Tan from a few of the veteran pilots. The North Vietnamese ace with the black dragons painted on the nose of his ship. But no one knew much about him. He left no witnesses. He was a mystery. A legend.

"What happened to him?" Vic asked.

"Don't know. He just vanished. Haven't seen him since the big fights over Thanh Hoa."

"Your Mig a '17,' major?" Vogle, a young first lieutenant, wanted to know.

"Right."

"How'd you get him, Vic? Sparrow?" Patterson asked.

"No. Sidewinder. Diving turn, left. Yo-yoed him.

If I had had a gun I might have got his leader too."

They lingered around him for a long time, milking him of all the details, vicariously experiencing the battle. He saw it in their eyes, the envy, the respect. He basked in the attention as they walked together in their heavy equipment, stopping now and then to go over the action again, Vic demonstrating with his hands the maneuvers that got him the kill. Other pilots joined the group wanting to get close to him, pay homage, offer their gift of congratulations. The excitement was heady and it wouldn't leave him for many days. They would celebrate in the club tonight. The tributes would continue and he would graciously accept. It had begun. He would not fail.

From nowhere came the cry of a baby. He jerked around. Then the pitiful and forlorn wail of a desperate mother. He wheeled again. The siren scream of falling bombs tearing the air around him. Wilting flowers. His feet turning red in the sand. Again, the shrieking infant. He shook his head violently and covered his ears with his hands.

The twisting serpent writhed on the ground, its undulating black body taunting him, defying him. The dragon's forked tongue darted forward from its cavernous, blood red mouth, sensing the air, smelling for him. The odious creature rolled its intelligent eyes, following every move he made, watching, waiting for its opportunity. The air reeked of fetid rot bubbling from the serpent's throat.

"Here beguiling, crawling thing. Eat," Vic said, holding out the mythical apple to the dragon. The obscene yellow eyes glazed over, the scaly neck arched high, and the dragon struck just as the heavy foot came down crushing its skull. And it remembered in the final fleeting second, ". . . it shall bruise thy head, and thou shalt bruise his heel."

The Man. Dragon. The Dragon Man. The name fascinated Vic as he rolled it over in his mind. Where had he gone, why had he disappeared so mysteriously? Would he be back? Vic felt cheated. He had come too late.

Suddenly, a turbulent, swift flowing river of emotion raged over him. He was overwhelmed with a burning desire to crawl back into his plane and scream north again, find Tan. Tempt him to rise again. Force the dragon to give him his chance. Just one chance to meet the champion. Maybe a scornful jeer would shame him into coming up again. No, a champion doesn't have to prove himself. Retiring from the fray is no wrongful act for a champion. He chooses his opponent. He chooses the place. He decides the time.

But, oh, to twist and turn with him for the briefest part of an eternal moment high and alone on the ethereal lists. To fight a champion and nothing would ever again be meaningless for him. He would reign forever between the tropics of Cancer and Capricorn. Ah, to be parched by the heat of battle with the prince of the air, to be scorched forever by the passion of combat with the singular most formidable knight-errant of the skies. The insensibility of it all. The clean, pure simplicity. All or nothing.

One pass. Two passes. Maybe three or four. But at least a chance. One chance to dethrone a champion. Come up Tan. Rise again, Dragon Man. Defend your crown one more time—give the newcomer a chance. I only recently arrived. I'm a beginner, only one Mig have I. How does that compare with your thirteen kills? You shouldn't have much trouble with me. Right? Come up Tan. Rise again from the pit, Dragon Man.

But the phantom was gone now, vacating his throne for a new champion. He hadn't been seen since the big fights last year, Colonel Johnson had said. He had carved his last contrail, no more to thunder through the formations intrepidly scissoring his foes, his icy, invisible breath consuming their courage, freezing them at their controls.

It was difficult for Vic to understand how this North Vietnamese ace could have reached such imperious heights of success in so brief a time. All those who had encountered him spoke in awe of his flying skill and resolute courage. Most felt he was invincible. He was legend.

Among the remaining veteran pilots in the wing who had gone against him, only a few had escaped his guns. One was Colonel Johnson. It had happened over Bac Ninh. A Mig sweep. The weasels had just finished doing their thing on the missile sites and the Thuds were pushing into the target area. Johnson, leading sixteen F-4s, spotted two Migs out about two miles. He put the enemy ships on his nose and climbed after them. Something wasn't right, though. He sensed danger hanging thick in his cockpit, inexplicable. He pressed the attack even though the strange emanation was almost unbearable. The closer he got to the Migs the greater he felt the presence. But the two Migs posed no threat. They were sitting ducks, just waiting to be popped off.

The North Vietnamese began a slow turn east. Johnson turned with them and selected HEAT on his fire control panel. The Migs tightened, then reversed left, headed directly into the sun as they climbed. Johnson pulled around with the Migs, losing some speed and distance in the reverse. Suddenly, the sun began reaching for him with long arms of red and yellow streams of light. Momentarily dazzled by the brightness he tried to focus on the source of the flashing rays which were arching out in parallel bursts of energy. He switched to Sparrows. Then, like a wild apparition, Tan's ghost ship exploded in fiery brilliance from behind the sun's protective glare, tracers spitting from gun ports, the black, intimidating dragons staring menacingly into the colonel's surprised face.

And he was gone. Tail pipe winking at him as he vanished into a thunderhead, climbing into the cosmos where Johnson said he lived, never touching earth. Their meeting had only been a flash in time but Johnson spoke of it reverently.

Now, each time he flies north, he watches the skies expectantly, waiting for the magic to brush him again, being pulled into the clouds of airy ramparts with the insidious magnetism of a delirious man laboring under a spell.

He was still up there. He had to be. Floating on the oceans of clouds, Turning among the billowing colonnades and battlements; through the high drifting gates he flew, eating his heavenly manna, waiting, watching. One more time. A champion must always return to the arena for one last conquest, to hear the exploding roar of the crowd cheering him again. The Champion. Hail Conqueror, victor of lesser beings. See his proud demeanor. See his exalted moves. None can compare. He alone is champion. Here was his food, in the arena, among his beloved. The charged air, the ionic bond, the complete transfer of energy, one to another, sharing in his greatness. Yes, he must return to the misty lists before it was all over. Even now he must be growing impatient for the arena, for a last joust, before the gates closed for the final time. One more fight before the war ended. He would return, of this Vic was sure. For Vic too had scintillated to the white hot heat of royal conflict and his blood was also aflame with the spark and flash of champion.

And when the enemy ace scrambled his Mig for that final taste of blood lust, Vic would take up his cudgels of war and enter the lists with the champion, infected with the dry mouth terror of the broil, thrilling to the wild excitement of modern jet warfare. And as destiny would have it they would clash in the regions of space that mingle with the earth's atmosphere, the cosmic DMZ, the high clear sky where only celestial beings venture unaided. Here was the all pervading ether, the infinitely elastic and massless bright air where Vic would meet the top gun in a last raving and fierce contest that would decide who was supreme champion, ace of aces.

"You okay, Vic?"

"Yeh, I'm okay."

Someone handed him his helmet and oxygen mask that had fallen to the tarmac. He headed for his hooch.

CHAPTER THREE

The oppressive tropical heat of the South Vietnam coast was an uncomfortable change from the air conditioned environment of the Phantom, and Vic was preoccupied with the thought of a shower and relaxing with a cool drink as he walked into his quarters.

A young Vietnamese woman was kneeling on the floor polishing his shoes to an immaculate sheen. He noticed his skivies and shirts, freshly laundered and folded, lying in a neat row on his bunk behind her. His uniforms, freshly pressed, hung neatly in the open closet and a bucket and brush sat at her side on the shining floor.

Upon his entering she quickly rose to her feet and respectfully stood motionless with her head bowed, only a glimpse of her almond eyes showing between strands of long, black, straight hair. Her tiny boneless hands were lightly clasped together below her small breasts, revealing perfectly sculptured nails. Her skin was of a tone resembling that of the golden Vietnamese sunrise breaking over the still rice paddies. Her small flat nose, high cheek bones and lovely long eyes accented her oriental beauty which contrasted so greatly to that of western women. She was dressed in the traditional Vietnamese *ao dai* which uniquely conveyed both her modesty and provocativeness at the same time. Its pink color with small white flowers accentuated the delicate tone of her skin and blended with the simple jade jewelry she wore around her neck and wrist.

"Chao ong," she softly said, lifting her eyes momentarily.

"Chao co," he responded.

He walked across the room to the window and gazed out over the base into the brown-green hills and the defense perimeter beyond. The girl assumed the Vietnamese squat and returned to her work polishing his shoes. He marveled at the suppleness of her body and how comfortable she looked sitting in this position. He had tried it once but only succeeded in straining a muscle in his leg. and falling over on his back to the amusement of the Vietnamese pilots who had encouraged him to try.

He thought that he should feel annoyed with the liberty she had taken with his quarters but her presence was a refreshing change and her manner so pleasant and reassuring that he found himself delighted with her. He pulled up a chair and sat opposite the girl. He tried talking with her but it became apparent that her English was as limited as was his

Vietnamese. After a few minutes of working in silence she put his shoes down and pulled out what appeared to be her lunch in a two level metal container, cylindrical in shape and having a carrying handle dangling from the top. The upper portion contained steamed rice and the bottom part held *chao gio,* spring roll, and pieces of salty pork in *nuoc mam* sauce. She ate in silence, occasionally stealing a glance at him through her long, narrow eyes and now and then brushing strands of her black hair over her shoulders where they cascaded down to meet her slim waist.

"Ong muon thuc an?" she asked, extending a spring roll toward him.

"Cam on co," he responded, thanking her as he took the *cho gio* from her tiny fingers.

He also tried a bit of pork and rice, fumbling with the chopsticks as she demonstrated their use for him. She giggled at his awkward attempts, covering her mouth in the feminine oriental fashion with her hand. She became more friendly and relaxed as they conversed in signs and haltingly exchanged words in each others language. She told him her name was Mai Lien and her village was in the hills a few kilometers distant. She pointed a delicate finger north.

He finished the spring roll and setting his chopsticks aside leaned back in his chair to study this hooch maid that base personnel had assigned him. This was the closest he had ever been to a Vietnamese woman. He was curious. She was embarrassed by his steady gaze and she diverted her eyes to smoothing her *ao dai*. He enjoyed her shyness.

Her presence had given him much pleasure in the

short space of time she had shared with him — a moment of refreshment from the turmoil of war. He had noted that for a peasant girl she carried herself well and demonstrated a remarkable poise and stylish quality that remained hidden from the casual observer. She had spoken very little, allowing her actions to speak for her. The simple meal, the sparkling clean room, his freshly laundered clothing, even his polished boots and shoes, had impressed him very much. But what had captivated him most was her quiet spirit and tenderness. There was a delicate softness about her and he found that he was unusually comfortable with her. Suddenly he was flooded with the emotion that this gentle girl represented all the loveliness and mystery in the oriental female that western men have found so irresistible throughout the ages. He marveled at the contrast between this comfortable scene and the violence he had experienced only a short time ago over Hanoi.

Unexpectedly he became very tired. He tried to fight back the numbing spread of fatigue as he watched the girl gracefully rise and begin putting away his shoes and clothing. He allowed her femininity to penetrate his protective exterior, calming his taut mind and tired body. He fell fast asleep in his chair.

Mai Lien placed the major's shoes and boots on the floor in the closet, being careful that they were evenly arranged side by side. She stepped back and admired their high gloss. She stacked the shirts, underwear, and socks neatly in the drawers, then glanced around the room to see that everything was in order before leaving. She noted that the windows were spotless with the exception of where the work-men had been careless and had splattered a few drops of paint. A bit of paint here and there also marred her otherwise perfectly clean and well polished floor. She had worked hard but she was used to working hard. She gathered strength from it. All her life she had been poor and it had always been necessary to work hard and long hours to provide the bare necessities. But lately, since working for the Americans, her meager income had improved considerably and she and her grandmother were able to live much more comfortably. They now had more to eat, even pork, fish, and duck became routine with their rice meals. Vegetables and fruit also. Mai Lien could even buy the Vietnamese gin for her grandmother now and then, though she preferred to make her own. For herself she had purchased French cologne, new shoes, underwear, and two new *ao dai*'s. She felt somewhat guilty about the two dresses. One should have been her limit. They were no longer exactly poor and as long as her job on the base lasted she could continue to send money to her mother in Saigon. She had even been able to save enough to buy some gold and hide it in the earthen wall of her bedroom.

But Mai Lien was still distressed by the recurring memory of the abject poverty in which she had lived throughout her childhood. Very few children of Vietnam lived a normal life, but hers had been particularly painful. She could vividly recall how every morning of her young life she would rise before the light of day from her poor bed of thatched leaves spread on the dirt floor and walk with empty stomach many miles to the train station where she would peddle bread and tea to the passengers. It was humiliating and embarrassing work begging the people to buy and she always avoided their eyes. But on occasion someone would recognize her and she would run away in a burst of tears. Sometimes she would sneak aboard the train and ride it to Hue trying to sell what she could along the way. The police were always chasing her from the depots and she often returned home without selling anything. The little she did earn she turned over to her grandmother who purchased what rice she could for the family. Sometimes they had nothing to eat.

Mai Lien had only two sets of clothes as a child, the pajama style pants and blouse of the Vietnamese peasant. She wore one set while her grandmother washed the other. She remembered always trying to keep herself clean and to keep her meager clothing in good repair, attempting to avoid the shame of being poor.

Mai Lien was a "new" girl. But there had been a time when the temptation had been strong to cast aside her better judgment and enter a life of prostitution. She had been very young when a *"Tu Ba"* had approached her to become a "working girl". She was told that she could make a good living and there was really no need for her to be poor when she was so pretty and could bring pleasure to men. The older and wealthier Vietnamese men were more than willing to pay handsomely, sometimes as high as 100,000 piasters, for a young virgin. It wasn't just passion that whetted their appetites, for they seriously believed that the strength and youth of the girl would be transferred to their own bodies and minds through sexual intercourse with her. Of course, the first to have her would have drawn away all of her virtue for himself, leaving none for those who might follow. Therefore, a new girl in Vietnam was highly prized and men, if they could afford her, would pay great sums of money to be the first of her lovers.

The *"Tu Ba"* had naturally been angry when she hadn't shown for her first customer. Mai Lien was a beautiful child and represented a rich income for her. But Mai Lien knew from the beginning that though poverty-stricken and her family desperately in need of money, she could not sell her virtue. She would find another way, for she had a strong faith in God and prayed often for her deliverance from her miserable condition. Also, it was common knowledge that in Vietnam once a young girl took up this sort of life she became indentured until she outlived her usefulness to the *"Tu Ba."* These children-women were often kept locked up in closely guarded rooms, seeing only their customers. They seldom returned to their families and friends, and eventually withered away into oblivion.

She turned her attention to the American major sleeping heavily in the chair. A handsome man she thought. Not very old, early thirties perhaps. She wondered if he was married or if he had taken a Vietnamese "wife" as was common among the Americans. She wanted to know more about this man and she felt an inner urging to draw close to him, to become his friend. He must be very brave, flying those big, fast airplanes day after day into

North Vietnam to be shot at. And he had to be very intelligent because the machines he flew were complicated. She looked down at him and studied him closely. She sensed that here was a sensitive and troubled man — a restless man capable of deep love and quick violence, but who chose to contain his emotions and spent a great deal of time with himself, alone, thinking.

She gathered up her cleaning things and quickly looked around one more time. Vic moved restlessly in the chair, still asleep. Something stirred inside of her, something generations old. Ancient. Instinctive. Genetic. Her Asian femaleness had been aroused by this American, and her need to serve a man, to exert her role as woman, rushed to the surface. She pushed it back.

"In due time," she said. "God will let me know."

She closed the door quietly behind her and went on to her next job.

CHAPTER FOUR

"Mold your flight into a precision combat team. I want Migs. Lots of Migs — we need more Migs."

Colonel Johnson pulled on his handlebar mustache, shaping the waxed red hairs between his thumb and forefinger.

"Which of your guys has it in him — I mean can get Migs if we turn him loose? I'd like an honest evaluation of your pilots, Vic."

"Sure — shoot."

"I understand that Pellegrini has the most experience but Davis is the better pilot."

"He's good," Vic said.

"Which one?"

"Davis."

"How about Pellegrini?"

"Davis is better."

"Then put him leading elements."

"I'm more comfortable with him on my wing."

"We need Migs, Vic."

"We'll get more Migs with him on my wing."

"How about Patterson and Moreno?"

"Both new."

"How are they shaping up?"

"Moreno still lacks aggressiveness — but he's dependable. He flies tight on his leader's wing and follows instructions closely."

"Patterson?"

"Overly confident. It's all I can do to bridle him when a fight breaks out. Pellegrini complains about him a lot. Has to watch him closely or he'll go off on his own . . . get his leader flamed."

"I'm going to need another flight leader soon, Vic. Butler's rotating back. I'm thinking of Pellegrini or Davis. What do you think?"

"Not yet, Colonel. I need them both right now. Maybe later. With those two I'll develop the flight into the leading one in the wing, with the most Migs. Split us up, especially right now when we're building spirit and pride and confidence in each other, and . . . well, you're not going to get your Migs. We're hot together and we're going to get hotter."

Johnson frowned and pulled his handlebars some more.

"I suppose you're right . . . but still . . ."

"I know I'm right, sir. Pellegrini has the eyes of an eagle and can spot a Mig or SAM at ten miles. Nothing can sneak up on us with him along. And Davis is dauntless and as loyal as a hound dog. The perfect wingman — he judges the break until the last moment and he's always right when he calls it."

"Okay, Vic—I'll let you keep them both, at least for the time being. But if you don't get Migs . . ."

"We'll get Migs."

"Encourage your pilots, Vic. Scold them. Motivate them. Draw them close together. Build their trust in you. Always be aware that you are their best example. Lead with authority and give them the model they need to emulate."

"I'll do my best, Colonel."

"I want more than your best, Vic. You're at home leading, just like your old man."

"I'll make it on my own, without the help of his reputation."

"Maybe. That remains to be seen. You have one Mig. Your old man had ten. A double ace."

"That was Korea. It was easier there."

"No, it wasn't. In some ways it was tougher. You've over-rated yourself, Vic."

Vic dreaded what was coming next.

"You've killed your first Mig and everyone's eyes have been opened. You've been thrust into a new arena, the arena of champions. But now you're being watched closely, being evaluated to see if you've got what it really takes to be a top gun."

Johnsosn paused and groomed his mustache.

"You're regarded as the newcomer around here. Two of your pilots have more missions than you. and there's resentment against you, Vic. You know it and I know it."

"What resentment?"

"I immediately gave you your own flight to command after only five missions. Some of these guys have nearly a hundred and are still flying wing."

"So why did you do it? Because of my father?"

Vic thought Johnson was going to hit him.

"No! Because I believe in your strong leadership ability and outstanding flying record — *that's why!*"

Johnson pulled a small jar from his flight suit pocket and adroitly waxed his mustache.

"You need victories now, major. Victories to prove . . . to prove to yourself and to prove to the others that you're better than . . ."

He stopped in mid-sentence and stood. "I wonder if you've got what it takes — to reach the pinnacle of superiority — like your old man. That superiority was carried proudly on his fuselage and on the claims board. The red stars set him above the rest of us."

Johnson twitched his upper lip, testing the cultivated hairs.

"Migs are everything. You walk at a higher level if you have one. If you don't, you're nothing, you don't stand in the light. You've become a member of a special group of men, son, but you've got a lot to learn about war. You've no right to discredit your father."

Johnson walked out of the briefing room into the black morning. After he had gone Vic sat down on the floor and stared at his clenched fists for more than ten minutes, bewildered by the whipping he'd just been given.

The air was dank and heavy even at 4 a.m. Vic's eyes pierced the darkness ahead as he walked to the locker room to dress for the early morning mission. His flight was scheduled to escort two reconnaissance ships making camera runs on North Vietnamese missile sites near the Laotian frontier. It was unlikely that they would encounter Migs, but the flak was sure to be heavy. He met Davis coming in from chow and together they walked into the room. It was already filled with other men, bantering with each other to release the tension that precedes a mission. Vic pulled his gear out of the locker and began to slowly dress. There always seemed to be too much lag time before they went out to their ships. He looked around the room at the other officers preparing for battle and watched their preoccupation with the tools of their trade. He wondered if they were thinking the same things he was.

"Think the Migs will be up?" Davis asked.

"Not for a reccy, especially not near Laos."

"Well, you're probably right. We've seldom seen them up this early anyway."

They continued to dress without further speech. He thought of the peasant girl, Mai Lien — her softness still lingered in his quarters. She was sure a pretty little thing. He strapped on his "38."

"Say, Drill, what do you think of that girl who cleans our room?"

"Haven't given her much thought. Does she say anything to you?"

"She's awfully quiet but she does say 'hello' when I notice her. Wonder why she waits at the gate for us after a mission?"

"Oh, come on, Vic. Are you blind?" He stepped into his g suit.

"She does command a kind of calmness doesn't she?"

"What do you mean, calmness?"

"She just strikes me as a symbol of sensibility in this otherwise inane war."

Drill looked at Vic strangely. "Symbol of sensibility in this otherwise inane war?"

It was time to go. They all walked out together, a slate gray half-light greeting them as they funneled out the door into the dawn. A clammy breeze drifted across the field refusing to give any refreshment. The Phantoms parked along the runway were cast in a pale light giving them a deadly, ghost-like appearance. Shirtless ground crewmen were making last minute inspections and ordnance personnel were fitting the last missiles into the wells and on wing pylons. Each aircraft commander and his WSO found their ship and clambered up the ladders into their cockpits. Open plexiglass canopies jutted skyward to allow entry.

Vic reached his aircraft and slowly walked around it, inspecting the exterior. Satisfied that everything was in order, he climbed aboard and let himself down into the confined pilot's station. Every bit of space was functional. Nothing wasted, a maze of instruments, switches, levers, and handles surrounding him within easy arm's reach. He began connecting himself to the Phantom, feeling the familiar uplifting transformation from ordinary man to dangerous cyborg. He joined himself to the armored seat, fastening the harness and inertia reel to his body. Slipping into his helmet, he fitted his oxygen mask to his face and plugged into the aircraft's life support and communications systems. Then he began a methodical and lengthy preflight cockpit check—radar . . . ECM . . . oxygen . . . armament . . . flight controls . . .

The sky had turned pallid and a few stars remained suspended in the fallow light, winking down at the scenario below. Vic inhaled a heavy dose of salt air through his nose, its biting fragrance clearing his head of any drowsiness that may have remained from the short night's sleep. Fully alert now and eager to begin the mission, he glanced down the line at the quiet F-4s. Squatting there in their green and brown combat camouflage, they reminded him of long nosed crocodiles silently poised for attack. He looked at his watch. 5 a.m.

"Dallas leader to Dallas two," he called to Davis, beginning his radio check on each aircraft.

"Dallas two. Roger," Davis signaled.

"Dallas three. Check." Pellegrini was ready.

"Dallas four. Okay." Patterson acknowledged.

"Dallas leader to Dallas flight, start engines."

One by one each commander fired up his two power plants, producing a deafening blast of energy. A tail of white hot flame erupted from the sleeping reptiles, awakening them from their slumber to become devouring predators once again. Slowly, the giants crawled out of their sandbagged dens and followed their leader single file, bellies low, to begin their search for early morning prey.

Coming up on line in elements of two, the pilots throttled up to full RPM, released their brakes, and rolled down the runway together, rapidly gaining speed, rudders flicking from side to side. Airborne, the foursome joined up and rendezvoused with the two reconnaissance ships.

Once again they had defied the laws of gravity and slipped the surly bonds of earth. Far below, the land remained dark in stark contrast to the blueing light in which they climbed, higher and higher, reaching for the tails of the sun, toying with the fringes of space. Through billows of cottony clouds they ascended, four metallic brothers riding fire into the heavens, traveling north, always north. Powerful hunters stalking their prey, knights in quest of adventure.

On they flew, floating on seas of air over a continent of antiquity where once only tigers and elephants ruled and where civilizations flourished and mysteriously disappeared, lost in history. Hue, the ancient capital of Vietnam and the River of Perfumes passed below them. Then Dong Hoi, Ha Tinh, and Vinh. Deeper into North Vietnam they penetrated. The danger increased with every passing mile as they neared the edge of the SAM rings that every pilot knew so well. Conversation was noticably absent. Nerves tightened, eyes probed and heads swiveled. "See them before they see you" was the first truth of the fighter pilot. They sailed ahead, buoyed up by oceans of atmosphere, high and alone, now bathed in the full light of the early morning sun.

Below, darkness had faded into sunshine and long shadows were cast along the ridges. The people of the earth rose from their slumber and looked up to watch the people of the sky pass over. The land came awake and so did the war. Silent black puffs began to appear above Vic. Then a few off to the left blossomed, and three or four below as the gunners felt for the range of the intruders.

Vic had positioned the two camera ships below and between his two elements. Now as the target loomed ahead and they began their run on the North Vietnamese missile sites, he pulled his flight into a weaving covering pattern behind the recon Phantoms, watching the ground intently for SAM launches and eyeballing the sky for Migs.

They were well into the target area flying at 425 knots and holding their escort position at 10,000 feet when suddenly the ground control intercept operator came on the air.

"Dallas one this Red Crown. I have two bandits bearing two seven zero, Bullseye sixty-one. Do you copy?"

"Dallas one, Roger Red Crown. What is their altitude?"

"Red Crown, bandits are in the dark, turning now to two seven five, Bullseye sixty-three."

The two Migs were flying a predictable intercept pattern on Vic's reccy flight. The communist GCI had pulled the "21's" out of Kep for a supersonic pass high over Hanoi, then sent them to the deck to make a run on the Phantoms from below and behind. It was an effective tactic, and without warning, devastating. But Red Crown had been able to track the bandits remarkably well "in the dark", at lower elevations where ground clutter masked the Migs from the radar, and Vic was ready for them.

The Migs were now sixty-three miles west of Hanoi, Bullseye, and closing fast. Vic ordered Dallas flight to punch off their fuel tanks and to watch their six o'clock closely. They continued their weave behind the camera ships, straining their necks to pick up the first glimpse of the approaching Migs.

"Red Crown, bandits two nine zero, Bullseye sixty-five."

"Red Crown, bandits low, now heading three two five."

"Bandits now angels five, three five zero, Bullseye sixty-eight."

"Red Crown, you should have visual contact Dallas leader."

Vic had followed Red Crown's data closely, timing the Mig's approach carefully. The North Vietnamese aircraft had made a near ninety degree turn and were at this moment climbing through five thousand feet at over Mach 1 in an attempt to sneak up on the flight from the rear. Vic split his two elements into a wide battle formation, keeping the two recon ships, now beginning their camera runs, in view ahead.

Instantly the air waves came alive!

"Dallas three and four, we have a Mig at our six o'clock! Break right *now!*"

Vic on the right of Pellegrini's element, and hearing his call, looked back over his left wing and saw a "21" rolling in on the two Phantoms. The Mig was about three quarters of a mile behind and pulling his ATOLs around for a shot when three and four made their break. Vic's instincts took command. Suddenly he was filled with wild aggression. His mind zinged ahead. He plunged into the fight, consumed with the determination to get the Mig.

Calling the Mig to his wingman, Davis, he hauled back on the stick and went to full afterburner. The F-4 now light and fast without its external fuel tanks, leaped into the vertical. Vic pulled the jet through the apex of its climb, rolled over the top, trying to scissors the Mig.

"You're clear, you're clear!" Davis shouted, keeping his leader protected.

Vic, rolling over the top, could see the Mig trying to

pull into Pellegrini's element. But they had too much angle off on him so the "21" reversed and tried to jockey around into Vic and Davis. However, they were too far above him now and he had lost his chance. The communist, deciding to break off the engagement, dove for home.

Vic continued on through the roll and came out behind and below the Mig, going supersonic. As he closed into position behind the "21", he called Pellegrini.

"Dallas one is padlocked."

"Roger, Dallas one. Am reversing."

"Clear me, number two," he called to Davis.

"You're clear."

Vic was worried. Red Crown had identified two Migs attacking and the second one hadn't appeared yet.

"Have you visual on bandit number two?" Vic asked.

"Negative," Davis answered.

"He's around here somewhere. Keep a sharp watch."

The Mig rolled right looking for the Americans, and spotted Vic. The Mig flier lit his afterburner and climbed straight up. Vic went up right behind him.

"This is Dallas four. I have a Mig at twelve o'clock high and starting a pass on lead element," Patterson warned, identifying the arrival of the second Mig 21.

"Do you have him, number two?" Vic asked his wingman.

"Roger. He's moving to eleven o'clock."

Still climbing after his Mig, Vic rolled, looking for the second Mig.

"Keep me clear, Davis. I'm padlocked."

"Roger."

The long hours he had spent training his flight were paying off. Working as a team, Vic had maneuvered his aircraft skillfully to thwart the enemy's attack. And now he was about to turn the tables on them. He had the advantage on the lead Mig and Davis was in good position to take on the wingman.

Continuing in the vertical the Mig began a 360 degree roll to the right, trying to get Vic to overshoot ahead of him. Vic counter-rolled, ending up at the Mig's blind deep six. He was well hidden from the Mig pilot's view. Both jets rolled out the top with Vic below and behind the communist. Obviously perplexed, the Mig pilot rocked his ship back and forth, attempting to locate the Phantom.

Meanwhile, Davis was becoming very much occupied with Mig number two. Vic had rolled out in time to see his wingman breaking hard into the Mig as it started to pull its nose around into firing position. Making a feint at continuing its pass into Vic, the Mig broke, then split between the two F-4 elements with Davis diving and turning hard after him.

Relieved of the threat from the Mig wingman, Vic bore in on the leader. Concentrating on the final phase of attack, he pulled the nose of the Phantom up on the Mig and placed his radar in boresight mode. Vic flipped the "Auto Acc" switch. The deadly radar strobed ahead to the enemy aircraft.

"You have full system lock on," Balinger said in the rear cockpit.

There was a moment's pause.

"You're cleared to fire. He's all yours, sir."

Vic pulled the Phantom's nose ahead a little to give the missiles some lead and touched the trigger two times. A pair of hulking AIM-7 air-to-air missiles fell out of the fuselage wells and a second later the rocket engines ignited, accelerating the projectiles ahead of the F-4. The two Sparrows, traveling at Mach 3 and leaving a great wake of white smoke sweeping behind, scented the enemy's trail and began stalking the Mig, guiding on a point ahead of the aircraft's flight path.

"They're pulling too much lead. Too much lead!" Vic moaned.

"No, the lead's good. It's good!" Balinger cried.

Too much lead! They're going to miss. Were going to get a miss. In front."

"No! No! We've got a good track."

The first missile slammed into the Mig's wing root sending a violent shudder through its vitals. Smoke and fuel streamed behind the mortally wounded enemy. The second missile hit the tail causing a brilliant explosion. The Mig nosed up, convulsing in its death throes, then lurched over in a long spiral earthward, trailing huge plumes of black smoke and burning furiously. Vic rolled his ship inverted and watched the Mig plummed down, down, until it merged with its shadow, silently bursting its innards on the open plain far below. A rising column of smoke marked its grave.

"I didn't see the pilot punch out. Did he get out?" Vic asked.

"Didn't see him go," Balinger answered.

"He was a good flier, better than the others."

"Yeh, he was good."

"Maybe too good."

"He didn't get out. Right?"

"Right, sir. He was good though."

"Dallas one, this is Dallas three. Good show. Congratulations." It was Pellegrini.

"Thanks, three. Where are you?"

"Off to your left, right below you."

Vic rolled out and began looking for the rest of Dallas flight. Far below, right on the deck and following the river, was a lone Mig being chased by three Phantoms, one out front and two trailing closely behind. A plume of smoke arched out ahead of the lead F-4. The Mig made a right turn, the smoke followed. The Mig reversed. The smoke closed. The Mig reversed again. The smoke caught up with the Mig. There was a brief delay, then a fireball erupted where the missile and Mig came together.

"Splash. I got him! I got him!" Davis was jubilant.

"Did you see him go in?" he asked.

"Right, he went right in," Pellegrini confirmed.

"Nice going, yeh he went in. I saw it," Patterson acknowledged.

"Good splash. You got him," Vic put in.

The recon planes had completed their photographing of the target and were now on a reciprocal heading. Vic and the others caught up with them and together they egressed the target area. Everyone was excited with their success and it was difficult for Vic to maintain radio discipline. The flak started up again and a few SAM sightings were called, bringing them back to the alert.

They headed out to sea, over the Gulf of Tonkin, and filled their fuel tanks. It was still early in the morning and the sun was low in the sky off their left wing as they cruised back to Da Nang. The sky was an intense blue and the large bulging cumulus cloud formations continued to build off to the west, deep in the interior. No one talked. An ethereal quietness moved between the ships as the returning conquerers slipped through space, titans of the heavens, sojourners among the Gods.

Vic was happy, proud. Not just for himself but for his men as well. After only twenty-five missions his flight had three Migs, two of them his. It was team work and good flying. He would continue to teach them, perfecting their skills. Alone they were vulnerable. Together, invincible. They would get more Migs.

CHAPTER FIVE

It was now seldom that Vic returned from a mission that the girl was not waiting by the security gate. He soon came to expect seeing her familiar figure shyly waving to him, looking frail and frightened. To his consternation he found that a sense of disappointment crept over him when she wasn't there. She always greeted him with respect and polite reserve, bowing slightly, head down, two tiny hands clutched together, and addressing him formally as Major Benedetti when he approached. This amused him. Her bright smile and shining eyes let him know that she was relieved that he had returned safely and that she had more than a casual interest in him. He stiffened at the thought.

Vic was cautious of her uncommon femininity. It dismayed him. He was used to American women, their large features, tall angular bodies, their aggressiveness and expressive behavior. He had no difficulty approaching them. But Vietnamese women were shy and much smaller, and had more delicate features. They made him aware of his coarseness and obtrusive direct approach. They were soft-spoken in contrast to his brusqueness.

The young woman commanded respect and she generated feelings in him that were new and confusing. It seemed incongruous that this peasant girl, so unsophisticated in worldly ways and whose background was so different than his own, could capture his attention. Disturbing.

But even though Vic was uneasy with the girl's attention, she had held his interest and as the days passed he grew more curious about her. The time came that he knew he must see more of her. So one afternoon finding her waiting by the gate looking fresh and pretty in a green and white *ao dai*, and wearing her wide conical peasant hat to shade her delicate skin, he decided that it was time to become better acquainted with Mai Lien.

"Good afternoon, Major Benedetti. I happy you come back safely," Mai Lien said in her practiced English. "You safe home now."

"Yes, Mai Lien. I got back again. Safe home."

"You see Mig today, Major?"

She smiled prettily. She was always smiling, Vic thought.

"No Mig," he said, finding that he had fallen into the habit of simplifying his sentences to accommodate her.

"Why no Mig, Major?"

"They're afraid of me, Mai Lien," he said with a grin.

72

Mai Lien smiled again, showing her even white teeth blending with the natural pinkness of her small full lips. She looked at the tarmac under her feet, waiting for Vic to continue. With a shake of her head she tossed her waist length hair over her shoulders. Her hair reminded him of black silk. He wanted to touch it.

"Mai Lien, would you like to go for a walk with me tomorrow and maybe . . ."

"Oh, yes, Major," she said excitedly, before he could finish. "I love to. I like walk with you. I talk to my grandmother."

"Will your grandmother object?"

"What please? I no understand," she said.

"Object. You know. Okay? Grandmother say okay?"

"Yes, yes. Grandmother say okay. She likes you. I tell her about you much. She say okay, for sure, Major. She say okay."

"Good. You have made me very happy, Mai Lien."

"You good man, Major. I like make you happy."

Vic looked away, brushing his loose hair with his hand, feeling unworthy and a bit ill at ease with Mai Lien's openness.

"We pray for you much. Grandmother and me, we pray for you every night before go sleep."

"You do?" Vic said with surprise, his brown eyes growing large.

"I pray in morning when you go on mission, too," she said, eyes glued to the black tarmac, her feet shifting nervously under her *ao dai*.

Vic cocked an eye at her, the beginning of a frown

growing on his brow.

"You pray, major?"

The question caught him completely off-guard. "Well, I haven't for some time . . . I don't remember the last time . . . Look, Mai Lien, this conversation . . ."

"You Christian man, major?"

"I suppose so . . ."

"You no Buddist?"

"Not Buddhist, no not me."

"Many Buddhist my country. Buddhist no know Jesus."

"No, they don't know Jesus."

"They pray Buddha, right, major?"

"Right, they pray to their Buddha." He was feeling very uncomfortable with the conversation. "Say, Mai Lien . . ."

"Buddhist no know Jesus, no pray Jesus."

"Right."

"You know Jesus, major?"

Vic felt the blood rush to his face with embarrassment.

"You will like my grandmother. She my mother too."

"Your mother too?"

"Yes. She my grandmother and mother."

"But how can that be, Mai Lien? *Ma? Ba ngoai?* Both?"

"Yes. *Ma* and *ba ngoai*. Because of war. You know."

He didn't know, but later he would find out, perhaps.

"*Ngai mai toi gap Mai Lien o nha phai khong?*"

74

he asked.

"Yes. You come my house tomorrow. We walk. *Ngai mai*. Tomorrow. *Ong muon an nha toi khong?* You like?" she asked him, slipping back and forth into Vietnamese and English in her charming style.

"*Toi muon co.* I would like that. Yes, I will eat at your house."

"I like too. I cook good food for you. Then we walk. Okay?"

"Okay, Mai Lien. I will eat your good food. Then we *di bo.*"

She clapped her hands happily.

The next afternoon Vic borrowed a jeep and following Mai Lien's directions, set out for her home. The sun was beginning its descent from its high point overhead and long shadows began to fall on the landscape. He passed through the main gate, the guards saluting him as he went by. He returned their salute, turned left on the main road and headed north through secured area. He was light with anticipation of a new experience and was eagerly looking forward to seeing the country under more natural conditions. The base and its interferences had a way of distorting the true image of Vietnam and the Vietnamese.

After a few miles driving the main highway, Vic turned the jeep onto a dirt road that wound through rice country and then straightened out to follow line after line of tall coconut palms. At a bend in the road, he pulled off to allow a slow moving ARVN convoy to pass. A short distance beyond he passed through a group of small houses where the road split. Continuing to follow Mai Lien's directions, he took the right track and proceeded through hill country. Breaking over the crest of a ridge, a most remarkable sight met him. Situated far below in a wide depression, bisected by a wandering river, and surrounded by profuse green vegetation checkered with rice paddies, was a small sleepy hamlet lying in the middle of the most pristine valley Vic had ever seen. It was inspiring. He parked the jeep and sat for a few moments taking in the spiritual quality of the scene spread before him. The war seemed ages away. He paused a few moments longer allowing the pastoral impressions to permeate his memory. He wanted it to last, to become permanent, to recall it again whenever he wanted to. Timeless valley. Pure and uncorrupted. A new dimension of Mai Lien began to take form inside Vic. He started the jeep and followed the track down into a hollow of bamboo thickets and then descended to the floor of the valley where the track widened into a road again.

The butterflies laughed with him and the good old earth sang its ageless chorus, rejoicing in plenty. Echoes of joyful music, sighs of mirth from the sweetened vine. Weep no more Vietnam. Your trouble has been long enough. Rejoice! The rice is in full measure. Does it grieve? Rejoice! Be glad with the sweet vine. Drink no more the bitterness of neglected pleasures. Eat, for the hills are unto harvest and there is room for laughing butterflies. No more travel the crying roads of pain. The lotus is in blossom.

The road followed the course of the river and then swung away for a few yards before passing through a plantation of mangos, bananas, breadfruit, and giant papaya. Coming out the other side of the plantation the road curved back toward the river and ran between individual plots of large perfectly round watermelons and row upon row of a variety of leafy green vegetables, all of which were strange to him. Beyond the vegetable farms were the rice fields and the hamlet proper.

Coming upon the scattered houses, Vic noticed Mai Lien's little blue 50 cc Honda parked in front of one of the homes set back from the river and on the edge of a grove of bananas. Large tamarind trees and tall bamboo shaded the yard. The house was constructed from bricks made from mud mixed with rice straw. It had several windows that were covered with wooden shutters, most of which remained open to allow free circulation of air. A heavy, planked front door hung from handmade metal hinges. The roof, made from layers of palm thatch, sloped toward the front of the house and terminated in an overhang of several feet of porch.

Vic pulled up in front and sat for a few seconds studying the house and its surroundings. A mixed group of ducks and geese waddled into view around the corner of the house. A family led their water buffalos home along the tree-shaded road. A strong sense of home, family, tradition, and love enveloped Vic and he felt the tension of months of war begin to drain away.

He hadn't noticed that Mai Lien was standing beside him. She had silently watched him lost in his thoughts and she wisely remained quiet until he had broken his own reverie. Vic looked at her without speaking. She read the peace in his eyes and understood.

"Hello, Major. *Chao ong*."

"*Chao*, Mai Lien."

"I glad you here now. Grandmother very excited. Me too."

He looked down into her happy eyes. Those lovely Asian eyes.

"What a beautiful place to live, Mai Lien."

"You like our valley, Major?"

"I love it. It's so peaceful."

"Yes, very peaceful. No war. No Viet Cong."

"No Viet Cong?" he asked, surprised.

"Sometimes at night. No Viet Cong day. No trouble. No soldier, very peaceful."

"*Moi ong vo nha choi*. Please come into our humble house and relax, Major," Mai Lien said, combining Vietnamese with English translation in her usual picturesque manner, and motioning to the open door with her hand. "We talk inside."

Mai Lien led the way through the door. They entered into one large room with a low ceiling and clay brick walls. The thatched palm ceiling was supported by several long roughly hewn teak beams set across the width of the house. The floor was red clay worked smooth and gave the appearance of manufactured tile.

"Please sit down," Mai Lien said. "I get grandmother." She disappeared into an adjoining room.

Vic was surprised by the size and comfort of the house, and by the quality of furnishings. The chairs and tables were built from black teak and jungle mahogany, some of which appeared to be Japanese in design and expertly crafted. What looked like a Japanese officer's sword hung in a prominent place on the wall. A religious altar stood at the far end of the room displaying objects of worship, not of Buddha, but of Christ.

A beautiful, small and ageless lady wearing long, bright green jade earrings, jade bracelets, and purple black *ao dai* appeared unexpectedly in front of Vic. Her long hair was rolled neatly on top of her head and held securely with a large comb. Her face was soft and smooth, almost timeless. Vic could see no blemishes. Only wisdom and experience spoken in her eyes betrayed her many years. Vic was captivated. He couldn't take his eyes from her. Here was Mai Lien in the twilight of her years. The resemblance was startling.

"Cam on Thieu-ta Benedetti den tam toi." Grandmother could speak no English.

"Grandmother thank you for coming visit her," Mai Lien said, translating.

"Tell her that I think she is beautiful, Mai Lien."

"Ong noi ba ngoai dep lam," Mai Lien told her grandmother.

Grandmother smiled at Vic and bowed her head slightly.

The three of them sat for a time conversing in this manner, Mai Lien translating for her grandmother and for Vic when his limited Vietnamese failed him. It amazed him that he felt so at home here, as if he belonged with these people. Maybe there was a genetic connection between his Italian ancestral lineage with that of the Far East, possibly through early travelers as recent as Marco Polo or as far back as Neolithic nomads. Mai Lien brought Vic and grandmother a misty colored drink.

"What is this?" he asked.

"Vietnamese gin. Grandmother make."

He tried it. It tasted something like saki. More Japanese influence—the furniture, the Samurai sword, and now the saki, he puzzled.

"Mai Lien, is that a Japanese sword hanging on the wall?"

"Yes, Belong my father. He Japanese officer. Major, like you."

"Your father was Japanese?"

"Yes, he Japanese officer, major like you," she said again, proudly.

"Where is he now?"

Mai Lien hesitated momentarily then turned to her grandmother, speaking to her in low tones. The lady's wise eyes grew distant in memory. Mai Lien turned back to Vic.

"Long time ago, big war. Japanese army come my country and my father marry my mother, Vietnamese girl. They live maybe one, two year together, then war end and Americans send my father back Japan."

"That must have been when Japan surrendered to the U.S. at the end of World War Two," Vic said.

"I born next year. Never see my father. No picture either. He only leave his sword for me," she said, pointing to the wall.

Mai Lien was speaking softly. Her head hung forward, long black tresses falling onto her hands, palms folded upward on her lap. Tear stains began to spread on her pretty *ao dai* as she recounted the story of the father she never knew. Vic felt awkward. Every girl wants a father. Mai Lien didn't even have a memory, only a story told to her by others. Grandmother placed a tender hand on Mai Lien's head, stroking her hair.

Mai Lien finished her story and dried her tears. "I sorry. No should cry."

"You cry if you want. Sometimes it's good if you cry. I wish I could cry sometimes too."

"You feel like cry too?" she asked, looking at him with widened eyes.

"Sometimes."

"If you cry with me I no care, even man no supposed to cry."

No, she wouldn't care, he thought to himself, looking at the honesty in her tear-stained face. Her eyes held him, all watery with dew. Vic stood at the divergence of two roads, sorry that he could not travel both. He recalled a stanza from Lin Wu:

When the women are young
    and the rice is green
The pangs of sorrow
    are not what they seem

"*Pho*," she remarked, suddenly bright and cheerful again. She pointed a small finger to the table on the opposite side of the room. Mai Lien moved lightly with short steps across the floor to where a steaming pot of hearty soup rested giving off a delicious aroma. Her eyes met his briefly, asking per-

81

mission to serve him. He nodded and she quickly set to work arranging the bowls, chopsticks, spoons, and chairs. She uncovered a plate of steaming rice and poured hot tea into cups that had no handles. A dish of green leafy Vietnamese vegetables, lemon slices, tiny green peppers, and a bottle of the inevitable *nuoc mam* also emerged. He was amazed at how fast and mysteriously all this food appeared and the manner in which the meal was so efficiently and attractively presented.

She motioned for him to sit, then she ladled the *pho* into his bowl. She chose a few vegetables from the plate and delicately picked the small leaves from their stems. She dropped the leaves into his soup and then squeezed the juice of a fresh lemon slice into it. Finally she spooned in the *nuoc mam*, added a few peppers, and evenly stirred the mixture together. She placed chopsticks in his right hand and a large porcelain spoon in his left, demonstrating with her own soup that he should use the chopsticks to eat the thin slices of pork, the long rice noodles, and the vegetables, and the broth he should eat with the spoon. Done properly, the spoon followed closely behind the chopsticks.

Her face beamed with pleasure as he settled down, with obvious satisfaction, to consuming the food she had prepared for him. She ate without talking, closely studying him through her almond eyes and now and then using her long fingers to brush strands of black hair from her face.

"You like?" she asked, pointing to the soup.

"I like," he responded, filling his mouth with more rice noodles.

"This North Vietnamese soup," she said, with a coy grin.

"North Vietnamese?" he said, surprised. "Don't you feel strange eating the enemy's food?"

"No. We all one country one time. South Vietnamese peoples eat North style all time. They eat like us too. My grandmother born North Vietnam. My mother too. They run away communists, Ho Chi Minh. Come South Vietnam many years."

Well, he had a great deal more to learn about the people of Vietnam. He had taken much for granted. Mai Lien was slowly opening his eyes to a number of things. Grandmother smiled at him across the table.

"You know, Mai Lien, most GIs don't know very much about your country, your people."

"GI fight Viet Cong, NVA. No time for learn people," she said.

"I suppose you're right. Most GIs don't care one way or another. They just want to go home as soon as they can."

Mai Lien remained silent, letting Vic talk, even though she had strong ideas concerning American-Vietnamese relations.

"I just wish every American coming to Vietnam could spend some time in a Vietnamese home like I have with you today. But of course that's impossible. Even so, it couldn't but help build understanding and confidence in what the U.S. and South Vietnam are trying to do together in this war."

"Yes, I think so. But very difficult. No speak language together and Vietnamese peoples no trust

American. American no trust Vietnamese. Maybe you, I, grandmother, we start something here today," she said laughing, pointing to the three of them.

"You like my soup?" she asked again.

"Never had better."

"*Nuoc mam* okay?"

"Strong flavor." He wrinkled his nose.

"I know. American no like. Too strong. But you like, yes?"

"I like it," he lied.

They finished their dinner and Mai Lien and her grandmother cleared the table while Vic remained sitting, at their insistence, and sipped a small glass of the homemade gin. Mai Lien placed the dirty dishes on a high table outside and proceeded to wash them in a large basin filled with water she had drawn from the well and had boiled on the charcoal stove.

"We go walk now, Major?" Mai Lien asked, finishing the dishes and drying her hands as she came back into the house. She poured herself some green tea.

"Yes, Mai Lien. Would your grandmother like to walk with us?" Vic asked, knowing that he would have to gain grandmother's confidence before Mai Lien would be allowed in his company alone. Also, for his own protection, it would be best that a long standing and respected member of the village like grandmother accompany him and Mai Lien. An American seen alone with a Vietnamese girl was not likely to be looked upon favorably, at least not until the villagers got used to him. Also, if any Viet Cong lurked in the area they were not apt to harm him, knowing he was grandmother's friend. The VC seldom risked drawing unfavorable attention to themselves when it came to their relations with the country people. For they wisely understood that whoever won the support and cooperation of the peasantry would win the war. Something that the South Vietnamese government and U.S. had bungled time and again.

"Yes, grandmother like come."

The sun was low in the valley, its rays filtering through the banyan and bamboo, causing reflected forest images to dance on the green waters. Mai Lien, Vic, and *ba ngoai* strolled together along the banks of the little river, enjoying the serenity.

"How long have you lived here, Mai Lien?" Vic asked.

"I born in this valley. I live here twenty-five year now."

"You are twenty-five years old?"

"Yes."

"You look only eighteen or so, Mai Lien," Vic said, remembering grandmother's youthful look. It was apparent that Vietnamese women aged well.

"We eat plenty vegetables and fruit. Good for skin and health. Too much meat no good."

She was probably right, Vic thought, as she had been on many points that he initially thought primitive and superstitious, but later upon closer examination proved legitimate. After all, being a practical people, hadn't her ancestors been testing these ideas and remedies for centuries, refining and selecting the most useful and discarding the unworkable and ineffective. Most modern medicines are traceable to common origins anyway, mostly plants.

Mai Lien stopped walking and looked pensively at the river, then toward the mountains in the distance. "River like woman. Gentle, beautiful. Also weak. Need protection. Often change mind, change path. Mountain like man. Protect woman. Strong, tall. Mountain make shelter for river, bring water, make road for river."

She then pointed to a house. "Woman is foundation for home. She hold home together. Make babies. Take care family. Give love. Support man. Man is roof. He protect foundation, keep family safe and strong. Without roof, foundation wash away. Without foundation, roof no stand up. Need each other. Yes?"

"I've never heard the principle of marriage described so well, Mai Lien. Simple, yet beautiful. You have a remarkable way of cutting away the underbrush and getting to the heart of the matter."

"What you mean? I no understand."

Vic smiled. "You speak the truth. Very wise. You make me understand. I agree, yes," he said, nodding his head.

She looked at him apologetically with her lovely sloe eyes.

"I go back school. Learn more English so I understand you better."

"No," he said. "I will go to school to learn Vietnamese better."

"You no have time. Major must fly Phantom. Fight communists. I will teach you when you come visit grandmother and me. Okay?"

"Okay. You teach me. I teach you. We no go school. Number one."

They both laughed together at this. Grandmother looked at them quizzically.

The three of them continued to walk along the river path for a while longer, then they moved onto the road, passing by houses with families sitting out front looking curiously on and nodding to *ba ngoai* and Mai Lien as they walked by. A few friendly smiles greeted Vic.

Coming to the outskirts of the village, they arrived at what was once a magnificent villa. Obviously built by the French during their rule, but now in disrepair and being taken over by the jungle, it was only a shadow of its original beautiful design. The old place reeked with intrigue.

Vic was fascinated. "What is this?" he asked.

"This where my father and mother live before I born," Mai Lien said proudly. "My father he big boss. Commander, Japanese Army in Da Nang."

"Big boss, big house," Vic said. He was still reluctant to ask about Mai Lien's mother.

She read the curiosity in his eyes. "My mother live Saigon now."

"Saigon?"

"Yes. With my brothers and sisters."

"Oh," he said, surprised.

"After father go back Japan, we very poor. Mother cannot take care me. She go Saigon to work. Leave me with grandmother."

Vic said nothing, afraid that he might bring on more tears. But Mai Lien went on.

87

"I see my mother very little now. Only when I go Saigon. Maybe once a year."

"Do you miss her?"

"Yes I miss."

From where they stood on a small knoll, they had an expansive view overlooking the valley. Mai Lien's home could be seen at the far end of the valley and grandmother was pointing out the individual homes and farm plots of friends and relatives. The air was heavy with the scent of mangos and bananas, and Vic breathed deep of the valley's fragrance. It was delightful here, a place of rest, a refuge from the disturbances of war. He would come here often to gather strength for the difficult times ahead.

The sun was setting, and extending dark shadows covered the hollow between the hills and mountains as they followed the road back. They walked in silence, feeling no obligation to talk. Vic noticed that Mai Lien was perfectly at ease with him. Twice on the way back to the house she had softly touched his arm with her gentle fingers, curiously examining him, as a child would, to see if he was real. When he turned toward her she said nothing, but her eyes spoke volumes. He felt that he could walk by her side for hours and never know the passage of time.

Too soon they had arrived at the house. It was time to say goodbye. Grandmother discreetly walked into the house leaving Mai Lien and her major alone.

"Mai Lien."

"Yes, Major Benedetti," she answered, cocking her head slightly and looking up at him. She toyed with a bamboo leaf in her palm.

"This has been the most enjoyable afternoon I have ever spent, and . . . I . . . well . . ." He stopped.

"Yes," she said, encouraging him to go on.

But his loneliness was overpowering and he just stood, unable to speak, drinking in her loveliness, thirsting for her like a lost soul in a parched and desolate land. He wanted to take her into his arms, press her close to him, smell her hair and soft skin, swim in her natural fragrance.

"Mai Lien . . . I would . . . I would like to come back again."

Imperceptibly her little hand reached out and softly closed around his fingers. Her heart began beating so rapidly that she thought it would leap from her chest. She delicately stroked the back of his hand, keeping her eyes shyly averted toward the ground at her feet.

The last rays of sunlight began dropping behind the hills and a hush fell like a blanket on the gentle valley. The curfew hour would soon be upon them, and the air grew heavy with danger, for the night belonged to the Viet Cong. Vic climbed into his jeep, still holding the bamboo pipe grandmother had given him as a token of her appreciation for his visit. He packed it with the strong black tobacco and lit up, drawing a few cautious puffs. I've tasted worse, he mused. He started the motor and headed back to Da Nang, trying to remember who it was that had said, "Watch out for those VN women. They're all milky sweet on top and vinegar sour underneath."

He drove slowly, soberly thinking of his visit. Enough light remained to see the variegated countryside veiled in greens and golds. I wonder how old this bridge is? He carefully drove over the ancient narrow span. Will you look at that! He slowed to a crawl, admiring the young women kneeling along the grassy banks of the river, beating their laundry with bamboo poles. I wonder if they'd run away if I stopped? They sang together, their high voices ringing clear against the sharp crack of bamboo on wet cloth. The catchy primitive rhythm fused with the scent of aromatic berries from spice trees sifting through the evening vapor. The girls lifted their heads when they saw the long shadow of the jeep cross the gentle waters. He could see their pretty, healthy faces mirrored in the jade surface. They smiled peacefully at him, bringing an ache deep in his stomach. Must I go against the guns tomorrow? Can't I stay here? Can't I? Forever?

Along the dikes between the paddies, children carried long bundles of rice straw to their homes. Water buffalo followed, the smaller children riding the peaceful swaying brutes.

"You know Jesus, Major?" Her question wistfully lingered on the back-burner of his mind. Was there some connection?

CHAPTER SIX

Rrr, the little 50 cc engine purred, accelerating the blur Honda out of the main gate and into the stream of bicycles, Vespas, and cycles bunching together, carrying the workers home. Mai Lien carefully pulled the loose ends of her yellow flowered *ao dai* over her lap to prevent them from catching in the wheels, and looked back at the huge dust covered base crowded with miles of parked aircraft, vehicles, stacked supplies, and mountains of ordinance.

She was proud of her job working for the Americans. She had come a long way from her childhood desolation and felt that she had a right to feel good about herself. No longer did she have to suffer the nagging humiliation of being untouchably, wretchedly poor, though sometimes she still felt frightened knowing that the hunger demon never strayed far from her door.

She swung into the center of traffic and was quickly swept into the clangor and rushing activity of the busy city. Da Nang. The French playground of the East, the world had known it before the ravages of these years of ugly war. Mai Lien looked around at the mixture of French colonial and oriental architecture clashing with the growing number of modern buildings. She loved Da Nang. It was an exciting city and she was very much a part of it. Sometimes the war seemed far away. When a child, she was certain that the war would never come to Da Nang. No, not here. Da Nang was safe.

But the war had come to Da Nang. To all Vietnam. The rattle of automatic weapons in the streets and rice paddies, and the terrible sight of charred and bloated bodies lying in the gutters and floating in the rivers were still vivid in her memory. At night she would hide under the bed while rockets crashed around her, and grandmother wailed and prayed relentlessly that God would spare them. The eerie glow of parachute flares flickered through the open windows and ghostly images danced on the bare walls. The noise was frightening and the smell of war was thick in her nose.

Nothing had been so bad, though, as having to search for her uncle among the dead and dying. A VC had booby trapped a bicycle and uncle had been one of the bystanders when it detonated. He was alive when she found him and she cried and cried upon seeing his torn and bleeding body. They took him away, to the hospital. She never saw him again.

Mai Lien's pet kongi crawled off her shoulder and took his usual place standing on the gas tank with his forepaws stretched forward clutching the handlebars. The friendly squirrel-like animal looked quite human leaning ahead, big, round black eyes watching intelligently, face pushed into the wind. Uncle had found the furry creature, just a baby, lying in a teak tree he had cut down while lumbering in the Binh Duong jungle. He had brought the little thing home to her as a present and she had been so happy to be given something alive, warm, and cuddly. Through the years she had lovingly cared for the affectionate kongi and they had become good friends. She reached out and fondly scratched his head.

Mai Lien turned the Honda onto Nguyen Thi Avenue, the kongi looking for all purposes like he was steering the motorcycle, and she nearly collided with a dilapidated bus pulling out in front of her, loaded with passengers, ducks, green coconuts, and bicycles. Mai Lien hit the brakes and skidded sideways along the pavement. People hung out the windows gaping. An old man threw a papaya at her. She kick-started the stalled Honda back into life with her high heeled slipper and roared around the slow moving bus.

"Quee-roo!" screeched the kongi, showing his indignation, drumming his little hind feet on the metal gas tank and nervously flicking his long bushy tail back and forth.

She zoomed down the narrow street weaving through traffic, past the open air markets, bicycle repair shops and sidewalk hawkers. At Ham Do Street she slowed to let three time-worn old ladies pass carrying overloaded baskets of yellow-red mangos and stalks of golden bananas hanging from bamboo poles bent over their shoulders.

"Xoai gia bao nhieu?" How much for the mangos? she shouted over the roar of traffic to the last woman.

"Tram dong ba trai," one-hundred piasters for three, she said, awkwardly turning under her heavy load to see where the question was coming from.

"Mac qua!" Too much!

"Sau chuc," Okay, sixty piasters.

Mai Lien reached into the leather handtooled Thai handbag dangling from her shoulder and pulled out one of the green Vietnamese fifty piaster bills and one blue ten, handing them to the woman. She chose three of the ripe fruit, dropped them into her purse and waved goodbye to a chorus of motorcycle horns and jingling bicycle bells. The kongi stomped his feet on the gas tank— "Quee-roo!"

She glanced at her watch "Hope Ngoc hasn't gone home yet," she said to the kongi, scratching his head again.

"Cheet! Cheet! Chrr."

Going a little too fast she banked around a corner and quickly reversed her turn into an alley. A pair of GIs in class "A" uniforms whistled their appreciation of her motorcycle handling skills. They stood rooted to the sidewalk, admiring the billows of black silky hair streaming behind her.

"Like wow, man! Did you see that?"

"Yeah, a real looker. Number one, huh."

Hearing their compliments, a pleasant glow passed over Mai Lien. She glanced around to see that no Vietnamese were watching, then hurriedly looked back at her admirers and smiled sweetly.

"Zowee! Sky-out. My day's complete," one of the soldiers said, dancing a jig.

Carefully threading her way through the press of scurrying, bundle carrying pedestrians, she puttered down the tight lane lined with swarms of stalls and small stores. She came to a stop in front of Ngoc's tailor shop and pulled the Honda's support stand down with her foot.

"Mai Lien! What a surprise," Ngoc said, seeing her good friend walk through the open door. She took the kongi from Mai Lien's shoulder, giving him an affectionate nuzzle with her nose. "Let me get us some tea and we can talk. So good to see you. I was just about to close up for the day." She took the *ao dai* she was working on from the sewing machine and spread it on the table in front of Mai Lien. "Isn't it beautiful?"

"I love the material," Mai Lien said, caressing the soft cloth with her hands.

"Thailand silk."

"Beautiful. Can I try it on?"

"Of course," Ngoc said, pointing to the ornate dressing screen. She disappeared into the back with the snug kongi nestled in the crook of her arm. "Mai Lien's here," she shouted to the family.

In a few seconds Ngoc's mother and father hurried out from the workroom followed by her five younger brothers and sisters walking behind in single file. Each took their turn greeting Mai Lien with a loving hug. The children bowed respectfully with folded arms across their chests.

"You're getting prettier everyday, Mai Lien,"

Ngoc's mother said, patting her cheek.

Mai Lien felt the blood rise in her face. She fidgeted with her jade bracelet. "Thank you, Mrs. Trong."

Ngoc returned carrying a tray filled with a tea pot, cups, and a dish of Chinese cookies. "I bought these fresh from Mr. Hai just this afternoon," she said proudly. "I know how fussy you are about food." The whole family laughed.

After a few minutes of polite conversation and family gossip, Ngoc's mother, sensing the girls' need to be alone for awhile, shooed the children off and pulled her fat husband from his chair. "Come, now, let's leave these two young ladies to their private matters. They have important things to discuss."

"Oh, you mustn't leave on my account, Mrs. Trong," Mai Lien protested.

"Hush, now. It's time I be getting home to making the rice, anyway. I can already hear the thunder," she said, pointing to her husband's stomach and smiling widely.

After hearing the back door close, Ngoc blurted out, "Have you seen him again, Mai Lien?"

"Yes, he came to dinner yesterday."

"Oh, I'm so excited," Ngoc exclaimed, grabbing Mai Lien's hand. "I think I'm more excited than you are about all this. Are you excited, Mai Lien?"

"Sure, I'm excited, but I'm also confused."

"Well, that's understandable. After all, he's a westerner. An American."

"Oh, that part doesn't bother me."

"It doesn't? I thought it would. So many Vietnamese despise the Americans."

"I don't. You know that, Ngoc."

"I know you don't, but others have their prejudices, and if they found out you were seeing an American . . . well, you may lose some friends."

"I haven't told anyone."

"Will you?"

"There's no need to at this point, is there? I mean, why should anyone know? Really."

"I suppose you're right. No need to get everyone excited until . . . well, you know. Do you think it can ever get serious? I mean, like marriage?" Ngoc suddenly put her hand over her mouth and looked around, feeling embarrassed.

Mai Lien laughed. "You know, I was so afraid of westerners when I was a child. The first one ı ever saw had blue eyes that looked like sea water. I thought he was a ghost."

"Really, Mai Lien?"

"And his long nose and blond hair made him even more strange and mysterious. I was so frightened that I started crying and ran into the house screaming for my grandmother. 'A ghost! I've seen a ghost, grandmother!' "

"What did your grandmother do?"

"Well, grandmother is very superstitious, you know."

"I know."

"And I think she believed me, seeing how frightened I was, at least until I pulled her outside to show her the 'ghost.' And then I learned that ghosts were westerners. This one a Frenchman."

Ngoc giggled, holding her hand modestly over her lips, looking typically Asian. She reached into the wicker basket and pulled the hand painted tea-pot from its insulated, quilted pillow bed. She touched the pot with her small hand. "More tea? Still very hot."

"Yes, please."

"Tell me, Mai Lien, what do you talk about with this American, Major Benedetti?"

"I tell him how I feel, my hopes and dreams. I try to explain the war. I talk about Vietnamese ways. And I ask him about America. His life there." She sipped her tea.

"I would like to go to America some day. Maybe to live," Ngoc said.

"Do you think you could leave your family and home so easily?"

"I don't know. Maybe not. How about you?"

"A Vietnamese girl goes where her husband goes," Mai Lien said stubbornly.

"But you don't have a husband," Ngoc said, tilting her head pertly, giggling again.

"If I had an American husband I would leave all that I have in Vietnam to be with him. That is, if I had an American husband," she said, looking shyly at Ngoc.

"Ahh," Ngoc murmured under her breath.

"What do you mean, ahh?"

"Nothing. Just that I sense something developing," Ngoc said with amusement.

"And what might that be?"

"Mai Lien, has he proposed to you?"

"Oh, Ngoc. Don't be silly. Of course he hasn't proposed. We are only friends. Besides, he wouldn't ever want to marry me."

"I'm not so sure about that. What's to prevent him?"

"Good sense, that's what."

"You don't think very highly of yourself," Ngoc said, taking a bite out of her cookie. "Don't you think you would make him a good wife? And don't you think you're pretty enough?"

"That's not the point."

"What is?"

"He's an American and American men marry American women. He's seeing me as a friend only, regardless of how good a wife I'd be or how pretty I am, or anything else."

"I'm not so sure about that either," Ngoc said.

"What do you mean?" Mai Lien looked surprised.

"He may have serious intentions. He probably already knows that we make good wives. Look at all the GIs and civilian workers that are marrying Vietnamese girls. He may just want to get to know you better."

"Ngoc! Do you think so? Do you think he might actually ask me to be his wife?" she said with excitement.

"It makes sense to me."

"But . . ." Mai Lien's face suddenly turned sad. "But there are many beautiful women in Vietnam. Maybe he won't want me." She looked like she might cry.

"Don't be foolish. Have you looked in the mirror lately? You have nothing to worry about, believe me."

"Oh, Ngoc. Do you really think so? I mean — really?"

"Of course. Did you give him a picture of yourself?"

"No!" Mai Lien's eyes widened in astonishment. "A picture?"

"Do you have any?"

"The ones you took of me at the fountain near the war memorial."

"They're okay. But let's go down the street and have a sexy one made by a professional photographer. There's one just a few shops from here."

"Won't that be too forward, to give him a picture of myself?" Mai Lien still looked amazed. "Vietnamese girls aren't supposed to be forward, grandmother keeps telling me," she said with upturned eyebrows.

"That was in your grandmother's day, when marriages were arranged."

"I think she is already arranging with someone."

"She is! With whom?" Ngoc said, dismayed.

"With Mrs. Ly."

"Oh, my God, Mai Lien," Ngoc said, covering her face with her hands. "Not Mrs. Ly's son!"

"I think so."

"Oh, you poor girl. That man's an imbecile. How do you know she's making an arrangement?"

"I overheard grandmother talking with Aunt Xuan when we were fishing in the canal last week."

"Do you still fish with your grandmother, Mai Lien? I thought you outgrew that."

"I love to fish. I'll never outgrow it. We caught six nice river eels like this," she said, indicating the size by patting her forearm.

"Well, anyway, what did you hear?"

"Grandmother was telling Aunty that Mrs. Ly's son was very intelligent and would someday become rich."

"He's an idiot. The only way he'll become wealthy is by inheriting his father's pharmaceutical business. He'd starve if it wasn't for his parents. But go on."

"I heard grandmother also say that Mrs. Ly has consulted a fortune teller and that the signs are favorable for a marriage between her son and me. Grandmother thinks that Mrs. Ly will send a family representative soon to see how she feels about the match."

"And she hasn't mentioned any of this to you?"

"No she hasn't. You know as well as I do, Ngoc, that the traditional way is not to let the children know until the preliminaries are completed."

"Well, there's no doubt about it, Mai Lien. Someday, Mrs. Ly's son will be a rich man, and based on that alone many Da Nang girls would like to marry into the family. But he's a fool. And you don't want a fool for a husband."

"I'll have to do what my grandmother says," Mai Lien said humbly, toying with her bracelet again.

"That would mean giving up Major Benedetti."

"I know." A tear trickled from the corner of her eye.

"Mai Lien. You're so . . . so . . . Oh, darn it, Mai Lien. You're so Vietnamese," Ngoc said, shaking her head.

"I can't help it. That's how I am. Besides, I'm proud of being a Vietnamese woman. You should

101

be too."

"I am, Mai Lien. I am. Don't be mad at me."

"I'm not mad, Ngoc. Just confused. I often think about this American, our growing relationship, and it seems so strange. And now with Mrs. Ly's son . . . and pleasing grandmother . . . and the war. I'm really very insecure."

"We all are, Mai Lien."

Ngoc put her arms around Mai Lien.

"I just want to do what's right. Do you think I'll make a good wife, Ngoc? Do you?"

"Yes, Mai Lien. You'll make a very good wife," Ngoc said, hugging her friend tighter. "It's all going to work out for you. You'll see."

Shadows began creeping across the red tiled floor and the two young women were soon clothed in the pallid glow of a magenta sunset.

It wasn't until the last vendor shuttered his shop and the lights winked on along the alley that Mai Lien, sitting knife straight on the Honda, the kongi facing into the wind, drove home to her village.

I waited too long—I can hardly see where I'm going—dare I turn on the light, Mai Lien groaned. She searched about uncertainly, feeling her way along the river road. The village is at least another ten kilometers. Whenever I visit with that girl I can't stop. Seems to be so much to talk about. She thought about turning the light on again. I should have watched the time. Oh, these ruts. Her hands automatically tightened on the handlebars, straightening the lurching motorcycle.

She talked to the kongi. "We'll be home soon. Grandmother will have rice and noodles for us and

I'll give you some sugar cane tonight."

The little mammal squirmed uneasily, trying to keep its balance on the bouncing Honda.

The night enveloped them. Only a few gray patches of light could be seen through the forest canopy. *It's getting so dark. I wish I was home.*

"Cheet, cheet." The little kongi was becoming more agitated.

"Are you frightened too, little friend?"

Then she heard it. A sound she had never forgotten. The hollow *"thunk"* of a mortar round hitting the tube. She broke out of the jungle cover into the open to see the first shell explode in the middle of the rice field. Then the explosions were walking across the paddy, reaching for her in bunches of hot bursts, longing to embrace her with spangled, convulsing arms of yellow and red. Terror gripped her heart.

The compression from the first round reaching the road threw her from the motorcycle. For a few seconds she lay stunned. She raised her head, looking at the Honda lying on its side, the rear wheel spinning crazily. *Got to get off the road. I will crawl.* She had lost her slippers. Her pretty *ao dai* was badly torn. She rolled over the edge of the road into a smelly ditch. A machine gun stitched a path of flying dirt to her front. *Karoom! Karoom! Karoom!* The mortars walked across the road, showering her with broken earth.

"Oh, God. Oh, God," she screamed.

Ping . . . Ping . . . Ping . . . Ping. Ricocheting bullets and hot shrapnel sizzled around her. *Pow! Pow! Pow! Pow! Pow!* The popping of an

103

M-16 on semi-automatic (or was it an AK-47) tattooed its message on the trembling night air.

Eerie incandescent parachute flares swung overhead, illuminating the paddies in a surrealistic half-light from another world. *Whomp . . . Wham!* The unmistakable firing of a B-40 rocket.

How long she lay shivering in the ditch, face pressed into the stinking mud, trying to flatten herself into the ground, she did not know. Even after the firing stopped she never moved. It wasn't until the first light of dawn that she stirred. And then only after she heard the familiar sounds of people at work in the fields.

Mai Lien rose to her knees and peered around with mud caked eyes. The Honda remained where it had fallen. A broken lump of fur lay a few feet away. Mai Lien tore a piece of material from her *ao dai* and carefully wrapped the shattered kongi in the soft cloth.

The motorcycle started on the first kick. She drove home. No one paid any attention to her.

CHAPTER SEVEN

Time passed slowly for Mai Lien. Vic flew his missions and she tried to keep busy with her job at the base. She studied English at the USAID school and enrolled in an office practice course to qualify for a clerical job with a Vietnamese government agency or, hopefully, with the Americans who paid much better. She didn't want to remain a cleaning maid forever, though that wasn't so bad as selling bread in the train station or laboring in the rice fields as she once had.

But where is my hope, Major? What is to become of me? Where do I place my dreams, my expectations to be fulfilled as a woman, she puzzled. I know it's too much to desire, a common girl like me becoming a U.S. Air Force officer's lady. But it doesn't matter. As long as you are here now with me. This is what's important.

As long as the dream lasted, as long as he remained in Vietnam, she would be happy. All she wanted was to be able to help him, do things for him. She asked nothing in return. She would love him forever, even if he left tomorrow. This was something she was more sure of than anything else. She couldn't explain it. It was just there. A one and only love. There would never be another man for her, of this she was absolutely certain. So for the short time she would have him before he returned to his American women, she would teach him her simple ways, bring him peace, and make his life as comfortable and pleasant as she could.

Mai Lien stood on the black tarmac, looking up at the leaden dawn, tears dropping from the corners of her long eyes. Her lips slowly moved but no sound was uttered. She turned her small face toward the scream of jet engines as his aircraft passed overhead clawing for altitude.

All these months I have watched you, waiting patiently, loving you, willing you to me, she mourned to herself. My life rises and falls with your missions, your coming and going, my darling. I hide. You can't see me. I watch you walk to your airplane, climb the ladder and settle into the seat. I see you put on the green and gold striped helmet and begin checking things on the inside while many men rush around the airplane on the outside. Then you start your airplane's engines, put on that funny black thing you breathe from, and pull the big sunglass down over your eyes. She wiped a tear away.

My heart leaps and my body shivers with excitement as the engines grow louder and the long Phantom jet pulls away from the parking area, rolling past me with you staring straight ahead. And the big plastic top, I forget what you called it, slowly comes down over your head and snaps shut, sealing you off from the world, from me.

Then you are gone, climbing into heaven, riding your ox cart of fire. And my vigil begins, expectantly waiting for your safe return, and not ending until I see the sweep of your airplane over the field. Her eyes fixed on the two disappearing fiery points of light burning a hole in the dawning night.

I wish I knew how you felt up there, dearest. Are you excited? Lonely? Scared? What do you think about? Do you ever think of me when you're flying north? I wish I could help you. I need a man to love. Are you angry because I have chosen you? She could still see the signaling tail pipes, faintly illuminating the F-4's vertical fin, carrying him away from her.

I love with all my being and with no reservations, my love. It isn't important that you don't love me now, I will be patient, she sighed. I will not allow my love for you to weaken because you do not love me. My faithfulness does not depend on what you do. I love you and that is that. She covered her face with her hands and wept openly. I can bring you the peace and fulfillment that you yearn for, if you let me. I will become your refuge from the turmoil of your world and I will be a source of strength to deal with this world, as you must. I will subdue you with my femininity and humble you with my submissiveness. I will encourage and strengthen your maleness. In my presence you will be a man and I a woman and there will never by any confusion in

107

that.

She remembered that once he had obtained permission for her to see his airplane up close. She had run her small hands over the smooth outer skin marveling at the awesomeness and beauty of the machine. He had lifted her into the cockpit and she sat in the very seat he was sitting now. She had placed her hand on the control stick and had envisioned his hand beneath hers as he guided the bird toward Hanoi. She scanned the maze of instruments before her, her eyes stopping on the fire control panel. She briefly considered the destruction he carried and watched in her mind's eye as he selected the proper switches for firing the rockets and missiles. She had fingered his seat harness and then grew momentarily still when she noticed the heavy seat armor and plating surrounding the pilot's station. The impact was complete and she fully understood that every time he went up, the possibility of him not returning to her was very real. This was something she had learned to live with. Her fear she held from him.

She caught a last glimpse of Vic disappearing into the steely sky, and turned away.

Oh, fill my mouth with thy sweet nectar, the drink of immortal dreams. For the lotus is in bloom on the pond and the rice is green again. The juice of the pomegranate is sweet on my lips — Ah, the honey liquid secreted by flowers. Feed me sweetmeats and sugar blossoms, my darling, and let me linger among the spice trees; let me dream under the tamarinds. What would I do if I could not dream; for thorns are found along the flowering paths wherever I walk. Press your lips softly to mine and fill me with thy nectar; let me dream, my love, of cloudless days and silky nights. Kiss away the light and put me to sleep; give me dreams — give me dreams. And when the dusky hours of desolation seek to wake me, I will remember thy sweetness in which I rejoiced and forget not the flaming moments that comforted me. Take my hand and walk me beside the quiet river: still the tempest — give me dreams, my love — give me dreams.

Vic lifted his eyes from the instruments and looked through the plexiglass at Moreno inching up on his right wing. The fiery orange dish, rising from its ocean bed of shimmering green jade, rested on the back of Moreno's ship, its long, shining silver rays cheerfully contrasting with the Phantom's stark battle camouflage. Vic went back over the briefing. "Four strikes today," the OPS officer had said. "Benedetti flies MIG CAP for strike one on Phu Xuyen along the Hong River, here . . ." he instructed, laying his hand flat over the target on the large wall map of North Vietnam.

"Call sign, 'Cobra.' Scattered cumulus. Bingo fuel . . ."

Vic looked back at Moreno again.

"Cobra one, Cobra two. Watch your distance."

"Roger, one."

He had to keep an eye on Moreno. A good pilot, but a bit too edgy. He wasn't as smooth and dependable as Davis, who had sat out this mission. He twisted his head to the other side of the formation.

Pellegrini and Patterson were lagging too far behind him.

"Bring it up three and four." The two ships nosed in tighter.

They circled over the rendezvous point waiting for the bombers. After a few minutes orbiting, the strikers appeared and together they began their ingress on the target at Phu Xuyen, eighty miles south of Hanoi. Vic felt strong and invincible, flying high cover for the bombers. It was a formidable force and he had a good feeling about the mission.

"The Migs will be up," he said to himself.

As soon as they crossed into North Vietnam, Vic's ECM equipment began picking up radar strobes from surface-to-air missile sites and from antiaircraft batteries. He called the strike leader.

"Cobra one, Blue leader. SAM and Triple A locking on."

"Roger, Cobra one. Will watch for launches."

"Cobra one, Cobra flight. Heads up, and *down!*" Vic said. "Call out SAM firings. Search your radar for Migs. Backseaters watch your six o'clocks."

To keep up with the bombers, Vic's fighter escort flew a weaving pattern over the much slower, bomb laden strikers. He kept alert, probing the ground for missile firings, knowing that the only way he could avoid the big "telephone poles" flying up at him was to see them early. The 600 gallon centerline tanks ran dry and he ordered them jettisoned.

"Cobra three, Cobra one. I have bogie contact." It was Pellegrini's backseater.

"Roger Cobra three. Range?" Vic asked.

"Eighteen miles."

Vic ordered a turn to put the unidentified aircraft on their noses. The bombers continued on toward the target, depending on Vic to take care of the threat.

"Cobra three, bogies fourteen miles."

"Cobra three, bogies eight miles."

"Cobra three, bogies . . ."

Vic picked them up visually at the same time the WSO called them off at four miles, two mottled green camouflaged Mig 21s. They were about three thousand feet above and heading in the opposite direction for the bombers.

"Migs one o'clock high! Blow tanks!"

Off came eight 370 gallon wing tanks, tumbling earthward, streaming fuel.

"Pellegrini, go high and protect my six."

"Roger."

The four pilots hauled their big Phantoms around, turning hard after the Migs, afterburners cooking. Vic was on the inside of the turn, putting him ahead of the rest. He looked at his instruments. Mach .95 . . . 1.0 . . . 1.2 . . . 1.3.

"Cobra two, Cobra one. We have company. Mig off port. Level."

Vic jerked his head around. His wingman had spotted a third Mig sneaking up from the deck and preparing for a rear pass on Pellegrini and Patterson. It was a good trap, one used often enough by North Vietnamese pilots, using two lead Migs as bait and holding another low and behind, hoping to pin the U.S. aircraft in between. But Vic had position on the attacking Mig. He called Pellegrini.

"Cobra one, Cobra three. You've got a Mig

climbing to your six."

"Roger. Tell me when to break," Pellegrini said.

"Negative, three. I've got him wired. You take the two lead Migs," Vic instructed.

"Roger, will take lead Migs."

The two elements split apart, Pellegrini and Patterson going flat out for the Migs ahead, and Vic turning into the lone communist. The Mig saw Vic coming, broke off his attack, and darted into a cloud. Vic went in after him. He tried to time his chase correctly, hoping to come out of the cloud below and behind the Mig. After about thirty seconds of flying in the cover, he pulled his ship up, emerging into bright blue sky once more. There he was again! The Mig was at eleven o'clock and a thousand feet above, climbing. Vic raced after him, climbing with the Mig.

The sun was behind him and he was pointed away from the earth.

"A perfect Sidewinder shot," he thought to himself. He selected HEAT.

"Moreno, I'm going to knock this guy down. Am I clear?"

"Roger. Nothing in sight."

He pulled the Phantom's nose around and pointed it a little ahead of the Mig. He pressed the trigger. *Nothing!* The missile didn't fire. He tried again. Nothing happened. Again. Nothing. He hurriedly went over the switches. He pulled the trigger. It was no use. The malfunction wasn't going to correct. He tried for a Sparrow shot but Balinger couldn't get a lock on. Moreno was wondering why Vic hadn't fired.

"Moreno, I'm passing the lead to you."

"Roger. I have the lead. Passing on your right," he acknowledged.

The Mig started down, Moreno diving after him, Vic following close behind. Moreno fired all of his ordnance, but the North Vietnamese pilot broke hard at the critical moment and skillfully evaded the missiles. It looked like the Mig was going to get away.

But the Mig had lost much of its energy in the breaks and Vic was in good position now for another try at him with his remaining radar guided Sparrows.

"Break left, Moreno. I'm taking the lead again."

As soon as Moreno broke, Vic turned inside, giving him clearance for a Sparrow shot. The Mig began dancing all over the sky, a real show of flying ability trying to shake the F-4s. But Vic was able to stay with him and he began closing the gap by flying inside the Mig's turn. He finally got the reticle centered on the enemy aircraft.

"Dick, I've got the Mig pinned," he told his WSO. "Lock him on."

The radar strobed ahead and the analog jumped out.

"We've got lock on, Major," Balinger said. A few seconds passed.

"Cleared to fire."

Vic didn't fully expect the Sparrow to come off after getting malfunctions on his Sidewinders. He pulled the trigger again and he felt the missile drop out of its well underneath him. A second later the AIM-7 fired and it leaped ahead of the Phantom, smoking after the North Vietnamese.

"It fired! We've got a hot one," he called to Balinger.

"Roger. Looks good," Balinger said, craning his neck to watch the Sparrow track the Mig.

"Looks good. Pulling good lead."

"Good lead, good lead. We've got him!"

The big Sparrow missile crashed into the Mig and huge chunks of metal began flying off the fuselage. A fire erupted and then the tail fell off trailing dense black smoke. Fuel streamed heavily from the ruptured enemy. The Mig stood on its left wing momentarily then lazily rolled over on its back, dead. After a few spins the pilot ejected, popping out in front of Vic just as his chute began to blossom, no more than fifty feet from him. He got a good look at the communist as he shot past.

"Dick, did you see him?"

"Yes, sir. Wow!"

"Did you see the surprised look on his face?"

"Roger. He didn't look too happy."

"Moreno. Did you see that?"

"Too much. He came out right in front of us!"

"Right. Right in front."

Vic rolled off with Moreno following close. He headed in the direction he had last seen Pellegrini and Patterson smoking after the first two Migs. He listened to the bomber pilots' conversation as they approached their target.

"Phu Xuyen on the left."

"Can you see the target?"

"Roger. Along the river. The rail yard beyond."

"Are we clear, Cobra flight?"

"Roger. You're clear." Pellegrini was on station with the strikers.

"Okay. Starting flak suppression run."

"Roger, right behind you."

Suddenly the voice of the air controller cut through the talk.

"Red Crown, bandits airborne out of Bullseye, one eight zero."

"Cobra leader, Red Crown. Range of bandits?" Vic asked.

No answer.

"Cobra leader, Red Crown. Bandit range?"

"Bullseye sixty, Cobra leader."

Vic looked down just as the Hong River passed beneath him. He quickly calculated that the Migs were about four minutes away. He flew on toward the bombers.

After about two minutes the controller broke in again.

"Red Crown, bandits turning to two seven zero."

Another minute passed.

"Bandits now headed three five zero."

"Red Crown, bandits behind you, fifteen miles and beginning their attack!"

Vic turned around, placing him and his wingman on a reciprocal heading with the Migs. He began "looking" with his own radar.

"Cobra leader, Red Crown. What is the altitude of attacking bandits?"

"Estimate angels 10."

Good. They were below him. With his nose pointed at the Migs he went to max burner to get rid of the tell-tale F-4 smoke. He pushed over, gaining energy for his second fight today.

Vic approached his task with machine-like precision. He went to his own radar, picked up the bandits at nine miles, and put Moreno out about twelve hundred feet in fighting wing formation. The Migs had faded to the right of the scope so he brought the ship around a few degrees. At five miles he saw them. The two Mig 19s were apparently still under GCIL control and hadn't yet seen the two U.S. jets. They began a slow turn east. Vic was now supersonic and called the Migs to Moreno.

"I'm padlocked, two. Clear me."

"Roger. Going high."

Vic pushed over, cutting down into the inside of the Migs' turn, boring in with afterburners full. He continued to roll with the Migs at full power, working his pedals and stick to bring the F-4 into position for a set-up. Moreno kept him clear.

"I'm boresight," he said to Balinger.

"Roger."

"Coming around onto the leader . . ." A few seconds passed.

"Reticle . . . centered . . . steady . . ." A short pause, then,

"Lock him on, Dick!"

"Good display. We have lock on!" Balinger shouted.

"Let's take him."

"Cleared to fire . . . wait! I lost it."

A few more seconds. It seemed like minutes.

"*Shoot! Shoot!* He's locked up."

Vic squeezed the trigger and the missile shot for the Mig. Incredibly the Mig fliers had not yet seen the attacking Phantoms. The Sparrow was almost to the lead plane when the pilot must have turned around and saw the big cloud of destruction high-balling for him. The "19" broke hard port and the missile smoked over his tail without detonating.

Vic recovered quickly, unloaded the plane, picked up more energy and locked onto the wingman.

"Where's that first Mig?" Vic asked Moreno.

"Headed home."

"I'm clear?"

"Roger. Clear," Moreno assured him.

Off came another AIM-7, smoking ahead, pulling perfect lead. It hit just below the pilot with a terrific explosion, pieces of the Mig flying in all directions, then fluttering earthward like confetti.

Vic watched the debris float down. He searched himself for emotion. There was none. For the first time, no excitement, no exhilaration, no feeling of triumph. He had destroyed two Migs within a few minutes. He should be elated. Shouldn't he? He rolled his plane around the remains of the Mig. Gray-black smoke drifted north and large pieces still trailing fire had almost reached their final resting place thousands of feet below. He felt a machine-like detachment from the death scene around him. Remote. Indifferent.

The guy didn't have a chance, he thought to himself. I wonder if he had any kids?

He rolled out of his turn and headed for the bombers to cover their egress from the target.

Suddenly he was cold. His mind reached back into the past — to his childhood. His brain tried to focus on words etched into his memory. Something still there—long forgotten. Beads of sweat broke out on his face and he shivered with cold . . . thine eyes are open upon all the ways of the sons of men . . . to give everyone according to his ways, and according to the fruit of his doing . . .

His head ached. His hand trembled on the control stick. Why was it so cold? The soft green lights on the instruments blurred into a pulsating glow . . . for the wages of sin is death; but the gift of God is eternal life through Jesus Christ our Lord.

He and Moreno joined up with the strikers and the other element. The air was filled with talk about his two kills and the success of the mission. Everyone except Vic was jubilant as they set course for Da Nang, pulses running high. Word had already reached the base and there would be celebrating, honors, more air medals, a party for him. His fame would spread, even reach Hanoi, Washington, Moscow. Four Migs, more than any other American. He was the hottest pilot in the air. His superiors were probably planning big things for him already. But all Vic could think of at this moment was the life he had just blown away. Someone had told him to go and he went, never to come back. Just like that, it was over for him. Gone with the smoke and debris. Poof!

Da Nang appeared below them. Vic led the ships around the landing pattern. He pitched off solo and flew his victory rolls over the field.

"Where was the meaning, the fulfillment?" he asked himself. Where? Where? The entire universe, the entirety of existence, the allness of experience

118

appeared to Vic an incomprehensible, purposeless joke—change without meaning. Climbing into the sun, he rolled the jet over on its back and let the nose fall off in a long twisting spiral back toward earth, recalling once more how destiny in the shape of an impoverished peasant girl had fortuitously embraced him. He remembered her sweet caresses and lyrical, flute-like voice, and his life hit him as terribly lonely, obscure, and wanting without her.

"Do you know Jesus, Major?"

CHAPTER EIGHT

A classic Vietnamese moon hung in the sky, large and full, illuminating the valley like day. A light wind stirred the coconut palms and banana leaves. The smell of the tiger was in the air.

Vic sat at the big table with Mai Lien, eating a country meal of green, unripened papaya soup and rice pork. *Ba ngoai* rested on the hand carved mahogany divan, legs crossed underneath her, back rod straight, reading her Bible by the light of a kerosene lamp. A guttural cough drifted from the jungle beyond the river, breaking the silence. Grandmother flared her nostrils, scenting the tiger.

"*Con cop,*" she said, looking up from her reading. She rose from the divan and locked the door.

Unreal, Vic thought to himself. One hour I'm flying a multi-million dollar technological marvel across the skies, the next I'm eating dinner with a beautiful Vietnamese girl, surrounded by jungle and Bengal tigers. He sniffed heavily of the damp air, wondering what a tiger smelled like, but all he got back was the sweet perfume of the mangos piled in a basket next to him on the table.

Mai Lien picked up a bite size morsel of pork with her chopsticks and dipped it in *nuoc mam*. Vic watched her intently. Placing her lips over the edge of the rice bowl held in her hand, she pushed rice and pork together into her mouth all in one graceful motion. It was an art form of its own — upwardly curved fingers, lightly balanced bamboo, delicate tilt of the bowl, swift neat motion — almost ceremonial. Not a grain was spilled as she scooped several mouthfuls in quick succession. With two fingers from her left hand she pulled threads of black silk from her eyes and placed the chopsticks neatly across the bowl, announcing the end of her meal. Her rhythm was narcotic, easing his spirit.

He reached over and touched her raven hair with his fingers, then slid his palm down the length of it. She shyly kept her eyes fixed on the rice bowl in front of her. He looked at her eyes. They fascinated him.

"Mai Lien, what do you think is the greatest difference between the face of an American and the face of a Vietnamese?" he asked, expecting her to say that the eyes were.

"Nose."

"What? Nose!" he exclaimed, surprised.

"Yes. Big nose. American have big nose."

"Well that's a surprise."

"Vietnamese have flat nose. Americans, big nose. Long nose," she said.

122

Vic looked at Mai Lien's nose. He reached over and touched it. It was very soft, seemingly boneless. He couldn't detect a bridge. Small and flat. He felt his own. The heavy bone structure and pointedness was obvious to his touch.

"Not pretty like yours," he said, still feeling his nose. "Western nose."

"I never see western nose until I nine years old. French soldiers come through my village. I very scared. Their long noses scare me. I run to my grandmother and hide. I think they ghosts."

Vic laughed. "Western people are much bigger than Asians. Bigger than Vietnamese," he said.

"Yes, men bigger. Women bigger too. I afraid them."

"American women?"

"Oh yes. I see them on base. They look mean at me. They very big."

"Do you think they want to hurt you?"

"I don't know. They talk very loud. Noisy. They scare me."

"You shouldn't feel afraid Mai Lien. After all, this is your country. Your home, not theirs."

"Yes, Major. My country, my home."

Vic wished she wouldn't call him Major all the time. But this was a habit she had gotten into and she felt uncomfortable calling him anything else. She had said that a person of her low status should address him with much respect, and besides, he was an Air Force officer, "great Phantom pilot," and deserved to be called by his proper title. For awhile she had tried to call him Mister Benedetti, but that didn't work out because mister came out as "mitter." She couldn't pronounce the "s" in mister. Also, she felt that calling him mister made him sound too common. At any rate, he let it go at that since it made her happy calling him major and after all these months it would seem strange to hear her address him as Vic.

He glanced around the house. Grandmother was still comfortably squatting on the divan reading her Bible by the flickering oil lamp, the Samurai sword hanging in its place on the wall behind her. The yellow moon rising above the forest canopy was visible through the open window. The tiger coughed again, more distant this time.

"You like my food tonight?" she asked.

"*Ngon lam,*" delicious, he said. "I enjoy your food very much, Mai Lien. I think I am beginning to like it better than American food."

"Oh, I glad. I want you like my food. Very important for Vietnamese woman." She poured him some tea.

"Mai Lien. Can I ask you something?"

"Oh, yes, major. You can ask."

"You have been good to me. You let me come to your home and rest, and you cook me your good food."

"Yes, I do for you," she said, looking at his face, studying it.

"You are always waiting for me at the flight line when I return from a mission."

"Oh yes, I waiting for you always," a look of concern appearing on her face.

"And you let me talk to you about things that bother me. Personal matters. You listen to my troubles."

"Yes, I listen you talk about trouble bother you."

"Why, Mai Lien? Why do you do all this for me. I've never done anything for you. I don't deserve your kindness."

There was a long silence. Finally Mai Lien spoke, her voice barely audible.

"You no know, major? You no know why?" a hint of sadness forming in her eyes.

"No, I don't."

"Because I love you. You are my man, you need me," she said, tears filling her beautiful eyes.

Shadows from the lamp moved irregularly on the wall, fluttering in the yellow light. Grandmother sat glued in her position, absorbed in her reading. Vic thought he heard the growl of the tiger, far away this time. The house was still and a full minute passed before either of them spoke. It was Mai Lien who broke the silence again.

"My heart belong you. You only man I ever love."

Vic wanted to say something, but the words wouldn't form. He wanted to say that he loved her too, but he didn't know if he did. He wasn't sure what love was, what his feelings were. He was very fond of Mai Lien. But love? Well, that was a different matter. He had to give it some thought. However, there was one thing he was sure of. Mai Lien knew she was in love with him and there was no thinking about it for her. Good grief, why couldn't he be as uncomplicated as her? Why was he always so darned analytical and cautious?

"I watch you when you come my home."

Vic looked at her. Her eyes were steadily fixed on

his as she continued to open her heart to him.

"You happy here. No sad like at base. You know grandmother and I love you. We care what happen you. We want you be happy. This your home. No killing, no Mig, no be afraid here. Only love. Major need much love. Much trouble in his life, need much love. You afraid Mig, afraid die. You feel bad kill man today too. But you always come to Mai Lien and you find her love. It take away hurt. Grandmother love you too. You like son to her."

Slowly something deep inside Vic began to churn. Mai Lien's words had moved him off his secure perch, off the fence of ambivalence, and had exposed his vulnerability. By her complete honesty, she was forcing him to be honest with himself, to take a long, hard look at who he was and where he had been. She had cut through the underbrush and laid the ground bare, announcing her love for him, revealing his weakness, and laying open his need for her. But what affected him most was that she had left no doubt that she and her grandmother cared about what happened to him. He was more than a visitor, more than an American passing through their war who would return home to his own country and soon forget about Vietnam. He was family. And this got to him. It kicked him hard, down where the hard shell was that nobody got through. He felt the cover breaking away, cracking sharply, painfully. Then the pain was gone and what was left melted away in a warm river of freedom. Years of loneliness and unhappiness, pent up frustration, and suppressed fears flowed out of him quietly, as he sat at the table, head in his hands, the hot tears burning his eyes.

Grandmother put her Bible down, walked over to him, and placed her arms gently around his shaking shoulders. Mai Lien held his hand and softly cried with him, feeling his sorrow as her own. It was a peculiar scene, these two little Vietnamese women bending over and comforting the strong American who had been sent to protect them. Distorted images cast by the dim light of the oil lamp danced on the dinner table. Deep in the jungle the tiger bent over his kill and coughed.

When Vic wasn't flying missions he was with Mai Lien, resting in her home, walking the pristine valley with its meandering green river and lush plantations, visiting with grandmother and the villagers. He had been fully accepted by the residents of the hamlet, and even the village chief would sometimes stop by grandmother's to chat with Vic and have a glass of *ba ngoai*'s homemade gin with him. It was normally dangerous for a lone American to be any distance from his base in Vietnam but Mai Lien's village and the surrounding countryside was militarily secured. However, the Viet Cong covertly roamed the area, especially at night, and the villagers, a few of whom were VC themselves, had arranged for Vic's protection.

Whenever Vic was free, he would meet Mai Lien after she had finished her work on the base, and climb behind her on the little blue motorcycle. He would steady the Honda with his legs while Mai Lien gunned the engine, and then with a push of his feet, away they would go, the little engine straining, the tires nearly flat from Vic's added weight. The guards would wave the familiar couple through the gate, enjoying the unusual scene as the two roared past, Vic holding tightly to Mai Lien's waist, his head and shoulders lost in her long hair sweeping behind. Sometimes he would drive, but it wasn't as much fun that way.

Whizzing down the highway and bouncing along the back roads, they laughed together and waved at friends and curious onlookers. Mai Lien would always want to stop along the way and buy fresh coconut milk, vegetables, a fish, or something. And of course there was always the gossiping while Vic patiently waited. Then they were off again to make a stop or two more at a cousins to pick something up for grandmother or to deliver a message or have some tea or soy bean milk. Sometimes they watched the fishermen catching eels and mudfish.

"Mai Lien, have you ever been to a dance?" Vic asked one day as they bumped along the road home.

Sensing that he wished to talk, she pulled off at a favorite spot of theirs overlooking the valley. They got off the Honda, walked to the crest of the hill, and sat in the shade of a large banyan tree.

"No. Country girls no dance. Saigon girl, Da Nang girl, they dance. I watch sometimes."

Vic thought for a moment. The annual American-Vietnamese military ball would be in a few weeks. He would be expected to attend as the Air Force's leading pilot and to help bolster U.S. relations with the Vietnamese brass and government officials. Many important people would be flying up from Saigon to attend. It might be risky asking Mai Lien to accompany him. Social status was important at this function and a country girl like Mai Lien might not be considered an acceptable date by his superiors or by the Vietnamese. They would prefer that he bring an American woman. Oh, what the hell, he didn't care about that. If he wanted to take her he would. This was as good a time as any to make a decision about Mai Lien. But the more important question for him was how Mai Lien felt about it. Would she feel comfortable in surroundings she had no experience with?

"I would like to take you to a dance, a big dance."

"Big dance?" she asked hesitantly.

"Yes, Mai Lien. Generals and other officers, District Chiefs, Province Chiefs, and U.S. embassy people will be there. Big dance."

She remained quiet, rubbing a bamboo twig with her finger tips.

"I country girl, not elegant lady," she said. "I not know how dance, I eat with chopsticks only, no talk well. I know you think about this before you ask me."

"Yes, I thought about it."

"And you decide you still want take me. Right?"

"Right."

"Okay I go."

"You will?" he said, surprised.

"Yes, I know you want me go very bad."

"Yes I do, very bad."

"I country girl, not elegant lady. Peoples maybe laugh at you. And you still want to take me. That

129

mean you want me go bad."

"Yes I do."

"Okay. I go. Look very pretty for you. I make new *ao dai*. You buy me cloth?"

"I will buy you a *new* ao dai."

"No, I make. Much better. You see. You buy me cloth?"

"Okay. You probably know best. I will buy you cloth."

She looked at the bamboo again and delicately stroked a solitary leaf extending from the twig.

"Bamboo," she said quietly, "mean love to Vietnamese peoples." She looked up at him shyly.

Those talking eyes of hers, he thought to himself. If she couldn't speak a word, her eyes would talk for her. He didn't say anything for a long time.

"I hope you will be comfortable at the dance. You won't be afraid will you?" he asked.

"A little, maybe. I be okay though. You stay with me? No leave me alone?"

"I will be with you all the time. Right beside you."

"I no afraid then."

There was one other matter. Grandmother. Except for their short meetings at the base, their rides home together, and walks in the valley, Mai Lien and Vic had never been alone with each other. Grandmother, relatives, or friends had always been present, and of course, that is how it was intended for a girl such as Mai Lien who had been raised in traditional Vietnamese ways. In fact, liberties had been allowed Vic in his relationship with her because grandmother in her infinite wisdom and ability to evaluate people had immediately discerned

Vic's sound moral character and his great respect for her granddaughter and her principles. Also, Mai Lien was deeply in love with Vic, and grandmother wanted her to be happy, to be with her man as much as possible, even if it meant stretching the old rules a bit.

"Do you think grandmother will let you go to the dance with me?"

"Oh, yes. She let me go."

"But it will be at night. It will be the first time you and I will be alone together at night. How will she feel about that?"

"*Ba ngoai* trust you, trust me. She know I very safe with you. You no let VC hurt me. You take care me, right?"

"Yes, but that wasn't exactly what I was referring to."

"What you mean?"

"Well, being alone together . . . I mean . . . well. Oh, never mind. It's not important." Her innocence overwhelmed him. He softly kissed her cheek.

It had happened so suddenly. He hadn't planned it, it just seemed like the natural thing to do. He was sure it was the first time she had ever been kissed by a man. She placed her finger tips on the spot he had kissed her.

"That how American kiss?" she asked bashfully.

"Yes. That's a friendly kiss, to show affection."

"Ah . . . fect . . . shun?" she said, trying to pronounce the word.

"To show kindness, friendship . . . between a man and woman."

"How you show love?" she innocently asked.

Vic stood up, drawing Mai Lien to her feet. She stood waiting, looking up at him, trust in her eyes. Like all noble revelations that come to men, springing forth from hidden places deep within, Vic suddenly realized his great love for Mai Lien. There was no analysis, no evaluation, not even a thought passed through his mind. It had been there all the time. It just needed something to draw it out, to allow its expression. His love for her had been suppressed for so long that it literally exploded inside of him in a release of happiness, penetrating to the core of his soul. Great waves of emotion washed over him, cleansing away past fears, doubt, suspicion, drowning his ego and anxiety. He rode the crest, free now to give, to love, to care. There was nothing restraining him to hold back any longer, no need to remain silent. He could tell her.

"Mai Lien, I love you."

She willfully gave herself to him, slowly and deliberately. He absorbed her into his arms, pressing her soft, warm lips gently to his. He submerged himself in the flavor of her body, inhaling her sweet natural fragrance, voluntarily losing his identity, drowning in her reality. She pressed herself into him and he could feel her lithe body melt into his. Her tiny hands and soft arms caressed his back. He was free-falling through a space of love. Mai Lien's love.

"I love you so much, so very much," he said.

He held her tightly, caressed her hair and buried his face in billowing clouds of the black silk. He placed her two hands together between his and kissed her red fingernails. He cupped her small face and looked long into her oriental eyes. He kissed her again, long, unhurriedly, gently. She accepted it all, humbly submitting herself to him.

They walked back to the parked motorcycle and drove down the hill into the plantations. Vic held onto Mai Lien a little tighter and snuggled a little closer. It was good to be in love with a Vietnamese girl, he thought to himself.

The time passed quickly for Mai Lien as she made preparations for attending the gala dinner dance with Vic. She wanted him to be proud of her and she intended to surprise him by learning to dance. Every day she would visit her cousin Hanh who worked as a cocktail hostess in Da Nang City and they danced the tango, cha cha cha, waltz, and other dances popular in Vietnam. Hanh would lead and Mai Lien would follow as the two girls danced around Hanh's living room, keeping time to the music being played on the little battery powered tape cassette. Curious and bewildered neighbors stood around watching in wide-eyed wonderment, marveling at the dancing girls, being entertained but not quite sure of what to make of this behavior. Being a very alert and intelligent young woman, Mai Lien rapidly picked up her cousin's instructions and was soon dancing smoothly and confidently.

Hanh also taught Mai Lien proper western table manners, how to eat with knife, fork, and spoon (having acquired a table setting from her place of employment to practice with), the use of the napkin, and introduced her to other refinements that would be expected of her.

"Watch the other women and follow what they

do," Hanh wisely instructed her cousin.

"Yes."

"And ask the major what to do when you are un-
sure of yourself."

"Yes, I will," she said obediently to the older girl.

Vic took Mai Lien into the city to shop for the
material from which she would make her *ao dai*. It
was to be a special creation and she shopped carefully for the fabric. After visiting several shops, her
eyes finally stopped on a distinctive, yellow-gold
gossamer cloth, smooth and luxurious.

Mai Lien remained silent while she kept her eyes
glued on the cloth, not wanting to ask outright for
Vic to buy it for her. Vic sensed that she had found
what she wanted.

"Do you like it?" he asked her.

"Thailand silk," she said, "very expensive."

"Very pretty," he said.

"Yes, very pretty."

"I will buy it for you."

"Oh, no!! Too expensive."

"But if you want it, I will buy it for you."

"No, too expensive. Thailand silk very much
money."

"It's beautiful though."

"Oh, yes. Very beautiful."

"This is what you want, isn't it?"

She said nothing, just stood there caressing the
material with her hands. Vic watched her long red
fingernails glide across the silk. This was getting
them nowhere, he thought to himself. He took her
by the hand and led her to where the shop owner
was arranging several bolts of material.

134

"How much for the Thailand silk?" he asked the man.

"Two hundred piasters a meter," he quickly said.

"Two hundred! My God!" Mai Lien cried at the owner. The haggling over the price immediately began, Mai Lien taking charge, talking rapidly in Vietnamese. The shopkeeper acting confident, argued with her, as is the custom, but quickly called Mai Lien back each time she started out the door. Vic had become an amused observer, watching a different Mai Lien in action. Here was a determined woman bent on saving him money. Well, that was refreshing, he thought, reflecting on his experiences with a few American women he had known.

After much storming about the shop and the owner following Mai Lien in and out the open door, a price was eventually agreed on. Half of what was originally asked! Friendliness and calm had been restored. Mai Lien smiled sweetly at the owner, and the owner smiled and bowed respectfully to Mai Lien as he handed the carefully wrapped silk over the counter to her. He smiled again to Vic as he shook his hand.

"Very nice doing business with you wife, sir."

"My wife! . . . Oh, yes . . . my wife. Yes, of course," he said, casting a reprimanding glance at Mai Lien, who looked at him coyly. They said goodbye and Vic took her arm, leading her out into the street.

"I tell him we married. Help bring price down," she said, watching him sheepishly.

"Oh?" he said grinning at her.

"You not mad?"

"No, I'm not mad." How could he be mad at her?"

Vic opened the door of the staff car and stepped out in front of Mai Lien's house. He took a deep breath of the balmy night air and gazed above at the star filled sky. Half the time you couldn't see the stars through the layers of smog in his hometown, Los Angeles. He didn't miss Los Angeles.

He took a cigarette from the pack and looked at it for a long time. He put it between his lips without lighting it. *"Nha toi* — my home," he whispered, looking at the house. Funny that the Vietnamese use the same words to mean wife. *Nha toi.* My home. Wife. Interesting — wonder who thought of that. Sensitive people.

He put the cigarette back in the pack. I swear I'm going to quit these things. He walked around the car, inhaling the perfumed night. Not all Vietnam smelled this good. He would never forget the smell that first day he arrived in Vietnam. Fetid rot. A mixture of dead bodies, spent ammo, and urine. Can't talk to an ordinary GI about the aroma of mangos and breadfruit or the sweet bouquet of tamarind blossoms and tea leaves. Never happen. No hiding place. All heat and stink.

It had been a week since he had spent any time with Mai Lien and he missed her very much. He was anxious to see her. He picked at a piece of lint on his formal dress uniform, then told the Vietnamese driver that he would be out in a few minutes. He walked under the overhang of palm and called through the open door.

"*Ba ngoai*. Mai Lien."

"*Chao con,*" hello my son, grandmother said. "*Vo nha choi,*" come in.

He took off his hat and walked into the house.

"*Ngoi day,*" sit here, she said as she brought him some tea. Grandmother sat beside him on the divan and smiled a knowing smile, sensing that he had missed Mai Lien and was looking forward to their first big evening together.

"*Mai Lien dep lam toi nay,*" Mai Lien looks very pretty for you tonight, she said.

Ba ngoai rambled on about the good rice crop this year and Mrs. Hai's ungrateful husband who wanted to take a concubine. Vic nodded his head, feigning interest. He felt guilty for not making more of an effort at the conversation. He politely sipped the tea. Just once he'd like to taste some sugar in it. Apparently Mrs. Hai got to choose the concubine.

"Good evening, Major."

He looked up, startled by the unexpected interruption. He couldn't believe what he saw. For a brief moment his mind fought to recognize what his eyes beheld. Standing before him was the most gorgeous woman he had ever set eyes on. She was stunning. Absolutely stunning. He had always thought Mai Lien to be the prettiest woman he had ever seen, but here she was looking even more fantastically beautiful.

Vic, you're a very fortunate man, he said to himself.

"Do you like me?" she asked, standing motionless, hands folded together in front of her, eyes demurely diverted to the floor.

She looked like a little Chinese princess, the kind he remembered seeing in an art book on ancient oriental culture. Her long hair was piled high on her head, held in place by two combs, and two long ringlets hung down in front of each ear. A wide lock of hair, tapering to a point at the end, curved forward over each cheek, framing her exquisite face. Long, golden pagoda shaped earrings set with jade hung from each ear lobe.

Vic's eyes moved downward, slowly drinking in her beautiful dress and lovely figure. The hours of attention she had put into making her *ao dai* had resulted in a distinctively delicate, feminine garment of high quality. The beautiful Bangkok silk modestly covered her graceful neck in a mandarin style collar, then flowed down over her shoulders to terminate at the wrists in tightly fitted long sleeves. The elegant yellow-gold material clutched at her slim waist and gently flared over her hips in two exciting splits along each side. The final result was a sensuous, aesthetic pleasure of exquisite taste and unique beauty. Vic's masculine senses reveled in Mai Lien's loveliness.

"Do you like me?" she asked again, a little worried look crossing her eyes.

"I like you," he said, rising from his seat to take her two hands in his own. "I like you very much."

"Em dep khong?" Am I pretty?

"Em dep lam," you are very pretty, he said.

"Cam on," thank you, she said, obviously very pleased that he was satisfied with her appearance.

They said goodbye to *ba ngoai* and walked to the car where the waiting driver stood by the open door. They drove along quietly with Mai Lien snuggled up close to Vic, holding tightly to his arm.

"Are you afraid?" he asked her.

"No," she said bravely, "you stay close with me, yes?"

"Yes."

"No leave me?"

"No."

"I be okay then." She slipped her warm little hand into his. He squeezed it.

They arrived at the posh Continental Hotel in Da Nang City. Vic could feel Mai Lien's little heart beating rapidly through her *ao dai*. Her grip instinctively tightened on his arm. But it was more from excitement than from fear. Her long eyes were wide with anticipation, studying the busy scene before them through the car window, intently watching the men in military formal dress and in tuxedos, and women in gowns and *ao dais*, as they stepped out of their cars and entered the hotel.

Their driver parked, and opened the door. Vic got out first and helped Mai Lien. He noticed that her nervousness was no longer apparent, having been replaced by her characteristic, intense curiosity. They walked up the well lighted path lined with ornamental shrubs, and entered the spacious ballroom built and decorated by the French in typical Louis XIVth style, complete with large hanging crystal chandeliers, and a profusion of love seats, sofas, and lounging chairs tastefully arranged in groups behind the dance floor. Paintings of the

French impressionists hung on the walls. The dance floor was large, circular, and sunken, with one hundred dinner tables placed around the outer edge. The twelve piece orchestra, already playing, was seated on the stage. Most of the guests had already arrived when Vic and Mai Lien entered. Mai Lien's eyes were flashing around the crowded room, taking in everything, watching the people, admiring the furnishings, studying the carpet. She was breathless with the richness of the surroundings.

"Very beautiful," she said.

"Yes, it is."

"So many peoples. All look so nice."

"You are the most beautiful."

Her eyes smiled at him. "You very handsome tonight."

Vic took her arm and they walked toward the dance floor and tables. He noticed several couples in small groups watching him and Mai Lien. He didn't know them. He looked around. Others were also looking closely at them, the men in particular, studying Mai Lien.

"Major Benedetti!" someone called behind him. Smiling from ear to ear, was his wing commander, Colonel Johnson. He had several people with him.

"Major, I'm glad you're here. There are a few folks I want you to meet. U.S. Vice Consul, Roger Dornbacher and his wife Marie — Major Benedetti, whom we are all very proud of."

"Hello, major. Very happy to meet you."

"Thank you sir."

"We've heard so many good things about you, major," Mrs. Dornbacher said. "Four Migs isn't

140

it?"

"That's correct ma'am." Mai Lien's heart swelled with pride. She lifted her downcast eyes to meet Mrs. Dornbacher's quick glance.

"And Vic, I'd also like you to meet U.S. Congressman Jerry Henderson and his wife Bernice," Colonel Johnson said. "The Congressman is here on a fact-finding visit. He'd like to ask you some questions later."

"Congressman, Mrs. Henderson, it's a pleasure," Vic said.

"The pleasure is ours, Major Benedetti."

"And who is this beautiful young lady, major?" Marie Dornbacher, an attractive woman in her late fifties, asked, smiling at Mai Lien.

"Yes, she's just darling," the congressman's wife added.

Vic proudly introduced Mai Lien to everyone present. It was obvious that they were all enchanted with her and Vic quickly accepted their invitation to join them at their table where more introductions were made. Many people stopped by to talk to Vic or just to meet Mai Lien, captivated by her beauty and charm.

Dinner was served and Vic suddenly remembered that Mai Lien had never eaten with western implements. But before he could ask for chopsticks, Mai Lien had unfolded her napkin and placed it on her lap, picked up the correct spoon and was eating her soup. He watched in amazement as she progressed through the meal, eating her salad, the main course, and dessert, always choosing the correct eating utensil, even buttering

141

her bread and smoothly cutting her meat.

"American food cook much different from Vietnamese food," she said to Vic.

"Have you ever eaten American food before, Mai Lien?"

"No."

"But how did you know how to use . . . I mean . . . well, you did so well . . ."

"We dance now, Major?" she asked excitedly, changing the subject.

"Dance! But Mai Lien, you don't know how to dance."

"Oh, we try, okay?"

"Well, I don't know . . ."

"Please."

"All right. If you want to."

Vic escorted her to the dance floor. The orchestra was playing a tango and he was about to tell Mai Lien they should wait this one out, preferring to start her with a simpler rhythm, when suddenly she was in his arms waiting for him. He began cautiously, but when he discovered that she was smoothly following him, he became bolder and together they flowed across the floor in perfect body motion. Vic felt like he was dreaming. This couldn't be happening. Mai Lien was dancing with him, gracefully following his every move. Vic forgot himself and the other dancers, and he became lost in Mai Lien, gently guiding her around the floor to the rhythm of the Latin beat. He couldn't take his eyes off her. Yes, he must be dreaming. Could he really be dancing with a beautiful Vietnamese peasant girl, with the Cinderella of Vietnam, at the grand ball? It was so good to hold her, so good to have her close, to dance with her. He really did love her, he thought to himself.

Throughout the evening many admiring men would approach Mai Lien and ask her to dance. Each time she would shyly but courteously refuse until Vic encouraged her to accept, and then she would do so only reluctantly. While dancing she would maintain a proper distance, not allowing the men to hold her too close, but close enough to give them some satisfaction.

One handsome army colonel in particular had been paying a great deal of attention to Mai Lien all evening, dropping by the table frequently to talk to her, or to ask her to dance. Vic had become irritated by the colonel's persistence, but because of his rank he felt obligated to remain silent. However, Mai Lien had been watching Vic's growing impatience and understood what was happening. She had no intention of letting her loyalties to her man fall into question. When the colonel made his play for her, she was ready.

"Mai Lien, you are beautiful," the good looking colonel said.

She said nothing.

"You are the most beautiful woman here tonight."

She continued dancing but pulled back from him slightly.

"I haven't been able to take my eyes from you all evening."

She pulled back from him further.

"I want to see you again. Can I meet you next week?" he asked, silkily.

Mai Lien instantly jumped back like being hit by an electric bolt, as if the man was a leper, contaminated, unclean.

"No! No! No talk me like that. No talk me no more. No more dance. You bad man."

What?" he said, completely taken off guard.

"You no respect Major Benedetti. You no respect me," she said, almost in tears.

"But . . . I . . . "

"I make big trouble for you. Tell general, big boss."

She was very angry now, more angry than she could ever remember. No man was going to talk to her that way. That was reserved for the major. He alone was allowed to talk intimately with her. How dare this man trespass on private domain. She had to be firm with the intruder. She had the responsibility to protect what rightly belonged to her man, to him only. This colonel was trying to steal personal property. He wasn't going to break her happiness.

"Please . . . I didn't mean . . ." he said, stammering for an explanation.

"No talk me no more. I have one man. No need two."

With that she fled from the dance floor and rushed to Vic who stood talking to several men near their table. Reaching him, she clung to his arm and glared back at the colonel where she had left him looking foolish standing alone in the middle of the dancers. He shrugged and walked

144

off.

The rest of the evening Vic mingled with the other guests, Americans and Vietnamese both, always with Mai Lien at his side, answering questions about the air war, discussing U.S.-Vietnam relations, and the latest developments in the war. They also talked about the ever present corruption, politics, and the no win policy of U.S. involvement. But the conversations always returned to the same theme — Vic's exploits. Migs. They pushed for details, wanted to know what the enemy was like, what tactics he used, his own emotions, comparisons between the F-4 and the Mig, his evaluation of the enemy as an adversary, how he had shot down his Migs, and what were his career plans after the war. They all seemed very interested in him and listened intently to everything he told them about his contacts with he enemy. Mai Lien listened closely and watched the reactions of the others. She remembered everything.

It was growing late and Vic wanted to be alone with Mai Lien. He excused himself from the circle of men and women and took Mai Lien to the dance floor. The orchestra was playing "Diem-Xua," a popular Vietnamese ballad that Mai Lien liked so much. He didn't pull her close to him at first, but instead, placed his right hand lightly on the small of her back, and gently held her right hand shoulder high in his left. She rested her free hand delicately on his shoulder. They danced slowly to the dreamy music, his eyes never leaving her, admiring the smoothness of her skin and its lovely light golden tone. He knew how much she had done to prepare for this evening so he would be proud of her. This was the time to show his appreciation.

"Thank you for looking so lovely tonight," he said.

"I Major's number one girl. Must look pretty."

"You learned to dance for me too, didn't you? And eat western style?"

"Yes, I do that for you."

"I'm a very lucky guy."

"Yes, you lucky find Vietnamese girl love you. You difficult man." They both laughed at this.

Mai Lien's expression changed and she became serious. The Vietnamese singer picked up the song again.

"Major, I love you forever. I no care you difficult."

"Mai Lien, I . . ."

"When you leave, go back States, you no forget Mai Lien. You remember her little bit?"

"When I leave? But I'm not going to leave you."

"Oh yes, you leave. Sometime. Must come back States. All American come back States leave Vietnamese girl. I know. But that okay. Mai Lien understand."

"No, I'm not going to leave," he said, trying to convince her.

"I cry long time maybe when you go. You remember Mai Lien little bit?" Tears were running down her cheeks now. "I love you forever."

Vic stopped dancing and took out his handkerchief. He dried her tears, holding her hand while doing so, trying to comfort her. He took her outside to the balcony overlooking the spacious oriental garden below with its fountains and pagoda. He held her two little hands and kissed her almond eyes, feeling her sadness, understanding her distress. He would feel the same way, knowing that he would someday lose her. He admired her child-like honesty.

"I love you. I'm not going to leave you. Please don't be sad," he said.

"Okay. I no sad no more. We dance again, before we go home?"

"Okay."

He took her inside. The orchestra was playing the last dance of the evening and people were beginning to depart for their cars. He held her close this time. She smiled up at him and he kissed her full on the lips. She was happy again.

On the way home, Mai Lien, exhausted from the night of dancing and excitement, fell peacefully asleep in Vic's arms. He closed his eyes and gently ran his fingers over her face, tracing the outline of her eyes, lips, nose, ears, and cheeks.

They arrived at the little house. The driver opened the door for him and he carried the little princess, still fast asleep, into the silent dwelling. *Ba ngoai* looked up from the oil lamp and smiled the smile of an understanding mother. She put her Bible down and led the way into the bedroom. Vic laid Mai Lien on the bed. He undid her long hair, allowing it to spill onto the pillow. He spread her hair evenly so she could sleep more comfortably, and placed the two combs on the night stand. He

147

kissed her lightly on the forehead. He put an arm around grandmother and they walked to the car.

"She had a good time, but she's very tired," he said in Vietnamese.

"I will let her sleep late. Good night, my son."

"Good night, grandmother."

CHAPTER NINE

Suddenly they were there, small specks at first growing larger as they loomed above the gentle landscape of Da Nang, bearing left in tight formation along the landing pattern, a concert of beauty and grace, each plane orchestrating its own finale. Mai Lien watched with excitement as the lead flight in close diamond formation made a pass over the field. Number one pitched off and swung in low with its three landing gears extended. Just before touchdown the aircraft folded its wheels and in a mighty show of power the pilot lit the afterburner, screamed over the runway in a series of victory rolls and continued on up into the vertical, still rolling.

One by one in intervals of three seconds, each Phantom broke off into final approach, placing the flight in a loose gaggle, echelon right. Flaps down, gears down, and nose pitched up, the F-4s followed each other down like a line of geese. The lead ship settled onto the runway, a large white flower blossoming behind it. The drag chute filled immediately, cutting the Phantom's ground speed. After rolling three quarters the length of the field the pilot applied pressure to his right wheel brake and the jet pivoted onto the secondary runway.

Mai Lien stood on the hot tarmac, her straight hair blowing freely in the tropical breeze. She shielded her Asian eyes from the torrid sun with her small hand and strained to see the aircraft's number. Her palms became moist and a quiet shudder passed over her. She began nervously pacing. Her legs felt limp. She waited.

"Is it always like this?" cousin Hanh asked.

"Sometimes it's worse," Mai Lien answered.

"You must love him very much," Hanh said, looking pained.

"Very much."

The two young women stood side-by-side holding hands, their sweet, musical Vietnamese tones strangely out of place among the harsh sounds of men and machines returning from war. They spoke in the low, lyrical rhythm of the northern provinces which they preferred to the discordant dialect of Saigon, Binh Duong, and the southern regions.

"It is so strange out here—exciting yet depressing," Hanh said. "I don't think I like it."

"You wanted to come, so I brought you. Don't complain."

"I was curious."

Hanh shook as each plane thundered past then broke low into the landing pattern.

"It's so noisy."

"Stop complaining, Hanh."

"When do you know he's back?"

She cringed and put both hands to her ears while another F-4 broke out.

"When I see him."

"Do they all come back?"

"No."

The high pitched whine of the twin engines intensified as the big jet drew closer, its red and white sharks teeth painted on the nose pointing directly at her. She gasped a small cry of joy mingled with relief as the plane slowly turned into its revetment flashing tail number "101."

"Major Benedetti *di ve nha,*" she sighed.

He was back, and her world came alive again.

The canopy lifted and she silently watched in fascination and with her highly developed woman's curiosity as Vic unplugged himself from the weapon. She noted that his missile rails were empty, indicating that he had been in a fight. He climbed down and the ground crew engulfed him and his WSO, all talking excitely and slapping him on the back.

"Major *ay ban ha phi co dich nam lan,*" she said to herself, holding up five fingers at him.

He grinned widely and nodded to her across the heads of the group which was fast growing into a crowd. Pilots and crews from other aircraft began descending on him. Congratulations were in the air and the word rapidly spread throughout the base that Vic Benedetti had gotten his fifth kill! He was the first American ace of the Vietnamese war!

Someone emerged with a case of French champagne, corks popped and bottles were passed around. Vic and his WSO were drenched in the wine and ceremoniously hoisted onto shoulders. With foaming bottles held high in the air the celebration marched off to the base officers club, its ranks swelling along the way.

Mai Lien watched in wide-eyed wonderment, her little heart pounding with pride and excitement.

"Nguoi My dien," crazy Americans, she whispered to herself.

She was not familiar enough with western ways to fully grasp the significance of the event. However, she did understand that the number *five* was somehow magical in the world of the fighter pilot and that her major had attained immortality among his battle compatriots by shooting down that many communist airplanes.

"Why is everyone so excited," Hanh asked, still covering her ears.

"Major Benedetti has shot down his fifth North Vietnamese airplane."

"He is a hero now?"

"I don't know—maybe," Mai Lien answered.

Hanh took her hands away from her ears. She looked sad.

"What's the matter, Hanh?"

"I think it's wrong."

"What do you mean?"

"The airplanes the major destroyed—did they have men in them?"

"Of course. Someone has to fly them, Hanh. Don't be silly."

"Those were Vietnamese men who had women, Vietnamese women like us who will never again feel

152

the comfort of their men's embraces."

"Oh, shutup, cousin."

"Even now a Vietnamese girl in Hanoi will be grieving the loss of her husband or sweetheart, the major's fifth victim."

"Just shutup."

Mai Lien turned away in disgust, deep in thought. So strange. Hanh has never acted like this before. What's gotten into the girl? Maybe she's just jealous. Or is she a Viet Cong? She stole a look at Hanh out of the corner of her eye.

"Our country has always been at war. Women must suffer the loss of their men," Mai Lien said angrily.

"The people have never gotten used to war," Hanh retorted.

"So?"

"It's as if each battle is a new experience to them and they weep just as loudly and feel as much pain with the loss of the first casualty as they do with the last. One would think that we Vietnamese would become progressively more callous with each ensuing year of war, but we don't," Hanh grieved. "We grow more sensitive. We see nothing philosophical about war."

Mai Lien turned from Hanh, looking away, sulking.

"Hanh, our grandmother and grandfather lived in the north."

"Yes. They were born in North Vietnam like many of our relatives and friends," she said, barely audible. She cowered away from Mai Lien.

"Do you think that they would ever return to Ho

153

Chi Minh's communism?"

"They may. I don't know. Grandmother has told us she is not pleased with the present Thieu regime. And she expressed displeasure with past Presidents Khee, Diem, and the others. She could go back north."

"But hasn't she also said that the freedom she has in the south is far better than the intolerable conditions she suffered in the north?"

The moan of aircraft touching down on the blistering runway suffocated the murmur of rustling rice gaily waving in the burnished fields.

"I did not hear her say it that way."

Mai Lien grabbed Hanh's hand and looked her in the eye. She's a Viet Cong. Surely she's Cong. But in her face I see the buffalo in the rice, and baskets of red mangos; yellow tamarind flowers, a pail of river water. The buffalo in the paddy, cutting the fresh earth; a farmer, the mud, a rice stalk. Kinfolk.

Mai Lien's countenance became severe. "With the defeat of the French in 1954, our relatives left their homes and possessions and fled south with over two million other Vietnamese. Do you deny that?"

Hanh's melodious intonations suddenly took on the harsh vocal sounds of the more severe southern tongue. "Why do you look at me that way, Mai Lien? I hate the communists too. I want to support our country. But I don't have to agree with this war and the killing."

Maybe she's not a Viet Cong. Mai Lien sighed. This war is so confusing. I don't even know if I can trust my own cousin. Does it really matter? She

154

turned and looked beyond the wire, across the defense perimeter where the hot wind pulled at the golden locks of ripening rice. She began to hum to herself:

Hear the cry of our poets who walk the bamboo shaded trails and eat the fruit of tamarind trees; listen to the word from our ancestors whose ears have heard and eyes have seen the rice of suffering and the rice of joy. Old Vietnam. New Vietnam. A delicate frenzy of images experienced, yet not experienced; leaving a misty form, knowable, yet unknowable.

"I'm sorry, Hanh."

She smiled and squeezed Hanh's hand. Hanh giggled and squeezed back. The cold shadow between them disappeared, carried away by the silent understanding between blood kin. Tender magic.

Mai Lien looked on after the parade whisking Vic away toward the buildings, gaining momentum with each step. This was his moment of triumph, and as knights of old returning after a great victory on the battlefield he would be made to relive the fight for the sake of his admirers who lacked the good fortune of being as skillful and courageous as he. They would enshrine him in glory, and legends would be built around his achievements. They would drink and be merry, each taking his turn in personally congratulating the conquering hero. To the younger and lesser experienced he would give encouragement to hopes for their own glory and to all he would bless with words of combat wisdom.

And it would not end until they lived every detail over and over again, satiating their appetites to identify with this man of greatness. Most would never fire a missile or experience the gut wrenching, mouth drying, excitement and fear of aerial combat. Many would never even see a Mig. But through this single individual now thrust into the center of their arenas they would live their dreams of glory as have knights of every generation. And as long as there are wars there will always be knights to emulate and none greater than the knights of the air, for it is only in the air that the one-on-one, man-against-man, single action combat still exists. When all is said and done, when the last contrail vaporizes over Hanoi, it will be voiced again that knights had mounted their steeds once more in quest of glory as they had in ancient times, but this time in jets over Vietnam.

You have the big head now, Major. But that's all right. I can wait, she reminded herself. You need your pride. You must have it to shoot down five enemy jets. Yes, Major, to reach high you need a big pride. It is what forces you to make one more break into a Mig when your fuel tanks are dangerously low, and what keeps you scissoring canopy to canopy with the enemy, to come over the top and go at him again. See, I've learned your flying language. I listen well, Major.

She watched Vic being raced down the flight line, bouncing on big shoulders, awkwardly trying to balance himself with a foaming champagne bottle clutched in each hand, arms outstretched, caught up in the ecstasy of his moment. You just can't avoid it. Always in the middle. Crazy man, she smiled wistfully. Always holding a slight edge of authority over the others. Maybe you are like all exceptional men, Major Benedetti, blooming from the blood of heroes, and requiring constant attention. Do you think so? She could still see him high in the air drinking from one of the bottles. The air was thick with the din of shouting men and parking jets, a medley of resounding and discordant noises. How long will you have this unquenchable thirst to excel? Always meeting the additional demand of personal sacrifice. Lifted above the masses. Driving yourself to reach high—sensitive and proud—to become a champion. Will it end? How, Major? How? How much longer can the discipline last?

Vic was totally engulfed by the mob, now. It was difficult for her to see him except for his dark, wavy hair. He had fallen off to one side and arms were trying to right him. The champagne bottles remained high, standing out like homing beacons. She stood on her toes and took a weary breath. I can wait for your pride, my crazy man. Women like me will always find their security in men like you. My ego is dead in yours.

"The pilots are so handsome," Hanh said in her flute-like Vietnamese.

"Would you like me to introduce you to one of the Americans?"

"No," she said firmly. "I'd be so frightened. They're too big."

"They are big, but very nice. Sometimes puffed up with their own importance."

"I'm happy with Minh," Hanh said.

"You seem happy with him. But are you? I mean really."

"With Minh I have learned a secret," Hanh said.

"I don't understand." Mai Lien looked perplexed.

"I don't know if I can explain it, but I'm sensitive to it just the same. Without him I feel like the rice stalks growing in the shade of the rain forest along the edge of the paddies in our village. They are thin, stunted, and weaker than the rice bathed in full sunshine. When the forest is cut back, this less developed rice grows stronger and reaches for the sun in an explosion of growth. Have you seen this?"

"Surely," Mai Lien answered.

"And so it is with me. I will burst into full womanhood through Minh's virility. The stronger his maleness the greater will be my femaleness. Do I sound foolish?"

"Yes, a little foolish—and incomplete as a woman."

"I am incomplete, without Minh."

"It is as simple as that with you?"

"It is as simple as that. I'm glad that God decided to create both men and women."

"And you're glad he chose to make you a woman?"

"I'm glad he chose to make me a woman and Minh a man," Hanh said.

And indeed she was a woman. Like Mai Lien, cousin Hanh was as attractive and feminine a creature that ever blessed the eyes of men. Her straight black hair reached her waist and had the sheen of polished teak. Her beautiful long almond eyes were set with sparkling pupils of deep black jade, and her nose and lips were dainty sculptures perfectly shaped to her face. Like the majority of Vietnamese women she was small and built like a beautifully proportioned doll, painstakingly handcrafted in a master's workshop. Her feet and hands were diminutive and delicately formed pieces of art. Though normally hidden by her *ao dai,* Hanh's legs were particularly attractive and would be considered inspirational by any man having the good fortune to gaze upon them. Her skin was clear and smooth, and her muscles well toned and strong. At twenty-six she was the epitome of oriental beauty and with each ensuing year new loveliness would unfold in Hanh. She would be exquisite at eighty.

The major disappeared into the officers club surrounded by the raucous cavalcade of admiring pilots. Mai Lien felt hurt, left out, and resentful in being nakedly ignored at such an important and memorable time in her man's career. But she was Vietnamese and had been taught that this was male country where women were not welcome. She stood motionless, clenching and unclenching her small fists in frustration. In due time, major, your ego will become fully saturated and you will tire of the celebration and congratulations, she thought. She blinked her eyes in surprise at how articulate she could be in her thoughts when angered. She could almost see the hot, fluid Vietnamese vaporizing in her mind. Then you will come, seeking refuge in me as you always do when you have killed, your tears soaking through my *ao dai* to my breasts; and in my young wisdom and long experience with war I will

159

understand and comfort you. You will tell me your secret thoughts, about your reluctance to fire the missile, your dreaded fear of being shot down, lost and lonely on the open escarpments of Mig Ridge, and the ever present torment that you must not fail. You will become embarrassed at your honesty but never uncomfortable in finding your comfort in me. I will dry your wet face with my hair and then feed you my good food. I will bathe your strong body in hot towels, walk on your back, and massage your bare feet while you stretch out on a palm mat. Your taut nerves and muscles will come under submission of my strong hands. Then you will fall into a fitful sleep while I vigilantly sit beside you soothing your brow and you break hard and fast into the Mig again and again, killing it over and over. She whirled on her heel, her long hair twisting in a wide comely curve across her shoulders, and spiritedly walked off toward the blue Honda.

"Mai Lien, wait for me," Hanh shouted, running after her.

Mai Lien kicked up the stand and sat astride the motorcycle.

"Are you coming?" she said tersely, patting the seat behind her.

"Don't feel so badly," Hanh said.

"Are you coming?"

"It won't work. You're too . . . idealistic . . . too romantic."

"Too romantic?"

"Yes. You should be more realistic about love."

"What on earth are you talking about?"

"It just won't work — it can't."

"What can't?"

"Between you and Major Benedetti."

"Why not?"

"He's American!"

"He's American?" Mai Lien nearly screamed the question.

"And you're Vietnamese. No decent Vietnamese girl would be seen with an American."

Mai Lien slapped Hanh. Hanh broke into tears.

"Everyone thinks you're so perfect, Mai Lien. Well, you're not. And you taking up with this American killer proves it."

Hanh ran off holding her hand to her red cheek.

"Cong!" Mai Lien shouted after her. "Sleazy Viet Cong!"

II

JUDGMENT DAY

". . . "The Struggle Has Ended."

CHAPTER TEN

It was Sunday morning. Mai Lien parted the mosquito netting and swung her legs over the edge of her bed and began rubbing the sleep from her eyes. The first rays of sunlight were reflecting off the rice fields into her open window and she could see the heavy mist lying low in the valley. Open patches here and there revealed the jungle and dim outline of low hills beyond. A gentle breeze rustled the bamboo outside her window and two small colorful birds chirped among the banyan leaves. The coolness of the night was already dissipating, being rapidly replaced with undulating waves of warming currents generated by the rising equatorial sun.

Soon it would be very hot. She must hurry while there was still comfort in the air, and prepare herself for a busy day. For today was Sunday and relatives and friends would be visiting her and her grandmother and she must do the shopping early, and attend to the cooking and cleaning to make her home comfortable for her guests. But first she must go to church and give thanks to her Lord for her many blessings and to pray for the major's protection.

Slipping her feet into open sandals, she twisted her long hair into a loose knot on top of her head peasant style, holding it in place with her Chinese comb. She walked quietly into the kitchen area, being careful not to disturb her grandmother. Normally cantankerous in the morning, grandmother would be in a scolding mood if Mai Lien didn't have the bitter Vietnamese tea ready for her when she awakened. Mai Lien quickly placed fresh charcoal in the stove and ignited it with kerosene. After placing the rice on to cook and the water to boil she made her way outside through the bamboo grove to the well for her bath water. As she approached the well the ducks and geese rushed from all directions to surround her, squawking for food and attention. She bent down, talking to them for a few moments in her melodious voice. They quieted down and listened attentively as she stroked their long necks. She gently parted the group with her lithe legs, drew water from the well and walked back through the bamboo into the house.

Grandmother was awake and demanding her morning sustenance, scolding Mai Lien as usual for not having her tea ready. Mai Lien quickly prepared the hot tea, poured a cup for her grandmother and served her a bowl of rice which she accepted with a smile and outstretched hands.

"Con gioi lam," you are a good granddaughter

166

she said to Mai Lien, sipping her bitter tea and pushing the steaming rice into her mouth with wooden chopsticks.

Mai Lien took boiling water from the stove and carried it to a small roofless enclosure adjacent to the house. Inside the bathhouse, the *phong tam,* a very large clay jar partly filled with water stood on the rough tile floor in the center of the room. Half a coconut shell with a short bamboo handle hung from the lip of the jar. She added hot water, increasing the bath to a comfortable temperature and poured in a few drops of French bath oil she had saved for special days. She slipped out of her pajamas and stood nude for a few moments, stretching her supple body and inhaling the perfumed fragrance in the rising steam. The morning sun, filtered by the swaying bamboo, streamed through the small window and cast moving mosaic patterns on her smooth, bronze skin. She completed a few stretching exercises then thoroughly soaked herself in bath water poured over her body with the coconut shell. After working at it for some time she was able to get a sufficient lather from the cheap Vietnamese soap to spread over her skin.

Like most of her lady friends, Mai Lien had been taught early by attentive elders to be very clean and meticulous about her body. She carefully bathed, then rinsed herself with fresh water from the jar. After drying, she wrapped herself in a large towel and stepped outside onto the grass. She sat in the sun with her jet black hair spread out like a giant oriental fan. Waiting for her hair to dry she painstakingly trimmed and shaped her long fingernails, then carefully painted them a fiery "Chinese Red." She did the same with her toenails.

Now came the most eventful part in her ritual, the combing of her hair. Mai Lien's lovely, long hair was her most important identifying physical feature, the mantle of her perfection, the capstone to her femininity that declared her preeminence as woman. Her hair now dry, she gathered it together and pulled it over her shoulder, holding in on her lap below her small breasts. To her large, Chinese wooden comb she applied a few drops of coconut oil that she had refined herself. She placed the comb at the back of her head and gently but firmly pulled the comb through her hair in broad sweeping curves, being sure that the oil became evenly distributed over each strand of hair. She repeated this procedure using a hair conditioner that Vietnamese girls make by rendering a special black bean found growing in large pods hanging from trees along the forest paths.

Mai Lien sang softly as she combed her hair. Her beautiful childlike voice carried across the yard to the edge of the rice paddy where the ducks and geese stopped feeding and arched their necks high to listen to her familiar singing. A young boy with a hoe over his shoulder and leading his water buffalo stopped for a few moments in the shade of the banana plants to listen to her Chinese ballads and ancient Vietnamese folk songs. Flying by, a large parrot changed directions and settled in the tamarind tree near her, cocking its varicolored head and large beak toward her. To be near Mai Lien was to be at peace. Even the flight of jets banking into their landing pattern overhead seemed to be acknowledging the tranquil scene below with their graceful sweeping motion and precision turn.

Mai Lien's rich bodied hair now shone like a raven's wing. She pulled her comb through it one more time and stood up as it cascaded down over her shoulders and back. She replenished the jar with water from the well then returned to the house where grandmother was busy tending to the stove. Mai Lien sat down at the long mahogany table, hand hewn from the rain forests surrounding her village and patiently worked by Da Nang craftsmen. The table had been in the family for many generations and it represented a chain of life continuous and rich with the ages. Mai Lien and her grandmother gave it the respect due a permanent member of the household. Her *ba ngoai* placed rice soup and a bowl of steamed pork and vegetables in front of her and smiled an ancient smile that spoke better than words of the deep love she had for her daughter's child.

Because of the many debilitating factors consistent with war and the poverty that it brings, Mai Lien's husbandless mother had been unable to care for her. The war and seven children drained her of any economic foundation that she may have once had and there came a time when Mai Lien, yet but a baby, was given to her grandmother for better or for worse. Not much better off, other than not having as many mouths to feed, her grandmother took Mai Lien as one of her own, even to the extent of having her own name placed as natural mother on Mai Lien's birth certificate. For in the ways of Vietnamese country people, births were carried out at home and it was sometime afterwards, maybe several years later as in Mai Lien's case, that the birth would be recorded. So through a quirk of war, Mai Lien's grandmother had become her legal mother.

Mai Lien finished her breakfast and went into her small bedroom to dress. She automatically chose her all white *ao dai,* for it was best that a Vietnamese girl wear white when attending church. She opened the side of the *ao dai,* then slipped it over her head, pulling it down snugly. The dress was designed to fit tight around her waist and upper body, effectively revealing the perfection of her femaleness underneath. She stepped into the white slacks and checked to see that the full split in both sides of the *ao dai* reached slightly above her hip. On her feet went a new pair of black, Bangkok open toed sandals with a small tapered heel and six rhinestones set in the instep strap.

A solid ring of pale green translucent jade covered her small wrist and tear drops of jade dangled from her earlobes. A highly polished blue-green jade ring set in gold glittered on an exquisite finger of one hand. The women of Vietnam regarded jade as an absolute necessity and they sacrificed a great deal to acquire this traditional jewel. It was an essential part of their femininity and its mystique had been worn for hundreds of years by each generation of women. Mai Lien's jade had been passed down successively through several generations and she was especially proud of these family heirlooms, treasuring them dearly.

Adorned with a provocative yet modest gleaming

white *ao dai,* black patent leather sandals, perfect green jade, mane of raven black hair, flawless sparkling red fingernails, and a hint of French cologne, beautiful Mai Lien anxiously waited by the open door.

CHAPTER ELEVEN

She saw the dust first, rising in the distance above the bamboo bordering the lane that led to her house. A few minutes later the familiar shape of a military jeep emerged from the covering and descended the short distance down into the picturesque valley, bouncing and weaving along the road, swerving to miss crossing chickens and muddy ruts filled with rain water. Vic pulled up in front and smiled openly upon seeing Mai Lien in the doorway. He leaped from the jeep and rushed up the remaining steps to her side. Mai Lien's heart ballooned in her throat as Vic took her hand in his own and gently kissed her palm, obviously very delighted to see her.

"*Thieu ta da den,*" she called to grandmother, announcing the major's arrival.

Grandmother poured Mrs. Ly more tea and smiled politely. "I hope the American's visit will not be an embarrassment for you."

"Of course not. Why should it? My business is with you."

"I just thought that in view of the nature of your business that the major's presence might detract from our conversation."

"Mai Lien is a very attractive woman and it is natural for her to have suitors. But you are a level-headed woman and we have been friends since childhood. I trust that good sense will win out." Mrs. Ly looked disdainfully in Vic's direction.

"You are not fond of the Americans?" asked grandmother.

"They serve their purpose. We need them for the time being. They are Americans and we are Vietnamese." She sipped her tea. "And that brings me to the point of my visit."

Ba ngoai waited patiently, teacup resting in her hand.

"Mai Lien is Vietnamese. My son is Vietnamese. The Ly family would be privileged to have your granddaughter as a member of the clan. We offer her security and a footing into polite Vietnamese society."

"How about love?"

Mrs. Ly ignored the question.

"You are a typical *ba ngoai*, sister Nghia. You are also very cautious concerning the training of children and other customs, particularly courtship between young people. I am surprised that you have allowed this to happen," Mrs. Ly said, pointing to Mai Lien and Vic talking in the doorway.

"You are resisting reality. The parents' influence

174

on their children's marriages has been severely weakened in past years, and only in the most traditional families are marriages still carried out in the old ways." Grandmother smoothed her *ao dai*, not daring to look at her friend.

"Many marriages are still arranged for the children by the parents, even to the degree of consummating the agreement when the future bride and groom are only babes. Have you forgotten that you and I are recipients of this kind of arrangement?"

"Yes, we were, but times are changing."

"For the worse."

Mrs. Ly looked like she would crush the teacup in her fist.

"I am proud to say that my eldest son has already made an arrangement with his best friend, swearing to a marriage between their yet *unborn* children."

"I'm not preoccupied with choosing a husband for Mai Lien. I've long ago decided that my granddaughter is fully capable of handling this for herself. I'm concerned only with her happiness, and if she has fallen in love with an American officer then let it be."

"The American's intentions appear honorable enough but only time and the war will tell how serious he really is about Mai Lien. He is American and she Vietnamese. This alone presents obstacles that will seriously hinder their relationship," said Mrs. Ly.

"I know little of the United States but I do know that people have prejudices wherever they may live."

"Forgive me for saying so, old friend, but a Vietnamese girl who marries an American is automatically labeled as an opportunist who has forsaken her country and traditional ways for the lust of money," Mrs. Ly said.

"Yes, and most think that she must come from a family of questionable repute and is no doubt a bar girl or prostitute."

Ba ngoai poured more tea, still smiling graciously.

"But even though many of the girls taking up with American men are seriously handicapped with bad reputations, they prove to be the best of wives when given the chance," she continued.

"Often they have no other alternative but to marry with an American since no Vietnamese man will have them." Mrs. Ly had a smug smile on her lips. She mopped off her sweaty face.

"But there are, good friend, girls from respectable families and with impeccable morals like Mai Lien who become wives of the Americans and settle down to happy and useful lives with their foreign husbands. I find it particularly satisfying to learn that the American men cherish their Vietnamese wives regardless of background, and that they give their women much more affection than would be expected from a Vietnamese husband."

"Are you insinuating that a Vietnamese man doesn't love his wife as much as an American?" Mrs. Ly sat up straight in her chair. *Ba ngoai* noticed that her teacup was shaking.

"Only that he is used to taking her for granted. The American male on the other hand looks upon his Vietnamese wife as being something special, a unique creature who is especially endowed with feminine qualities that are new to him and of which he is experiencing for the first time, and who gives him far more love and attention than he is used to."

"Well, sister Nghia, we have talked long," Mrs. Ly said tersely. "Do you have an answer for me?"

"Time will tell. It is too soon."

"Too soon is it?"

"Yes, too soon. These things shouldn't be rushed."

"We are growing impatient, dear friend," Mrs. Ly said.

"I can understand."

"The Ly family cannot wait forever. I'm afraid that you have forgotten your status. There are many well-to-do Da Nang families willing to make an immediate arrangement."

"I'm sorry, sister Ly, but it is yet too soon."

"I will delay for a while longer—but only because of our long friendship," she added.

"I am grateful," *ba ngoai* said.

With that she concluded her visit and hotly waddled out the rear door, leaving grandmother with much to ponder.

Watching Mrs. Ly disappear through the bamboo, *ba ngoai* recalled a poem her mother often recited:

The stupid have their wisdom
The ungainly their grace
The poor have their riches
But the proud save face

Ba ngoai stood silently musing over the past and watching the American and her granddaughter talking quietly to each other in an odd combination of Vietnamese and English. The scene brought back memories of another time, another war, and another language when two lovers stood talking in this same doorway. Mai Lien's mother, like Mai Lien, had been an exceptional young woman and the conquering Japanese officer had been captivated with her beauty and charm in much the same way as this American major had been enamored with Mai Lien. In the beginning, *ba ngoai* had severely objected to the Japanese officer taking her daughter as his wife. But as time passed, she became resigned to the union, especially when it became apparent that the garrison commander's in-laws were entitled to certain benefits that would make the family's life tolerable in spite of their captivity.

They lived comfortably throughout the Japanese occupation but there came a time when *ba ngoai* decided that she had had enough of Japanese rule. She waited until her son-in-law was away on a field operation, and with the help of a villager and his ox cart, she had stolen into the commander's home and brazenly kidnapped her daughter who was now heavy with child. With hopes of a new life with relatives in the province further south, grandmother and her daughter made good their escape until they encountered, on the same road they were traveling, her daughter's husband and his troop returning from the field. Upon recognizing the small entourage and immediately comprehending the significance of their travel, *ba ngoai's* son-in-law leaped from his lead vehicle with drawn Samurai sword and in one blow severed the oxen's head from its body. The driver fled into the surrounding rain forest, abandoning his decapitated animal and cargo. *Ba ngoai*, fearing for her life and that of her daughter, screamed like a banshee and pummeled her son-in-law with her small fists. The enraged Japanese commander ignored her, picked up his wife and carried her unceremoniously back to his vehicle. The convoy resumed its march leaving an exhausted and sobbing *ba ngoai* alone in the dust, slumped over in an ox cart with a beheaded animal.

Not to be denied, the dauntless *ba ngoai* made a second attempt to steal her beautiful daughter from the Japanese, this time with the aid of the Viet Minh. These guerrilla fighters commanded by a young Ho Chi Minh, operated from their jungle redoubts and were dedicated to the destruction of all foreign domination and to helping the Vietnamese people in their struggle against the invaders. Their motive was the same as that of the present day Viet Cong, to establish communist rule in all Vietnam with Ho Chi Minh as leader. *Ba ngoai* and the small band of armed Viet Minh approached the Japanese commander's villa under the cover of darkness. The guards were more alert this time and had to be distracted by a diversionary ploy. When the Viet Minh began firing at the opposite end of the villa, grandmother and her husband quickly entered the rear of the house and raced through the rooms in search of Mai Lien's mother who was now being held prisoner in her own home. Coming upon her in an upstairs hallway, the surprised guard was unable to respond fast enough as *ba ngoai's* husband shot him in the head. Carrying their pregnant daughter between them, the two parents ran downstairs and under the covering fire of the Viet Minh, sped across the expanse of front yard to be swallowed up by the jungle beyond.

The family escaped to relatives who hid them and it was the last they saw of the Japanese. A few months later grandmother heard news that a big bomb exploded on Japan and all the foreigners were leaving. The rumor proved to be true and she returned home with her family. Shortly thereafter her daughter gave birth to Mai Lien. When new occupants took over the villa outside the village, they discovered a Samurai sword, a gold watch, and gold ring. Attached to this collection was a note written in both Japanese and Vietnamese, and addressed to *ba ngoai*. It read:

"Please give these gifts to my child that I shall never see."

Grandmother slowly returned from the past and she stared at Mai Lien still talking to the American major outside. Her gaze shifted to the heavy Japanese sword on the wall. It was a work of art hanging there in its finely engraved scabbard. She wondered if any ox blood remained on its blade.

CHAPTER TWELVE

Vic walked beside Mai Lien, his attention being drawn to the sights, sounds, and smells of Da Nang City. The open rawness had a beguiling attraction for him.

"Hey, Major."

Vic turned in the direction of the familiar voice.

"Out for a Sunday stroll, Vic?" Davis said, pushing his way through the street crowd. *"Manh goi,* Mai Lien?"

"Manh, Captain Davis," Mai Lien answered demurely.

"You're looking very pretty as usual."

"Thank you, Captain." She bowed politely.

"We're going shopping, Drill. Want to come along?" Vic asked.

"No thanks—have to get back to the base. You and I are the only ones in the squadron not flying today's mission. Someone has to mind the store,"

Davis said, winking at Mai Lien.

Vic faked a punch at him. "Okay—don't rub it in. I can't fly them all—neither can you."

"Who's leading? Pellegrini?"

"Who else."

There was an awkward pause.

"Johnson wants you to lead elements, Drill. I told him no."

"I know it."

"Well?"

"You're the boss, Vic."

"He thinks you'd make a good flight leader. So do I."

"I'm ready whenever you are, Major," he said, winking at Mai Lien again.

"Soon, Captain, soon."

They watched a cyclo pull up to the entrance of a well trafficked bar. An attractive girl stepped from the bicycle powered rickshaw and wiggled her way through the crowd and disappeared into the bar's dim interior.

"I really feel sorry for these young women," Davis said, nodding toward the girl, happy to change the subject.

"Why's that?" Vic asked, only half interested, studying the noisy Asian street scene swirling around them.

"The really pretty ones drift into cities like Da Nang and Saigon and get seduced right away—they don't have a chance."

"Yeh, I know. But I don't feel sorry for them. It takes two to tango."

Vic wasn't paying much attention to Davis. He

was intrigued by the swarm of humanity scurrying like busy elves toward some unknown end.

"The way I see it, most of these Vietnamese girls are pretty and poor, the Americans, lonely and wealthy — at least by Vietnamese standards. This is a natural setup and the native girls fall into the trap with ease."

"Trap? Do you really think they're being trapped?" Vic was becoming interested.

"Sure it's a trap. It's legitimate and instinctive with Vietnamese girls to expect a permanent relationship, which includes marriage. Their basic insecurity, spawned from the depths of war and poverty, together with their inborn dependence on men, is a deadly combination and makes them particularly vulnerable to the Americans' persuasions."

Vic looked at Mai Lien uneasily.

"No trap. Girls go with GI because they want to. Love GI money," Mai Lien interrupted.

"That's just it." Drill was getting excited. "With the coming of the American GI and the money he brought with him, the Vietnamese suddenly encountered problems and temptations with which they had no past experience."

"Maybe you're right. I've been pretty stupid about all this. Didn't even care until Mai Lien opened my eyes to the struggle of the individual Vietnamese. If it hadn't been for her I'd never have known the real Vietnam."

"The real Vietnam? What's the real Vietnam?"

A covey of young women in swaying *ao dais* swung around Davis. One turned and frowned at Mai Lien.

"Delicate and lovely creatures," Drill said. "Do you see that one there, the beauty that frowned at Mai Lien?"

"Mmm."

"I bet she was dropped by her first lover just like most of them."

"Like most of them?"

"Then a predictable and unfortunate pattern of an ever tightening circle of unhappiness and despair developed. This gave way to hopelessness and withdrawal. She probably went from affair to affair in search of lost love and security, led on by the ever present promises of the men who toyed with her."

"With her? That wholesome looking girl?"

"And hanging over her head is the unrelenting specter of poverty and the return to her family home where she is no longer wanted. If the cycle continues long enough and she becomes desperate enough, she will turn to prostitution and pills, if she hasn't already, and then suicide."

"Prostitution, pills, and suicide—come on!"

"No, really. To complicate matters, if she has been seen to hold frequent company with an American man, she has little chance of ever attracting a Vietnamese husband. Furthermore, once she has allowed herself to be violated out of wedlock, a Vietnamese man upon discovering this fact on their wedding night, has the legal right to cast her away. Moreover, it is his moral duty to uphold the reputation of his family by sending her back to her parents with the announcement that she is not a virgin."

"Seems unfair to me," Vic said.

Mai Lien's long eyes were wide with child-like

fascination at Drill's surprising knowledge of Vietnamese customs. She wondered how he could have such accurate information concerning these things. He must have a Vietnamese girl friend.

"Additionally, the girl, who was no doubt born and raised within the usual strict code of modesty and moral principle, now finds that because of her wayward ways her relatives and friends reject her and she no longer has the comfort and security of a family which is so much a part of her life and without which her hopes quickly evaporate."

"Yes — true, very true," Mai Lien said.

Davis warmed to Mai Lien's encouragement. "From the beginning her heart never accepts her unbecoming behavior and she is continually persecuted by guilt feelings. Her natural instincts, carefully inbred and passed on to her by generations of the world's most faithful and morally principled women, rebel against what she knows is a violation and degradation of womanhood. Because of this she doesn't make a very good bed hopper or prostitute. End of lecture."

"Thank you professor."

"You come walk with us, captain. We talk more. Maybe you come my home have dinner with us." Mai Lien was still in wonder over the well delivered dissertation and was reluctant to let Davis go.

"Sorry, Mai Lien. I'll have to take a rain check."

"Rain check?"

"Next time. I'm behind in my letter writing. Wife and kids. But ask me again. Okay?"

"Seriously, Drill. Come on out to her home with us. I'm sure you'll enjoy yourself. Get a slice of the real Vietnam you seem so interested in. How about it?"

"Please, Captain Davis," Mai Lien begged. "You will like Mai Lien family. For sure they like you. You come. Please, Captain."

"Best food in Vietnam, Drill. You don't know what you're missing."

"I'd sure like to, Vic, but I really miss my family. I need to write to them."

"Okay," Mai Lien said. "Your family more important. You take care them first. Rain check, okay?"

"Okay, see ya."

Mai Lien and Vic passed through the market entrance and were quickly swallowed up by the bustle of activity. Vic felt conspicuous but it appeared that no one was paying any attention to him. But upon closer inspection he noticed that curious oriental eyes were subtly being cast in his direction as Mai Lien led the way through the press of the crowd. It was natural for these people to be interested in his presence, he encouraged himself. After all, he was the only American in the whole place and U.S. servicemen were seldom seen rubbing elbows with the Vietnamese at their level. Just the same, he felt uncomfortable knowing there were Viet Cong present. He casually brushed his side to be sure his .45 was still intact.

"You like chicken?" she asked, picking up a brightly colored jungle fowl and holding the squaking bird up for him to inspect.

"Sure."

She nodded to the toothless vendor who quickly

lopped off the hen's head with a single swift blow from her *dao phay*. Vic stood aghast as the headless animal popped loose from the vendor's outstretched hands and raced down the aisle, wings flapping, blood gorging from the open neck. He recoiled with revulsion at the shoppers' gleeful shouting and giggles, being openly entertained by the bird's adrenalitic Saint Vitus' Dance. He turned away.

Vic carefully watched Mai Lien gracefully moving from vendor to vendor skillfully haggling over the price of vegetables and meats she was purchasing. The arguing was customary and when agreement was reached over one commodity they would begin haggling anew over the next item. Mai Lien would rub and poke the pork until she found just the right piece that satisfied her. She was very busy with her shopping and chatting with friends but she never for a moment neglected Vic, buying him a glass of sugar cane juice and making sure she never got too far ahead of him as they walked through the myriad displays of colorful fruits, vegetables, and fresh meats and fish.

Suddenly Vic's fighter pilot instincts brought him to the alert and he felt the immediate urge to check behind him. He slowly turned and his eyes fought the crowd in search of a clue that would signal danger. All seemed normal enough, even peaceful. A woman untied a cord holding several chickens by their legs and she handed two of the bright jungle fowl over to a customer. A man passed carrying a heavy bag of rice on his back, and people squatted on their haunches bartering, drinking tea, and eating from bowls. Children ran to and fro chasing each other.

Then he saw the bicycle pull up outside the entrance and the rider nervously dismount and glance around. A cloth suspiciously covering the bicycle's carrying rack fell away exposing the ugly silhouette of the claymore. As if caught in a slow motion nightmare, Vic's mind struggled to set into motion the muscles and coordination necessary to avert the impending disaster. He pulled his pistol and plunged headlong into the mass of humanity screaming, *"Tranh ra! Tranh ra! Chat no! Chat no!"*

"Explosive! Explosive! Out of the way! Out of the way!" The crowd parted for him, scattering in every direction as he raced like a crazed man for the bicycle. The Viet Cong, no more than a boy in his teens, was in full flight down the road. Vic fell to one knee, pulled down on the Cong and squeezed off a round. The heavy slug hit the VC in the shoulder, nearly tearing his arm off as he pitched forward into the street mud. In one motion Vic leaped onto the bicycle and furiously began blindly pedaling in search of an open area to abandon the claymore. He careened through the streets of Da Nang yelling his warning all the way. The Vietnamese vanished before him fully aware of what was taking place, encouraging him on with their own shouts. His mind raced ahead scanning its memory bank for a familiar landmark, a side street, anything to direct him away from people before the damnable thing detonated. He asked his computer how soon it would be before the timing device triggered the explosive. Ten minutes? Five minutes? Negative! The VC always set them for just enough time to make the plant and safely withdraw. The risk of the bomb being discovered increased proportionally with the passage of time. He knew he had only seconds left. Suddenly he was on the outskirts of town. Still shouting his warning, he drove the bicycle off an embankment and rolled over into the ditch on the opposite side of the road just as the mine went off ripping the air with a violent explosion. Shrapnel zinged over his head and the ground convulsed, throwing him over on his back. Then all was quiet. He opened his eyes to see a pall of dense smoke and dust drifting over him. The acrid smell of cordite filled his nostrils. His ears rang. Vic lay there for a few moments sucking in lungfuls of air and gathering his strength. In the distance he heard the clamoring of approaching Vietnamese. He pulled himself to his feet and climbed out of the ditch. Knees wobbling, he stood in the center of the road. People streamed out of the town and crowded around him, jabbering and patting him of the back. A few tried to dust off his clothing, one gave him tea from a container on her back. Several men passed pieces of the shredded bicycle around. A cyclo appeared and he was helped into it.

The crowd of several hundred, with Vic seated in the cyclo, paraded him back over the route he had carried the deadly load. Cheering Vietnamese lined the streets, crowded around him, waved to him. Vic was embarrassed but at the same time the appreciation from the people for what he had done in saving many of their lives gave him a comfortable feeling of worthiness.

Mai Lien was certain that Vic was dead. Like Vic, she had in a flash discerned the threat and watched in wide-eyed horror as the major incredibly ran directly into the face of certain disaster, shot the VC, *Then raced off to his doom*. Then there was the explosion and she had fallen to her knees weeping uncontrollably. Now, looking up through tear filled eyes and seeing the returning procession with Vic enthroned in the cyclo, surrounded by a throng of townspeople, Mai Lien stood up in disbelief. When the truth finally impacted on her, that this was indeed the major, she dried her tears, tidied herself, and thanked God for keeping him safe.

"Nguoi My dien," crazy American, she whispered to herself.

The police and military arrived and the investigation was underway. The boy was identified as a hard core Viet Cong agent and Vic was asked a few questions regarding the attack. However, in their excitement the witnesses took over answering for him and Vic was allowed to go about his business. He looked around for Mai Lien and found her standing on the edge of the crowd looking like an orphaned child. He touched her shoulder. "Afraid?"

"Em lo so cho anh, khong phai cho em," not for myself but for you, she answered, tears brimming to the surface again.

"I'm all right."

"You crazy."

"Aren't you going to give me a kiss?" he said playfully.

"No can do. You crazy."

Vic stood in front of her, grinning. She reached up and tugged at his sleeve." Promise you no do crazy thing no more."

"Give me a kiss first."

"No can do."

Two young mothers, each with a baby seated on her hip came up to Mai Lien and held her hand in the characteristic fashion that Vic had seen these tiny women do when they wished to express their understanding and affection. They appeared to be close friends with Mai Lien and talked loudly with her in rapid Da Nangese, now and then stealing a glance at Vic. It was obvious that they were talking about him but their Vietnamese was too fast and he was unable to get the gist of their conversation. Eventually they stopped and Mai Lien explained that the women had been chosen as a delegation by the people in the market to speak their appreciation to the major for his act of heroism. She went on to say that the people wished him good fortune and long life, and that they would pray for his continued safety and success in battle. The two women, smiling prettily, bowed respectfully and departed. Vic was touched. He felt a warm glow of humility spread over him.

Mai Lien completed her shopping and he helped her carry the freshly caught fish, the pork, and variety of vegetables and fruit to his jeep. She insisted on carrying most of the food herself and Vic had a difficult time persuading her to let him carry anything at all. She gave him the decapitated chicken.

"Vietnamese way," she argued. "Man no carry, woman do."

He finally relented, realizing that he was putting Mai Lien in an awkward position by usurping her female role. It was important to her to be able to carry out her responsibilities as a woman and he was interfering with the satisfaction she received when doing her work well. Moreover, other women would not respect her for allowing her man to do work that was clearly not becoming to him.

Women are women and men are men, and there is no confusion in that over here, he said to himself.

While Mai Lien tended to her dutiful chores, Vic pondered his close encounter with eternity. The frightening incident had proceeded with such lightning force that he scarcely had had time to consider its consequences. With respect to all logic and rules of probability he should at this moment be scattered in little pieces across the countryside and not healthy and whole, admiring the diligence with which his Vietnamese sweetheart was filling the jeep with produce.

"Mai Lien."

"Yes," she answered, not looking up, her attention fixed on her work as she placed the last basket of food into the jeep.

"Do you still pray for me?"

"Always."

"What did you mean when you asked me if I knew Jesus?"

"What you say?" She stopped arranging the baskets and stared at him.

"You know. The day you invited me to your home to have dinner and meet grandmother. You asked me if I knew Jesus. Remember?"

"Yes, I remember."

"What did you mean?"

Mai Lien's countenance grew serious and an air of serenity enveloped her. Vic sensed a resolve in her that surprised him.

He felt a heaviness in his chest. He stared up into the puffy vertical stacks of cumulus building in the east. He looked back into her deeply earnest face. She remained taciturn.

She nudged him into the driver's seat, finished securing her baskets, and climbed in beside him.

"We go home now, *cung oi*."

CHAPTER THIRTEEN

Vic shifted out of second gear and accelerated around an overloaded melon truck swaying on broken springs. He carelessly leaned back in his seat and looked out over the countryside, enjoying the drive. The sky began filling with towering white pillars of giant cumulus, announcing the arrival of the daily tropical shower. Vietnam was a picturesque country and Vic welcomed the opportunity to absorb its beauty, free from the interference of the war.

The jeep bounced along through groves of orange red mangos, coconut palm, breadfruit trees, and golden yellow bananas. The ever present rice paddies shimmered in the noonday sun and the rice stalks waved gently in anticipation of the coming rain. Here and there a farmer trailed behind his water buffalo pulling a plow. They passed through tall banks of bamboo gently curving inward high over each side of the road, meeting to form a swaying, living arch. Bamboo, the people's symbol of Vietnam. It was imprinted on their money, always in their art, they made their homes from it, and used it to make toys for their children. They found sustenance in its leaves and roots, and built their furniture and containers from it.

Vic slowed the jeep and shifted into low gear, turning off the main road, crossing over an irrigation canal and onto the secondary road leading to Mai Lien's village. Women carrying water jars and baskets of food walked at the sides of the road and along the levees that separated the rice fields into individual paddies. They wore scarfs folded on top of their heads or were covered with the typical conical straw hats of Southeast Asia to protect themselves from the intensity of the tropical sun. They were dressed in pajama style black pants and the usual long sleeved white cotton blouses with "V" necks and short splits along each side at the bottom. Most were barefoot and some wore sandals. The people of Vietnam, Vic mused, sensitive, resourceful, and hardworking, all struggling for a place in the sun. It occurred to him that these people asked only to be allowed to labor untroubled in their private world, where their ancestors had before them. Where life is easy there is no necessity for complexities or complicated habits of living. So these simple people, so inferior to America in elaborate systems and technology, live successfully their innocent lives.

Further on they came upon an interesting and colorful procession of men, women, and children.

The women were dressed in the most beautiful *ao dais* Vic had ever seen. Even the little girls wore the traditional Vietnamese dress. At the head of the procession two men carried a long tray upon which lay a roasted suckling pig wrapped in red cellophane. Immediately behind the roast pig followed two rows of adults and children transporting smaller trays laden with what appeared to be gifts also wrapped in red cellophane. An old lady walked behind the trays and behind her were a younger man and woman. A long column of people followed. At the very end, lagging a few feet behind everyone else, trudged a rather subdued looking young man dressed in a well tailored western suit.

Vic shifted into second gear and studied the line of people as he and Mai Lien drove past. His curiosity aroused, he turned to Mai Lien and asked her what was going on. She explained that this was a wedding procession headed for the bride's home where the groom and his parents, relatives, and friends would receive her. She went on to say that the suckling pig and objects carried on the trays were gifts from the groom to the bride and her parents. The gifts were wrapped in red for long life and good fortune and consisted of earrings and jewelry, money, ceremonial rice wine, tea, the traditional *trau* (large bitter green leaves containing a mild narcotic) and *cau* (palm nuts), and other offerings for the hand of the bride. The people were arranged behind the gifts in order of importance. The first person in line was the marriage arranger, or agent, an individual (usually a friend or relative) who introduced the couple through the parents or sometimes directly, to each other. Then came the parents, followed by senior relatives, junior relatives, guests, and finally bringing up the rear was the least important of all, the groom. Mai Lien further explained that when the groom's entourage arrived at the bride's home, the parents of both sides, with the arranger and the more important relatives, would sit down together at a table and share the tea and wine. The parents (or representative) of the groom would speak for their son in presenting their gifts and asking for the bride's hand in marriage. The bride's parents would present her dowry and then each of the groom's relatives would take turns presenting their gifts and offering their congratulations to the bride's family. The entire ritual would be overseen by the agent, who, after both parties were satisfied would consummate the agreement. After all this, with the groom standing silently to one side throughout, the bride having been hidden someplace within the house, is informed by a sister or another female relative that she has been accepted into the groom's family. She then makes her entry in traditional Vietnamese dress of red and gold *ao dai* and small open centered hat, and takes her place beside her husband to be. The groom places jade earrings and ring on his bride, and the wedding ceremony is now free to take place. They are then married in the Christian or Buddhist manner, depending on the couple's faith. A wedding feast that could go on for two or more days follows.

They left the wedding procession behind and continued on through open farmland, followed along a meandering green river for a short time, then dropped into the lush shallow little valley where Mai Lien and her grandmother lived, surrounded by low-lying forested hills. Pulling the jeep up to the front of the earth wall house, Vic noticed that a few of Mai Lien's guests had already arrived. Grandmother's two older sisters and a younger woman of about fifty sat just outside the open front door chewing *trau* and *rau* in the manner of all elderly Vietnamese country women, and occasionally spitting the red juice into their brass cuspidors. The two sisters recognized the major and beckoned him to come and sit with them. Mai Lien was already busily unloading the baskets of food and carrying them inside where a group of women were talking with *ba ngoai*. She would soon be fully occupied cooking with the other women and rather than risking being reprimanded again for doing women's work, Vic resisted the urge to help and ambled over to chat with the old ladies.

"*Cac ba manh khoe khong?*" he addressed them, asking how they were.

"*Manh khoe*," they answered, indicating that they were strong and healthy.

Vic seated himself on a stool beside them and watched the younger of the three begin spreading a white lime paste on a broad, green *trau* leaf. She folded the betel over into a tight rectangle then reached for a *cau* nut. With a crude knife she cut through the soft betel shell, about an inch in diameter, and pulled a section of the meat away, handing it with the leaf to Vic. He watched her demonstrate how to bite off a piece of *trau* and chew it with the *cau*, motioning for him to try it himself. He hesitated for a moment wondering what he was getting himself into, then took a healthy bite of the bitter leaf and popped in the nut. He chewed the mixture for a few moments. Suddenly he began to feel the blood rising to his face followed by a buzzing in his ears and a tingling sensation in his head. Grandmother's sisters smiled knowingly as the narcotic began taking effect. Before too long he was chattering away with the old girls in Vietnamese he never knew he had, and gesturing and laughing loudly along with them as if he had known these people all his life. Their frivolity attracted the other guests and one of the older men handed Vic a glass of homemade Vietnamese gin and invited him to join the other men inside.

By now the house began to fill with relatives and friends. Half a dozen women were relaxing among the pillows on the carved mahogany divan, which looked more like a wide short legged bed than anything else, fervently discussing their husbands' habits, complaining about a variety of ailments, and gossiping about other women of the village. The men separated themselves from the women (or maybe it was the other way around), and along with Vic, most of them sat at the long dining table drinking the cloudy gin and glasses of beer, talking about the weather and its effect on the rice crop, president Thieu's policies, local hamlet news, and money. Vic noticed that they didn't talk about women or the war and he wondered if that was significant.

Vic was unable to enter into the conversations to any great extent because of his limited facility with Vietnamese, but he had a fairly good comprehension of the language and was able for the most part to pick up the main ideas flowing through the group. Now and then a few younger men, Mai Lien's cousins, would speak with him in English and help him along with his Vietnamese. They showed keen interest in Vic's earlier experience at the market place.

At this point in time, Vic had been accepted pretty much as a member of the family and it was generally understood that he and Mai Lien were to become betrothed. To be sure, feelings about him were mixed and in the beginning, when he first began calling on Mai Lien, there was considerable negative discussion concerning his intentions and suitability for Mai Lien. Feelings still ran high among the Vietnamese against Americans marrying their women, and Vic had to go to great lengths to win over grandmother and the relatives before Mai Lien was allowed in his company. Vic in his naivete about Vietnamese ways, had not realized the impact that his presence had made on this family. Nor had he understood how fortunate he was to have gotten so close to a Vietnamese girl from a good family, a Vietnamese girl, who though poor, was respectable and morally strong. Virtually only a handful of Americans in Vietnam had ever talked with such a woman, let alone be invited to her home.

The storm broke and the rain began pattering among the banana leaves and running off the matted palm leaf roof onto the ground below. The lush little valley was enveloped in the downpour, causing a comfortable drop in temperature, and stirring the air with a refreshing breeze. The house was constructed to take advantage of every bit of circulating air and Vic noted that from where he sat he could look through the entire length of house to the outside by way of door openings. The wooden window shutters were propped widely open, upward on their hinges, and lizards clung to the wall and ceilings taking advantage of the shelter.

Large pots of steaming rice unexpectedly appeared on the table as Mai Lien and the other women began serving the men. Bowls of sour fish soup and platters of roast duck were placed at each end of the table along with fresh bean sprouts and leafy vegetables that Vic could only identify as being typically Vietnamese. Every two or three people shared a saucer of *nuoc mam*, the popular salty fish sauce that is found with every meal, given an unnecessary added kick by mixing in the notorious and famous torpedo shaped bright green peppers. Beer was served in the usual Vietnamese fashion, poured over ice in a tall glass. The strong and zingy Vietnamese coffee was served boiling hot, not in a cup, but also in a glass as was the very bitter green tea. Stacks of *banh tranh*, rice paper, and plates of pork slices filled out the table fare.

The women were constantly moving among the men, replenishing the food as it was consumed, and generally tending to the gastronomic needs of the fellows. Frequently, the men shouted for more beer or rice and it would be instantly supplied. The cooking continued, children were tended to, and a controlled tone of conversation covered the busy household as the meal progressed.

Vic admired the efficiency of the total operation. Each woman filled in where she was needed most and all were diligently occupied cooking, serving, cleaning, or tending children. Each was enthusiastic in her role and took pride in performing her job well. They were especially concerned over their individual men, and saw to it that they were given special attention. Now and then a wife would select a particularly appetizing morsel of duck or pork and with her chopsticks place it on her husband's rice, or pour him soup, or fill his rice bowl before he could ask. Vic attempted to fill his own bowl and it was snatched from him by a passing lady, quickly heaped with rice and returned to him with several slices of meat neatly decorating the mound. Mai Lien paid close attention to him and encouraged him to eat more, reminding him that he was too thin. Actually he wasn't underweight, and it amused him that Vietnamese women felt that a fat man was the image of excellent health and that a thin man was considered sickly. Most Vietnamese don't gain an ounce regardless of the quantity they eat, their physiology and diet being much different than that of the westerner.

Eventually the men finished eating and the women took their turn. The serving bowls and platters were refilled with food and the women seated themselves around the table enthusiastically discussing their children, the price of food, and other matters that concerned their daily lives. They ate daintily and with impeccable neatness in contrast to the table manners of their men. Mai Lien now and then glanced Vic's way to be sure he was comfortable, and on one occasion rose to serve him a glass of cold soy bean milk.

Eventually the table was cleared, dishes washed and put away, and a new phase of activity begun. Many of the women formed around the big table to gamble. Tiny playing cards with miniature Chinese characters and figures imprinted upon them emerged, and the popular game of *tu sac* got underway. The game was characterized by a considerable amount of enthusiastic betting and excitement. Some of the men sat behind the women, encouraging them in their betting and offering advice, which was generally ignored. The remainder of the men sat in a group smoking strong country tobacco and drinking homemade gin while they continued their conversations.

Vic was feeling pleasantly content, having been pampered and filled with food, when a U.S. Air Force jeep unexpectedly splashed up outside. Drill Davis jumped out and rushed to the protection of the overhang. He worriedly peered inside and seeing Vic relaxing on the wooden divan, motioned him to the door. The curious Vietnamese noticing the arrival of another U.S. officer immediately hushed their talking and stopped their activity. Vic saw the concern in his wingman's face and he knew from Davis' unprecedented visit to Mai Lien's home that something serious had happened.

"Have you heard?" Davis asked Vic.

"Heard what? Have Russia and China entered the war?"

"There was a big fight. We lost five ships."

Vic felt his legs go limp, his mouth began to dry.

They had never been hit this hard before. An engagement of this magnitude meant that there had been many Migs aloft and he had been here peacefully being entertained, missing the action. He was disgusted with himself. He knew he should have gone on this mission. He had had a gut feeling about it this morning, before he left.

"Five ships! Five!" Vic repeated in disbelief. "Who bought it?"

"Moreno from our flight for sure," Davis said sadly.

"Moreno? Oh no! How did it happen?"

"Don't know for sure. A Mig 17 gunned him in close. He and his WSO bailed out. Somebody saw two chutes open."

"Where did they get hit?"

"Right over Mig Ridge."

Mig Ridge. Suddenly it all seemed like a dream, as if he had become detached from it all. Moreno, alone and exposed. Helpless. Had he been captured yet? Was he being stripped right at this moment by communist soldiers and loaded into one of their trucks? Or maybe some farmers had gotten to him first. Killed him on the spot! Alone and trembling on Mig Ridge. One moment dangerous and superior, then in one terrible instant falling from the safety of the heavens to become helpless booty for the pack, a vanquished knight.

"Did they get any Migs?" Vic asked.

"Nine."

It was absurd. His chance of a lifetime and he had remained in Da Nang. He had to sit down.

"Good Lord, the sky must have been filled with them."

"It was plenty crowded up there. Yeh, filled. But there's more."

"More? Man, what else could have possibly happened? Did you get promoted to major?"

"Not quite."

"What then?"

"Colonel Tan is back."

Vic felt his pulse rate climb. Beads of perspiration formed on his forehead. He rose on unsteady legs, heart pounding. Tan! The legend. He had returned to change his whole life. The black knight had come back to silently challenge him. Ace against ace, champion against champion. Tan the dragon man, with thirteen confirmed American kills! In the distance Davis was rambling on about a dragon painted on the Mig's nose. The words were lost. Vic was already racing to his own jeep. If he hurried he could meet them when they landed. Davis was still talking.

"I'll see you at the base. Tell Mai Lien I'm sorry."

CHAPTER FOURTEEN

Vic was soaking wet by the time he passed through the main gate. He glanced at his watch.

"The lead ships should be on radar approach about now," he said to no one.

He drove out to the operations building, stopped the jeep, and peered up, his eyes fighting the monsoon pour. He heard them first. He strained to see where they were, then he saw them dropping out of the soup on initial. He looked on as their gear came down. One element, followed by a single. Then a flight of four. His sight was dimmed by the falling rain and he couldn't identify the jets as they banked into their landing pattern. He began walking toward the revetments through the sandbagged positions and lines of parked aircraft. He waited for what seemed like an eternity. Then came the distant whine of idling engines. He started running now. A line of Phantoms following each other closely like giant lizards swung onto the apron and taxied by Vic. He recognized the pilots now. Patterson, Pellegrini, Jacobs. . .

The first F-4 turned into its parking position, wings blackened, missile wells empty, and came to a halt just as Vic reached it. He climbed up to the cockpit, panting. Patterson shut down his engines and the high pitched cry of the twin General Electrics slowly began to fade as the turbines dropped their RPM. Patterson didn't bother to take off his helmet. He just stared straight ahead through his windshield at the rain, not even looking at Vic.

Before Vic could say anything, Patterson began, slowly at first, then picking up temp as his fear turned to anger.

"We ran into Tan, coming off the target. He and six of his pals. They smoked two of the Thuds before we knew what was happening. Never saw them."

"Where?" asked Vic.

"Crap I don't know. Somewhere on the way back, about two minutes south of Haiphong maybe. There were Migs everywhere. We were getting calls from every direction."

"What happened to Moreno?"

"I had just rolled out over the 105s, the last of the four of us, when Moreno's ship, second out of the turn, exploded in a sheet of flame and smoke. He and his WSO punched out at the same time. Man, then this dragon devil got on my tail and I couldn't shake him. I tried everything. I pulled twelve or more Gs. Everyone was screaming at me to turn tighter. I broke everything, flaps, panels, everything, trying to shake him. But he stayed right there. I reversed and rolled the ship one hundred twenty degrees, pulling hard, and that Mig turned inside of me! I looked over my head and got a canopy full of Mig belly."

Patterson took his helmet off and fumbled with his seat harness. Vic noticed his hands were shaking. He finally looked up at Vic.

"Oh, he's good, Benedetti. I tried everything I knew but he stayed with me turn for turn. I just about tore the ship apart. He just hugged my rear toying with me. Never fired a shot. He could have smoked me anytime. But he just hung in there. I swear I gave up. Just waited for him to drop me. I couldn't get away. All the rumors you've heard about him are nothing, Vic. Nothing! He's better. Better than all the talk we've heard."

"I believe you Jim. He's got to be good. You tangled with him."

"I tangled with him all right, but . . ."

"How did you get away?"

"He just broke off! Let me go. It was as if the lesson was over and he wanted me to live to tell the story. To tell you maybe. I don't know. All I know is that I was lucky. By all rights I should be on my way to the Hanoi Hilton right now."

"Let you off. Didn't fire a shot. Was that it, anything else?"

"F-4s were falling all around me. I saw Vogle streaming fuel, losing altitude fast. Don't know what happened to him. Maybe he had enough power to get to the sea. A few moments later another F-4 bought it. Went straight in. Butler and

Richards, I think."

"Did they get out?"

"No one called any chutes."

"Butler and Richards too. Vogle. Moreno . . ." Vic said looking away, rain dripping from his hair. The downpour continued. "Did you get any Migs?"

"I saw Pellegrini crank in behind a '21'. His first sparrow went ballistic, the second one nailed him. 'A '17' jumped in on Pellegrini. I told him to drag the Mig out about a mile and then break left. I came in at about 20 degrees angle off. The missile went right over Pellegrini's tail and caught the Mig in the turn. Blew it all to pieces. The pilot didn't get out."

Patterson unbuckled and followed Vic down the ladder. Men were milling around, some in groups discussing the big fight. More Phantoms were returning. Most had fired all their ordnance, some were heavily shot up. Five never came back.

God. I wish I had been there, he said to himself.

Vic was empty. Exhausted from the ordeal. Bewildered and confused, he watched the ships straggling in. Everywhere there was talk of Tan, the dragon colonel. The black knight had returned to reaffirm himself, to stake out his turf. Like the lobo wolf of the North, he had announced his territory to all. He had established the boundary markers with his victims, then sent one of the beaten back to the enemy camp as a witness to his invincibility.

But the North Vietnamese ace could be taken. Even though Vic had never seen him, others had. He would talk with Patterson again and with the others. He would drain them of all information they possessed on the colonel. Facts, he needed facts. He felt better now that he knew the legend was human, not just a fleeting image, a deadly mist that could never be touched before it disappeared, to reappear again somewhere else. But this was a man, a Mig flier, who had weaknesses and could be taken.

That night Vic went to the club alone. He took a seat off to the side where he wouldn't be easily noticed and ordered a beer from the waitress. He let his mind go blank. He wanted to rest, to be free this evening from confusion. He had to get himself straight. The girl brought his beer.

"*Cam on co*," thank you, he said.

"*Khong co chi*," you're welcome, she replied, giving him a sweet smile.

Vic sank back into solitude, pulling an envelope of repose around him. He became absorbed in the haunting ballads of the pretty Vietnamese singer. He permitted her soft, enchanting voice to penetrate to his vital core. Nothing relaxed him faster than a slow, romantic Vietnamese song. The singer moaned on. He was soon completely tranquilized by her sinuous movements, the poetry in her eyes, the honeyglazed voice.

Vic had retreated into the distant corridors of his mind. He was alone now and he would remain alone until he had accomplished the task set before him. Nothing else mattered. From here on he would feel the dark knight's presence wherever he went, and he would train himself for the day when they would meet on the ethereal plains over North Vietnam. Drawing off into his own world, his every action would be disciplined to honing his reflexes

211

and skills to a fine edge. And when the time came, he would be ready. He would take Tan disdainfully, high up and alone where it was only appropriate that two champions meet. He would stalk him, hunt him down, let him know the fear and the dry mouth terror that comes with knowing you are doomed, unable to shake your adversary. Then he would press in. One clean, swift blow and the legend would be destroyed. He would hold the severed head up high for everyone to see, and he would know the sweet savor of total victory. The final statement. He would be enthroned supreme champion.

CHAPTER FIFTEEN

Vic flew every mission he could. He was limited to twenty-four a month over the North but he flew as many as two or three a day. When he wasn't flying he was withdrawn with his thoughts. His mind was fixed on his objective and there was no changing it. He had one purpose now dominating his life. Search out Colonel Tan and destroy him. Kill Migs, excel, anything less would be failure. Being an ace was not enough. He must be champion.

The dragonman was seen everywhere, sometimes simultaneously in different locations, miles apart. The pilots talked of him with admiration or with scorn. All searched the skies for him, knowing that he could fall upon them anytime, unexpectedly, surprising them in his inimitable style, flashing, scissoring, cutting the formation apart with his wingman.

Yes, that's how he came, Vic said to himself, scissoring through a formation with his wingman, flashing silver across the sky, riding his stallion, guns blazing, never breaking off until the last moment.

The runway ended and Vic stepped off onto the dusty red earth.

"Kind of late for a stroll isn't it, major?" The young second lieutenant didn't bother to salute. He insolently tipped his steel helmet to the back of his head.

"Yeh, couldn't sleep. You marines have everything under control out here?"

"Don't we always?" he said arrogantly. He remained leaning against the gun pit wall, looking up at Vic, stroking the barrel of a fifty caliber machine gun. The pale moonlight glinted off clenched teeth that held a stubby dead cigar.

"What brings you out slumming?"

"Like I said, couldn't sleep."

The marine spotted Vic's wings. "You fly one of those," he said, pointing to a row of Phantoms.

"Uh huh."

"You couldn't get me in one of those for a million bucks." He pushed away from the parapet and spit in the dirt. He stuffed the stub back into his teeth. "You've gotta be crazy to haul around sitting on exploding kerosene. Why do you do it?"

"I'm looking for a guy." Vic jumped down into the gun pit. The marine's cigar fell out of his mouth.

"You're doing what?"

"I'm looking for a guy."

"Who?"

"Doesn't matter—just a guy—North Vietnamese."

The lieutenant looked spooked. He edged backward.

"Oh, just a guy — a North Vietnamese."

"Yeh — a North Vietnamese — just one," Vic said.

"Just one?" The marine's eyes were very wide.

"You ever felt like a man suspended for his duties, lieutenant? Like a boy expelled from school?"

"No sir. Can't say that I have." He took another step backward.

"Patterson got his second Mig, you know."

"No I didn't."

"Drill's now leading elements. He has three Migs — the colonel wants to take him away from me — give him a flight. I can't let that happen."

The lieutenant unwrapped another cigar and began nervously chewing one end.

"Even the newcomers are getting their first Migs — and they're beginning to talk about me." Vic stepped closer to the lieutenant, head thrust forward. "They say I've lost my touch, that I'm avoiding the action — afraid. That's what they're saying, lieutenant." He thumped the marine's chest with a stiff finger.

"Oh, I wouldn't pay any attention to them, sir. What do they know?" He began looking around.

"The others — the ones who know me better, who have been with me from the beginning — they try to console me. They say I'm in a slump and that I'll be back in the thick of it soon."

"Sure, major, sure. All you need is a little time and you'll be back in the thick of it." Vic had him pinned to the wall.

"You think so? I don't know. Do you know what it's like to feel your confidence slipping away? You fight it, but depression sets in. You begin to think that you'll never see another Mig. You withdraw, lieutentant. You avoid the other men. You can remember when your reputation was un-challengeable. But now the glory has faded like a vapor trail."

Vic moaned and made a sweeping motion with his outstretched hand, wiggling his fingers to symbolize the disappearing contrail. The young marine stood transfixed.

"The days wear on into weeks but you never catch sight of them."

"Who?"

"You fly more missions, but they continue to elude you."

"Who?"

"So you begin choosing your missions more carefully. But nothing helps. Whenever you fly they won't come up."

"Who?"

"*The Migs,* Lieutenant! *The Migs!*"

Vic swung around and grabbed the handles of the 50 caliber.

"No, major! No—don't! There aren't any Migs around here."

Vic menacingly brandished the big gun in mock battle, pivoting it back and forth, making shooting noises. He abruptly stopped and slowly stepped toward the marine who was spread-eagled flat against the sandbags, eyes bugging as if Vic were an appari-tion.

"Lieutenant," Vic said softly, putting his arm around the marine's thin shoulders. "Do you have a girl?"

"Yes, sir, I do."

"An American girl?"

"No — Vietnamese."

"Vietnamese — well, isn't that nice," Vic said suspiciously.

"Is there something wrong with that, sir? I mean, shouldn't I have a Nam girl?"

"Is there something wrong with our American girls, lieutenant?"

"Oh, no sir, it's just that . . . well, I'm kind of . . ."

"What's your girl like?"

"Well, she's not well educated and she comes from a poor family. But she understands me."

"Yes, sounds like someone I know. Go on, marine." Vic still had his arm around the lieutenant's shoulders.

"The land, the rice, the people, and the heart are her books. She has a special corner on tranquility — God himself would find rest under her roof."

"I know what you mean. Yes, I know what you mean, son," Vic said paternally, patting the young man's shoulder.

"Do you love her?"

"Yes."

"Are you going to marry her?"

"Yes I am."

"Hmm. You're really going to marry her, are you?"

Vic took his arm away and stepped aside, looking

at the silhouetted mortar emplacements behind him dully illuminated in the clouded moonglow. The marine relaxed.

"Have you ever bailed out over North Vietnam, lieutenant?"

The lieutenant tensed again. Vic turned and faced him, anxiety etched into his face.

"Would you be afraid of bailing out over North Vietnam? Would you have enough courage to survive as a prisoner of the communists? It takes courage, lieutenant?"

"I . . . I . . . don't know, major."

Vic's voice became somber.

"Shot down deep in enemy territory to be hunted like an animal; put on display and paraded through the streets like some sideshow freak. An oddity that fell out of the skies and had to be exhibited — then punished."

Vic made a face like a ghoul. The lieutenant fell back against the machine gun, deathly pale.

"Moreno and Butler and Richards."

"Who?"

"They never got out of their ships."

"Yes, sir."

"Have you ever felt fear — I mean their fear? There's no kind like it."

The lieutenant's cigar was chewed to rags.

"Feel that fear, lieutenant. The Migs out-turning them, pulling to the inside and slashing at them with their hot tracers and ATOLs. Listen, marine, and you can hear their frantic cries for help, for someone to get the pack off their trail. Turning, twisting and diving. Anything to break the grip!"

Vic was performing with full ceremony. The young officer stared at him incredulously, as if he had just plundered a grave and was feeding on its corpse.

"And then that awful thud, the convulsive jerk of the aircraft. The controls not responding, the fire, smoke, and then . . . nothing. Silence. Eternal silence."

Vic heaved a deep sigh and smiled to himself. This guy really thinks my brains are scrambled. He fought back a primordial urge to scream.

"See ya, lieutenant. Got to get some sleep."

"Y . . . y . . . yes, sir." He snapped a rigid salute.

Vic lay on his bunk in the darkness, naked except for his skivvies. He shivered in the tropical night heat. Thanh Thu weeped her dirge of passion. I wonder if the powder is deep at Mammoth. Betty and the kid will be up.

The moon had dissolved in the open window. It would soon be dawn and the early morning strike would begin. He went over it in his mind. Pellegrini would fly number two slot on his wing. Drill would lead the second element with Patterson flying his wing in the fourth position. Briefing at 0530. Weather probably clear. With any luck at all the Migs should be up today. They had been active lately and several big fights had developed over the past few days. The reccys over Kep, Hoa Loc, and Phuc Yen had spotted many more Migs on the ground, a large percentage being new "19s" and "21s". It looked like the NVAF was beefing up for a max effort to slow down the bombing raids.

He closed his eyes and became immersed in the dreamy Vietnamese song playing on his tape cassette. He always listened to Thanh Thu when he wanted to think, her brooding voice relaxing him into pleasant reverie. Most of the men listened to the usual rock beat and popular standards sung by American artists. But he preferred the moody and unique style of the Vietnamese female vocalists who expertly blended the traditional and modern oriental rhythms into their music. Thanh Thu, like most Vietnamese performers, sang of the war and lost love. These were the songs of the people. Vic listened intently to the girl's sweet childlike voice and let his mind float with her to the villages and hamlets that she sang about. The young girls, the young men, their love, the war, their separation, the long wait, the heartache and anguish. He thought of gossamer *ao dais*, waving fields of rice, flowering tamarind trees, and stately groves of bamboo. And he saw the young, wise women comforting their men in frustration. Sweet Vietnam. He drifted off to sleep with Thanh Thu's lamentations lingering in the heavy air.

CHAPTER SIXTEEN

The satisfaction of leading. Nothing compared with it. The first place, the foremost position. In command. Guiding, directing your men, at the head of it all. Leader. The sleek Phantoms followed him out of the parking area, Davis, Pellegrini, Patterson, knights aboard their steeds, preparing for battle. Eagles mounting to the attack, lances tucked under their wings, they swung evenly onto the runway. Two by two, accelerating slowly at first, then more rapidly, the F-4s overcame their inertia and rose into the early morning Asian sun.

Vic called for a climbing left turn and they wheeled around, heading northeast to meet the tankers. The sun, rising out of the sea, shot its long rays westward, changing the water to a sheet of glistening blue-green jade. From his perch high up, he watched the ancient spectacle of the sun chasing the darkness across the firmament, bathing this land of antiquity in light once again. Four arrows, propelled by their own momentum, shot across the face of the sun, independent free forms heading north to their rendezvous with destiny.

They hit the tankers on schedule and with a full load of fuel; the flight began their climb to altitude. Vic felt the tense excitement begin to build as he approached the DMZ and crossed into North Vietnam. He could feel his palms start to sweat through his gloves. The butterflies in his stomach became active, on schedule. All senses came to the alert.

His mission this morning would be somewhat different from the usual MIGCAP operations. The Thailand based F-105 Thunderchiefs would soon be coming in over the Gulf of Tonkin and swing down Mig Ridge for a strike on their target near the Mig base at Kep. Lately, the North Vietnamese were putting more Mig 21s in the air and using them effectively with a new tactic. Carefully deployed and under complete GCI control, the Mig pilots drove in on the strike force at 6 o'clock at close to Mach 2, launched their missiles, and dove for home. If the F-4 cover was not warned of the attack, and if they were flying at the same speed as the strikers, between 400 and 500 knots on the bomb run, they had little opportunity to mix it up with the

Migs.

Vic was even more uneasy about another communist tactic that was proving successful — the Mig 17 attacking from below in a high speed pass, forcing the Thunderchiefs to jettison their bombs. At lower altitudes the Mig 17 was difficult to spot by the fighters who held their norman escort positions high above the strike force. On this mission Vic was going in ahead of the bombers and sweep the lower elevations for Migs hanging around on the deck, hoping to engage them before they could position themselves favorably for a pass on the Thuds.

"Ha Tinh off to the left." Another checkpoint was called off matter-of-factly by his backseater, First Lieutenant Dick Balinger.

"Roger."

"Flamingo leader, this is Flamingo three." It was Drill.

"Flamingo three, Flamingo one. Go."

"I can't get tones on my Sidewinders and my radar doesn't seem to be working right."

"Abort, three. Go home with him Patterson." It was Air Force policy to abort in pairs.

He felt naked without Drill. Maybe Johnson was right. But he couldn't allow himself to believe it.

They climbed past twenty-one thousand. He looked across at Pellegrini, expecting to see Drill. He wouldn't believe Johnson. He fought the feeling. Come back, Drill.

When had it happened. Don't know. Maybe it was on that dawn strike . . . had just returned from the mission . . . climbing down the ladder . . . Johnson waiting below on the tarmac. The colonel's voice echoed through the cockpit:

"It's time we had a talk."

Vic knew what was coming. It had to be said.

"I've delayed discussing the subject with you because it's loathsome. Let's walk over to the blast shield," Johnson said.

They stood behind the parked Phantom looking into the twin tail pipes; the smell of burnt kerosene effused from the hot metal. Johnson rested a boot up against the blast shield and pulled a pack of cigarettes from his survival vest.

"You know, Vic," he began. "You haven't seen a Mig in weeks."

"That's not my fault, colonel, I'm . . ."

"Shut up and listen."

Johnson changed boots on the blast shield and lit a cigarette. He took a deep drag and exhaled the thick smoke through both nostrils. Vic thought he looked like a fire breathing dragon.

"The men you're leading are growing impatient with you. They want Migs. They're hungry. You're getting a reputation in the wing as being the 'milk run' flight leader."

Vic said nothing. Johnsom put both boots on the tarmac and stood straight, looking into the tail pipes.

"I'm thinking of giving you a desk job—

shipping you back to the States."

Vic was stunned. His eyes dimmed for a moment. No! He couldn't end his career this way. He had to convince Johnson. He had to say something. His mouth was cotton dry. It weakly came open.

"I know there's something wrong . . ."

"Wrong!" Johnson bellowed. "You bet your sweet buttocks there's something wrong. You're so paralyzed with fear you've lost your sense of perspective."

The colonel shifted his feet again and leaned against the blast shield. Vic looked down the flight line. He wished he was dead.

"I'll tell you what's wrong, Vic. You think there's some sort of cockamamy divine plane for you. That you have been created for a special purpose, to accomplish something of great importance. That the world is supposed to be waiting breathlessly for you to fulfill your destiny, whatever that's supposed to be."

Vic's soul ached for a smart retort to salve the stinging pain.

"You're so out of touch with reality you're endangering your own life. You're going to get shot down, Vic!"

The colonel ground out his butt. Vic stared at the tarmac.

"Your old man always felt that you could be anything you wanted to be, do anything you set your mind to. I don't agree with him. You're frustrated, confused, and shaken. You lack confidence. You aren't sure what your goals are anymore. Flying had been your whole life and excelling as a combat pilot was your top priority. Now you aren't sure. Your past performance is insignificant to me. What matters is how you are doing now, right now, not yesterday. Refuse to live on your laurels. You must produce. Everyone is watching you—your superiors, your fellow pilots, and your . . . old man. You need another Mig."

He walked off and never talked to Vic again.

Vic listened to Davis and Patterson egressing the area. Further north a fight was developing. SAM calls intensified. And from somewhere, yet nowhere came a still, small voice.

". . . my soul thirsteth for thee, my flesh longeth for thee in a dry and thirsty land . . . to see thy power and thy glory, so as I have seen thee in the sanctuary."

He made a slow turn east and passed through thirty thousand. ". . . Because thou hast been my help, therefore in the shadow of thy wings will I rejoice. My soul followeth hard after thee; thy right had upholdeth me."

He began leveling off but continued the turn. Colonel Johnson's frenzied, mustachioed face filled the windscreen. ". . . But those that seek my soul, to destroy it, shall go into the lower parts of the earth . . . They shall fall by the sword; they shall be a portion for foxes . . . But

226

the king shall rejoice in God; every one that sweareth by him shall glory; but the mouth of them that speak lies shall be stopped."

Vic and Pellegrini continued driving north, deeper into enemy territory.

Out over the Gulf of Tonkin they flew, a sea of jade below them. It was a beautiful day, the visibility perfect. In the distance further north and east he could see the coast of China. Haiphong harbor was coming up fast to the west. He began a slow turn, descending toward the mainland of North Vietnam. His belly tightened like a fist. Pellegrini nudged up closer on his wing as if to comfort him. Together they closed on the dark green mass where the most awesome concentration of air defense weaponry in the history of warfare waited for them.

Vic decided to brief Pellegrini on their battle tactics. He flipped over to discreet frequency.

"Flamingo two."

"Roger."

"We'll begin our sweep at the east end of Mig Ridge. Triple A should be heavy. Watch my six."

"Rog."

"We'll be right on deck going in. Once through flak we'll climb out and head for Bac Giang. Stick tight. Watch for Migs above. They could try and slip a couple in on us."

"Will do."

"The strikers should be coming in right behind us."

He checked his fuel.

"Red Crown . . . Flamingo is at base plus four."

"Flamingo . . . Red Crown. We have you."

"Vic, did you copy Red Crown on the Migs?"

"Those are Phantoms."

"Roger."

"All right, let's blow tanks."

"Roger Flamingo lead. Tanks gone."

"All set? It's going to be heavy."

"Roger that. Set."

"Okay, here we go," Vic said with determined voice. "Remember, keep tucked in. *TIGHT!*"

The two aircraft commanders pushed the noses of their Phantoms over and began rapidly gaining energy for their dash into North Vietnam. By the time they hit the coast they were ripping through Hon Gai at Mach 1.6 and had descended from 40,000 feet down to tree top level. They flashed through the valleys, jinking from side to side to throw off the gunners. Pellegrini kept closely tucked into Vic.

"We're being watched," Balinger said in the backseat.

The ECM equipment showed that they were being sectored by the North Vietnamese AAA and that they were being tracked by SAM radar. Vic knew from experience that the communists would draw his attention to their radar, keeping his preoccupied with watching for antiaircraft fire and SAM launches, then trying to slip a Mig in on him unnoticed.

"We're drawing fire on the left," Balinger yelled.

Then muzzle flashes erupted on the right. A wall of flak blossomed out in front of them like a black flower.

"Light your AB and let's get out of here," he called to Pellegrini.

Simultaneously the afterburners of both F-4s ignited and the two jets accelerated down the narrow canyon. Vic gunned his ship forward. He was remotely aware of brown and green flashing by the canopy, his eyes rigidly fixed on the horizon and flak ahead. With only two vectors to compute, he knew that it wouldn't take long for the gunners to get their range. He called for a climbing turn to the right, out of the valley, giving the gunners three vectors to work on. The flak dissipated. He breathed easier. His body went limp for a few moments. Pellegrini closed in on his wing again and they both throttled back.

"Your too nervous," Vic repeated. ". . . calm down." He had learned that by talking to himself he could usually drive away this uneasiness when under strain. But lately his anxiety stayed with him on missions. It was becoming harder to shake each time he went up.

He leveled off at 5000 feet and began searching

for Migs. They headed west along Mig Ridge and then turned north at the flat lands near Bac Giang to sweep the area around Kep. Without their wing and centerline fuel tanks the ships were much lighter now and handled a great deal easier. He checked his armament switches. He was carrying four Sidewinder missiles and two Sparrow missiles. His F-4E also had a 20mm gun mounted in the nose. Pellegrini was flying the F-4D model which didn't have the cannon.

He continued north and turned slightly east in the direction of China. The strikers' leader came up on the radio, checking their position on the ingress. The four flights of Thuds escorted by several flights of Phantoms were entering North Vietnam along the corridor that Vic and his wingman had swept clear for their run on the target. He was about to turn back for a final sweep around Kep before joining up with the Thuds when his experienced eye caught a hint of a reflection at 11 o'clock. His eyes continued to pierce the blue, straining to pick up the glint again. There it was! A momentary shimmer of light once more. Then two almost imperceptible dots appeared, growing in his windshield, moving to 12 o'clock. He continued driving toward China, his heart pounding in his chest, daring to hope that after these long weeks of drought . . .

The dots continued to grow and he could now discern the faint outline of airplanes. They couldn't be F-4s, no smoke, he thought to himself. The F-105s were all behind him beginning their run on the target.

"I've got two bogies," Balinger said.

"I see them, Dick," he quickly replied.

"Two bogies. Roger," Pellegrini acknowledged.

Just a few more moments and he would have them identified. The seconds became eternities. They drove on. Was it too much to hope for. He wondered if they had seen him yet. Friendly or enemy?

"They're Migs!" barked Pellegrini.

"What?"

How could Pellegrini have identified them at this range? They were still no more than specks on the plexiglass. His eyes stretched again, probing the space ahead.

"They've punched off their tanks, Flamingo lead. Do you have them?"

Tanks, where? Good grief that Pellegrini has good eyes, Vic thought to himself, nervously.

"They're rolling in on us Vic!" yelled Pellegrini.

A sudden surge of adrenaline shot through him. Fear and confusion clawed at him. Lord, what was happening? Was he dreaming?

"Get ready to break!" screamed Pellegrini.

In a flash it all came clear. How could he have been so stupid? Already it was probably too late. He had waited too long. He instinctively shrank in his cockpit trying to make himself smaller, waiting for the hits that were about to come. He snapped his head around to three o'clock in time to see two silver Mig 21s slashing down at him from the sun. He had been concentrating so intently on the airplanes ahead of him in the distance that he had failed to see the approach of the two attacking Migs. Worse, he had been caught up in his hope, his emotion, and had not responded to his wingman's warnings. And now he was about to pay for his mistake.

The two ATOLs left their platforms at the same instant that he muscled the stick over, breaking hard into the Migs. The F-4 was designed for taking an 8 g load but he was pulling 9. His cockpit turned gray then black, then turned gray again in time for him to see the white plumes of smoke pass behind him. His mouth felt like cotton. Rivulets of perspiration trickled down his limbs soaking through his g suit. He tried to pull himself together, gather his resources, but his reflexes wouldn't respond. This wasn't like him. He had to get hold of his wits.

"Shake it off, Vic," he told himself. "Let's bring it around and go after them," he shouted to Pellegrini.

They reversed, lit their burners, and with a jolt the two jets went supersonic. The two Migs, having made their firing pass, had no intention of sticking around to engage the Phantoms. They were going flat out in a straight line for Laos, attempting to outrun Vic. But he knew that the

F-4 had the advantage of speed and acceleration and as long as his fuel held out he would overtake them. He set his teeth in determination, glanced at his fuel readout, made a few mental calculations, then settled in for the chase. The Migs could not continue their westward dash very long. Eventually their fuel would run low and they would have to turn back to their base.

Vic was already planning his attack for the moment when the North Vietnamese pilots began their swing back to Hanoi. He would have to time his intercept so that he wouldn't overshoot the Migs and come out of the turn too far ahead, nor could he afford to pull in too far behind them. He lost visual contact with the Migs and quickly switched to radar. The steering dot was off to the right so he brought the F-4 around a few degrees, centering the Mig in his scope. Then suddenly the dot shot off to the left. The Migs were starting they're turn! Vic made a hard break left.

"Flamingo one is padlocked!" He was bringing them under attack.

"Honeymoon Flamingo one." Pellegrini was covering him.

"Go boresight, Dick. Get me a lock on."

The Migs continued their turn. It all seemed so easy. The enemy ships hung there, pinned to the radar.

"Can I shoot?" he asked Balinger.

"Negative. I don't have a lock on."

The Migs were still out too far, somewhere around thirteen miles, the maximum range of his Sparrows. He kept turning with the Migs, cutting them off, reducing the distance. Just a little more time is all he needed. He lit his afterburner again and the Phantom jumped, rapidly closing the distance.

Then he caught sight of the Migs, their silver bodies flashing brightly in the sun, like two fish streaking across the sea of air. He turned hard into them bringing the pipper onto the lead Mig. Balinger immediately got a good attack display.

"I have lock on!"

His heart swelled. This was it. He was about to drop number six. He was on top of the mountain again, king of the Mig killers. Free. Exonerated. His finger settled on the trigger.

"Break!"

It was Pellegrini screaming into the radio.

"Break hard right, Vic. *Now!*"

"Shoot! Shoot!" shouted Balinger in the rear cockpit. "He's yours!" Balinger shouted again.

"Break!" pleaded Pellegrini.

He sat frozen at the controls. Not now, no not now. Why? It was as if a conspiracy of supernatural forces was working against him, preventing him from fulfilling his destiny, pulling him down into the abyss, away from triumph, down to defeat. Deep inside a thin voice wailed, crying for recognition, for someone to listen, to understand, to explain to him.

He pulled hard full rudder, breaking off in time to see the gaping maw of a lone Mig 17 roll in behind him. The nose lit up as tracers erupted from its guns. Cannon balls whizzed past his canopy, forcing him to shrink in the seat for the second time this morning.

"I can't shake him," he called in desperation. "Where are you number two?"

"Hang in there. I'm rolling in on him . . . Break left. Now!"

He broke, glancing over his shoulder as he did. Pellegrini was cranking in on the Mig, firing a missile in desperation to scare the pilot off. The tactic worked. The pilot did a Split-S and broke away for home.

Vic rolled out, driving straight ahead, indifferent to where he was or in what direction he was flying. He was despondent and unnerved. Twice Pellegrini had saved him. The word would spread throughout the wing that Migs had sneaked in on him, outclassed him. Further evidence that he was washed up, through as a fighter pilot. He heard the Thud pilots conversing as they egressed the target. He was so vulnerable to his thoughts. His feelings of inferiority were overwhelming at this moment, high up and alone.

"Let's go home."

"Roger that."

CHAPTER SEVENTEEN

"You want to talk about it?" Davis asked him.

"No."

"Are you sure? It might help."

"Could be," he said.

"It could happen to anyone. You shouldn't feel so badly."

"You're a good friend, Drill, but this is something I have to work out for myself."

The waitress brought their drinks.

"Have you ever had a primeval urge growing deep inside, calling you to bust away from the routine of everyday responsibilities and live among the sandpipers and gulls, to ride the shifting currents of free spirit, buoyed up by your own energy and initiative, dependent upon no one?"

Drill looked at him with a cocked eyebrow.

"Did the waitress slip something into your drink? You sound like a frustrated poet."

"Poet, no. Frustrated? Maybe. At least Johnson thinks so. He's washed his hands of me, you know."

"There's been talk."

"What do you think?"

"Me? My opinion doesn't count," Davis shrugged.

"It does to me."

"Okay — I'll tell you." He leaned toward Vic, both elbows on the table.

"You're an idealist, subject to your fantasies. The colonel is a pragmatist, subject to nothing. You're digging for answers to larger questions — yourself, the war. Johnson wants Migs — Period! He doesn't have time to hold your hand."

Vic looked startled. Davis settled back into his chair. Both took a long pull at their cognac.

"Drill, I want to tell you something. I have a father who's much like Johnson. In fact they flew together in Korea."

"Yes, I've heard. They still keep in touch don't they?"

"They do." He swirled the cognac and inhaled the aroma. "I had always wanted to be like . . . well, he was my hero . . . I wanted to outdo . . ."

He looked into the brandy.

"But something went out of me when I got my fifth Mig. Maybe it was sooner than that."

He swirled the glass again. He looked directly

at Davis.

"Drill, do you think you could ever again rediscover the light hearted freedom and sense of well-being that you experienced as a child? Or enjoy the purposeless use of your time—I mean doing something with no objective in mind—directionless?"

"No. My training has killed that idea. I'm too much like Johnson now. I can't sympathize with you, Vic. Sorry."

"Okay, let me try another one on you. Imagine yourself a passenger on the subway of life, seeing only what immediately surrounds you as you speed through a tunnel of time and darkness unaware and not caring that only a few feet above in a different direction is so much more to be discovered and enjoyed."

Davis put his elbows on the table again and leaned forward.

"There you go again, pontificating. You sound like one of those bleeding-heart liberals. Let it be, Vic. Can you imagine having a conversation like this with Johnson?"

Vic took a deep breath, puffing his cheeks as he loudly exhaled. "I'm washed up, Drill. I wouldn't give you a nickel for my future right now."

"Come off it, Vic. You're motivated by challenge, being the best, climbing the mountain, defeating Colonel Tan. If you quit now you will be going against all your principles, the code you have lived by. You'll prove the others right, that you're washed up, have lost your nerve, incompetent, no longer capable of leading men."

"I've had my moment of glory. Now it's someone else's turn. Maybe yours, Drill."

He whiffed the heady fumes again, smiling dourly at Davis.

"It was a brief passing interval—a slight, gentle gust of perfume—like the spicy odor from this cognac."

He held up his brandy glass in salute and gave it a spin.

"Can anyone find their peace in war, Drill?"

"What are you talking about?"

"Success turned bittersweet."

They stared across the table at each other. They had reached their understanding.

"North to Hanoi, Vic." Davis raised his glass to Vic.

"North, always north—through the towering gates—and into the fray."

He clinked his glass against Davis'.

"All you need is a rest, old buddy. Get away from flying for awhile, away from the base. You need to sort things out."

"You think so, huh," Vic said sarcastically.

He eyed Drill doubtfully.

"Have you been to Saigon?" Vic asked.

"A few times."

"What's it like?"

"A diversion. Sex, gambling, excitement."

"Can a guy relax there? Think?"

"Hardly. You're better off getting out of the

country."

"Like where?" he asked.

"Manila, Hong Kong, Singapore, Malaysia."

"Sounds like more of the same to me."

The waitress arrived with more drinks.

"*Cam on,*" Drill said to her.

"*Khong co chi,*" she responded, smiling shyly.

"Nice, huh?" he asked Vic.

"Nice, yes. You're married, remember?"

"Right. I don't forget it either. I'll be on my way home to her in only twenty-five more missions."

"You like being married, don't you?"

"It makes a difference when you have the right woman."

"Yeh, it does make a difference."

"You want to go to Hong Kong for a few days?" Davis asked him.

"Might be a good idea," Vic said.

"We have leave time coming. We can probably get away with no sweat."

"I'm not sure I want to."

"Oh, come on. We'll have a great time, Vic."

"Maybe. But I'm not looking for a great time. Not now anyway."

No, he didn't want to go to Hong Kong, or Malaysia, or any other place. There was only one place where he could go to heal, before it was too late, before he ended up on Mig Ridge with his airplane a smoking pile of rubble. In the morning he would go see Johnson and ask for a few days off to stay with Mai Lien and grandmother.

As soon as he made his decision he felt much better. He checked with the two women, and grandmother in her wise ways broke another rule for him. Mai Lien was naturally delighted with Vic coming to stay with them. She and *ba ngoai* immediately set about preparing for their guest, making a soft bed for him on the wooden divan, setting in stores of his favorite Vietnamese foods, including *chom chom, pho* noodles, and sweet rice, and borrowing an extra oil lamp and other conveniences from relatives for his personal use.

Vic departed the base with only a bag stuffed with a few personal belongings. On the way he asked Drill to pull the jeep off the road at a squat market, a convenient assembling point where women had come to sell their food. Reed mats were scattered over the ground. Umbrellas protected the women and food from the blazing sun.

"My lord, Vic, do you eat this stuff?" Davis asked, glancing over the assortment of peculiar meats, vegetables, fruits, and an odd assemblage of eels, snails, frogs, and other crawling and creeping things.

"You bet. Rather good when prepared right."

"Mai Lien a good cook?"

"Sure. It's impossible to find a Vietnamese woman who doesn't cook well."

"Does she ever cook you American food?"

"No."

"Why not?"

242

"I don't want it. I can get that any day at the base. Besides, all I would have to do is ask her to and she would find a way to cook it. And it would probably be the best American meal I ever ate."

The curious, squatting village women jabbered noisily in their excitement and carefully eyed the two Air Force pilots going from vendor to vendor comparing foods. After about ten minutes of looking and haggling in the manner he had learned from watching Mai Lien shopping, he chose black salty eggs, crystalized ginger, dried jellyfish, and sour plums, all special favorites of Mai Lien and grandmother.

Davis dropped him off in front of the house. Vic noticed that the little blue Honda wasn't parked outside.

"Have a good rest, Vic."

"Will do. Take care of yourself while I'm gone."

"Roger."

Vic waved goodbye and watched Drill wheel the jeep around and head back to the war. He stood for a moment in the middle of the road watching the dust rise from the jeep as it disappeared over the rise. An aching loneliness rose in the pit of his stomach. He walked into the house and set his bag down, calling for Mai Lien and *ba ngoai*. Finding no one home, he picked up one of the small bamboo cups kept stacked on the long, carved dinner table and pured himself some of grandmother's homemade, country gin. He

243

tucked a big pillow under his head and stretched out on the wide backless divan. He lay there looking around the house and letting the warm rice liquor relax his body. He wished Mai Lien or grandmother were home.

He stared up at the matted palm ceiling supported by teak beams. The sun filtered through breaks where the weave was loose and cast pencil rays of light on the rough, red tile floor. From where he lay he could see the bundles of sticks and rice straw used for cooking fuel stacked in the kitchen near the mud brick stove. A broom made from rice straw and bamboo leaned against the stove. A large white goose poked its head through the kitchen door and curiously looked around. Satisfied, it waddled off through the bamboo. The goose was quickly replaced by a brightly colored male jungle fowl accompanied by his hens. Finding nothing that interested them, the group followed the goose through the thicket.

Vic got up from his comfortable position on the divan and walked to the table. He took a clay bowl and chopsticks from the pile and peeked into the pot on the stove. There was still some warm rice left. He filled his bowl and then reached with his chopsticks into the open jar resting on the stove and added a few large pieces of pickled cabbage. He dropped a few bean sprouts into the bowl, poured a spoonful of *nuoc mam* over it all, and sat down at the table with another small glass of gin.

At this moment he felt more Vietnamese than American. He looked out the open window to the rice fields beyond and the water buffalos and farmers working the paddies surrounded by green hills and forested mountains in the distance. He felt that he could settle down right here with Mai Lien and grandmother, working the fields with hoe and buffalo, never climbing into another cockpit again. The thought fascinated him.

He finished his humble meal, enough to keep a Vietnamese going most of the day, but only whetting his appetite. He walked out into the open air heavy with the fragrant scent of the rich valley and its productive farms. He scanned the unobstructed view. Gentle green waves of new rice growing quietly and effortlessly in the ancient soil that had been nurturing crops for centuries, spread out before him. Yes, he thought to himself, he could easily make this his home. If it wasn't for this rotten war. . .

The familiar rapid purring of the little Honda's engine reached Vic's brain, breaking his thoughts. He walked around to the front of the house and saw Mai Lien coming down the river road as fast as the motorcycle would carry her, ebony hair waving in the wind like a long black cape. Seeing Vic, she put a hand high in the air and waved. She pulled the Honda off the dusty road and came to a stop in front of him. She got off, kicking the support stand down with a pretty foot.

"I see Captain Davis at base. He tell me he bring you here already. I come fast," she said, almost out of breath.

He had forgotten in his hurry to get away that it was Friday and she would be working late.

"That's all right. I forgot that you would still be at the base."

"*Ba ngoai* not home too," she said apologetically.

"Yes, I noticed."

"She at elder sister farm. Catch fish."

"Fish?" he asked, curiously.

"You want come catch fish too? Much fun. We eat tonight," she said clapping her hands, her eyes widening, hoping he would say yes.

"Do you have poles?"

"Poles? What that?"

"You know, fishing poles, to catch the fish."

"We catch with hands. No use poles," she said matter-of-factly.

"Hands? You catch fish with your hands, without a pole?"

"Oh, yes. Catch many."

"This I have to see," he said with interest.

They went into the house and Mai Lien let out a squeal of happiness upon seeing the tempting foods Vic had placed on the table. She examined it all carefully.

"*Cam on*," she said, thanking him and bowing toward him with folded arms.

"We eat salty eggs tonight with fish we catch."

"Okay. But you must show me how to catch

fish with my hands, like you."

She critically examined the clothing he was wearing. "Uniform no good for catch fish," she said. She disappeared into the bedroom and he heard her rummaging through her chest. She came back with several yards of black cotton cloth and began measuring him with her yellow tape.

"What are you doing?" he asked.

"I make you black pajama like Vietnamese country man."

"Oh . . . Mai Lien, I don't know about this."

"Hold still please. I make, you like," she said intently. "You put Air Force clothes away. Stay Mai Lien house you wear comfortable clothes. You like, you see."

Well, maybe she was right. Why not shed his skin and become Vietnamese while he was here? It might be just the change he needed. At any rate, the new clothing would be more practical for what she had planned, and it appeared from her tone that she had more for him to do than fish during his stay.

She finished measuring him and quickly went to work skillfully cutting the soft cloth and sewing the pieces together. Within thirty minutes Vic had his new clothes, which she instructed him to try on behind the dressing screen. He did so. When coming back out she examined him with an approving eye. Looking at his bare feet, she disappeared into the bedroom where he heard her once more searching for whatever it was she wanted. A minute later she reappeared with a pair of sandals, the soles of which he saw were made from U.S. Army truck tires and the straps made form inner tubes. He put them on and found them surprisingly comfortable, the elastic bands easily adjusting to his feet. One more critical look over by Mai Lien, a changed button, a conical basket hat placed on his head, and she decided he was ready.

"Vietnamese man," she said, smiling. She changed out of her *ao dai* into her own pajama peasant clothes and straw hat, and they rode the Honda down the dusty river road to grandmother's elder sister's rice field. When they arrived he was surprised to see most of Mai Lien's relatives were there. They had gathered in a group along an opening in the levee where the field was being drained. A large screen had been placed over the opening.

Vic knew most of the people present with the exception of some of the children and a few cousins. He dismounted from the motorcycle and all inspected him curiously, smiling and nodding their approval, telling him in Vietnamese how well he looked in his new clothes, and pointing to the draining field and the fish already beginning to jump and struggle in the shallow water. In their humble way they were expressing their friendship toward him, drawing him closer into the family.

Elder sister shouted something, and everyone rolled up their pajamas and walked into the mud and water, scrambling excitedly about grabbing the slippery, flatheaded fish with their hands. There was a great deal of yelling and splashing as the five gallon oil tins began rapidly filling with the black fish. Vic was knee deep in the mud, thrashing about chasing the elusive quarry, Mai Lien at his side pointing out which fish she wanted.

By the time the sun had settled below the forest canopy, the family had harvested the field of its crop of fish, and were returning to their homes with full cans. Mai Lien left the Honda at elder sister's home, to be picked up next day. She, *ba ngoai*, and Vic started home carrying their cans of fish on bamboo poles slung over their shoulders, one can at each end of a pole. Vic was covered with mud, having fallen several times into the sticky ooze, and he smelled like a swamp. The three of them laughed and joked about his misfortune, and he was keenly aware of being happy and more alive than he could ever remember.

In the ensuing days, Vic planted and harvested rice with the family. He built levees and dikes, and engineered waterway systems. His mind was finding its rest in work, in the good earth, in the people of the land.

Drill, being the concerned guy he was, dropped by to check on Vic.

"I just thought you might want some company or something. How's it going?"

"I'm okay. Come on, Davis. I want to show

you what I've been doing out here," Vic said proudly.

"You look rested. Where did you get those crazy pajamas? You look like a VC."

"Never mind. They're comfortable."

They wandered out along the narrow paddy dikes toward the green fields.

"Look at that. Will you just look at that." He pointed to a large impoundment of water.

"What is it?" Davis asked, shading his eyes from the sun.

"What is it!" Vic frowned.

"Yeh, what is it?"

"That, my friend, is the Benedetti-Thua Thien community water project."

"It is, is it?"

"Yes it is. You know, Davis, you have a problem."

"*I* have a problem?"

"Yes. You don't seem to have a grasp on the aesthetic values of life."

"Is that a fact."

"That is a work of art." Vic pointed to the dam again.

"That—is art?" Davis scratched his head.

"See what I mean? No appreciation for beauty. No refinement. Your tastes are on the level of a baboon."

Davis managed a wry smile.

"See all those interconnecting irrigation ditches?" Vic went on.

"Yeh."

"See the main feeder canal?"

"Yeh."

"See that flood gate and the secondary shunts?"

"Yeh."

"All designed and engineered by yours truly." He paused for Drill's reaction.

Drill thought Vic looked like a school boy waiting for the teacher's praise after correctly spelling "Mississippi" on the blackboard.

"Not bad, not bad," Davis said.

"The village now has a reliable, controlled, labor saving and nearly automatic irrigation system."

"The marvels of western technology."

"And the enterprising genius of one tired soldier."

They both laughed loudly. Vic playfully grabbed Drill around the neck.

"Thanks for coming by." He punched Davis lightly on the shoulder. "You know, Drill, I enjoyed helping these people."

"You've helped yourself in the process. How's Mai Lien?"

"Just great. She feeds me well and during the early evenings, after dinner, we take walks through the valley. She seems to instinctively know what I need. And she works right alongside of me in the fields."

"Count your blessings, Vic. She's teaching you her secrets."

"She has a lot of common sense. Unorthodox

in many ways to my thinking—but intelligent."

"Have you told her what's bothering you?"

"No," Vic said.

"I don't think she needs an explanation. Women like Mai Lien know intuitively what's troubling their men."

"Think so?" Vic pulled the conical peasant hat lower to shade his eyes.

"Sure. Don't forget, she's had more experience with war than you. She's already figured out your problem."

"She's a good kid."

"She's more than that, Vic. She might not be able to articulate her feelings very well but I bet she can make you understand when she wants to."

"She can."

"She's a peasant girl and doesn't have much education but her young wisdom is worth more to you than what you could get from a hundred intellectuals."

"Hey, you sound like you're in love with her."

"Don't be silly—I just don't think you appreciate her and what she's doing for you."

Vic took off the straw hat. "You don't think so?"

"No I don't."

"Maybe you're right," Vic said pensively. He put the hat back on. "Maybe you're right."

"If I wasn't already married I'd be looking for my own Mai Lien."

"She tells me stories," Vic said.

"Stories?"

"Vietnamese stories. Old parables she remembers from childhood."

"No kidding." Drill looked amused.

"She's really funny. So serious, and she tells the stories in that peculiar vernacular of hers."

"You mean combining Vietnamese with English."

"Yeh, you know how she does when she gets excited."

"What stories does she tell. This is fascinating."

"They're all moralistic—you know the kind—man's peace and fulfillment can't come from pursuing achievement and fame, or you can't satisfy the expectations of others, and so on. They're all Chinese fairy tales."

"Maybe she's trying to send you a message. Maybe you ought to listen to her," Davis said seriously.

"Oh, I listen, but when she starts telling about that Jesus of hers . . . I begin to feel uneasy. I watch this young Cochinese woman slowly form her words, pondering each one carefully, her hope for me showing through her engaging, slanted eyes, and I feel uneasy."

"I'm probably out of line in saying this, Vic, but I'd pay attention to what she says and reflect on the care she's given you over the past days. I don't think you really yet understand Mai Lien's rare and unselfish love."

Vic looked embarrassed. He nervously readjusted his hat.

"It's a sacrificial love that gives and asks nothing in return, only the opportunity to love. You're a fool if you don't do something about it."

"Think you're pretty smart don't ya." He punched Davis again.

CHAPTER EIGHTEEN

By the time Vic got back to Mai Lien's home, he was very nervous. What if she said no? What would he do then? She had to say yes. But first he must talk to grandmother. That was the proper thing to do. Ask *ba ngoai* first. Mai Lien would ask him to do that anyway, before giving him her answer. She would obey her grandmother. That was the Vietnamese way. Oh, brother, he breathed. This wasn't going to be an easy matter. He wondered if he could persuade *ba ngoai*.

Grandmother motioned him to the table and brought him tea and sweet rice. He watched her, not knowing if the timing was right to discuss the subject. His Vietnamese had improved considerably and he had little difficulty in getting *ba ngoai* to understand him. Mai Lien was visiting her cousin Hanh and wouldn't be returning for awhile. It was the right time, but he hesitated, realizing that he wasn't very good at this sort of thing. Adding to his nervousness was the gnawing thought that he may have to learn to live without Mai Lien, a possibility that he felt totally unable to deal with.

He sat at the table sipping his tea. It's over for me. A few more missions and I'll be on my way home, he brooded. He picked up the chopsticks and pushed some sweet rice into his mouth. He sipped more tea.

Nervous, he got up from the chair and walked to the back door. He peered out through the bamboo thicket toward the well and playing children. Several women were filling their jars and cans with the cool well water. I wonder who they are. The cute one in the middle looks familiar. He leaned against the cracked wall, eating from the bowl in his hand.

He turned his gaze to the farm land and rice paddies, the dikes and tree lines, orchards of fruit trees, farmers bent over the soil, water buffalos working the fields, all merging into a panorama of peace, harmony, and beauty. I've been lucky. He poured more tea and returned to the doorway.

A heavy swell of cooling air from the northern highlands dropped over the encircling hills and drifted through the valley, rustling the bamboo and rice, sweeping the fragrance of mangos and bananas across the land. The days were temperate in the valley, the nights now chilly. Beyond the rice and over the hills beyond his vision lay the bush where the air was fetid and dust choked, the infantryman cursed Vietnam and the day he had arrived.

The girl at the well was looking at him. She kept her head up so she could watch him while she dipped her lithe, brown arms into the sweet water. Young tree, just a sapling she was. Some of the water from the can splashed on her bare legs, turning the dusty skin to polished copper. One of the older women gave her an empty can to fill. She accepted obediently, her doe eyes never leaving his. When the cans were filled she cupped her hands and scooped water to her flower petal lips. She moistened her brow and golden cheeks, water dripping from her elbows. Her eyes continued to talk to him. Then she was gone, swaying down the path with two sloshing water cans slung on a bamboo pole across her thin shoulders. She stopped in the middle of the path and turned around to look at him one last time. The flower petals parted into a lonely smile and she waved. Sweet Vietnam.

Clear, blue, sun kissed sky
Blackened napalm burned tree
The perfumed garden of Hue Linh
The stink of body bags at Phu Chi
Flower petal lips, golden cheeks
So be it, lonely smile — FINI

Grandmother was squatting on her haunches outside the kitchen door, turning and gently shaking a wide, flat bottomed basket filled with loose rice. As she worked the basket, the heavier grains migrated toward the center, separating themselves from the lighter chaff that collected around the edges. Vic squatted beside her and transferred a handful of winnowed grains to the rice bag. He began talking to her in slow, deliberate Vietnamese.

"Grandmother, I have something important I wish to talk to you about."

She nodded and added more rice, continuing to turn the basket, not saying anything.

"I will soon be leaving Vietnam. I will be returning to my country."

She collected the chaff that clung to the inner rim of the basket and threw it to the ground at her feet. She did not look up at him.

"I am sad because I must leave you. This has become my home and I have learned to love Vietnam. I love you too. I am also happy because I no longer have to kill and I can return to the home of my birth."

Ba ngoai stopped her work and set the basket down. Vic admired her beauty. She was ageless. Time had been good to her. Her hair was raven black with only a touch of gray in it. Her skin was still smooth, that of a young woman's, and her body was firm and strong. He eyes were Mai Lien's, long and sensuous, happy and full of wisdom from a complete life. He had grown very close to this exquisite lady. He loved her like his own mother. He would miss her.

"I wish your permission to take Mai Lien as my wife. I want to bring her to America with me," he said with sincerity and hope in his voice.

He knew he must abide by her decision. Mai Lien, though she loved him with all her heart, would not go against her grandmother's wishes. That was the nature of things in her world.

"Mai Lien is not an elegant lady like your American women," she said, her eyes looking out toward the farms and plantations, scanning the countryside. "She is wise for her young years and she learns fast, but she is a peasant girl and will remain so in her heart all her life. You or America cannot change that."

Vic nodded. "Yes, and I would not have it different. This is her strength and my comfort. It is from her simple ways that I have learned how to be at peace with myself. No, she is not a worldly woman. I am not concerned with this. There are many worldly women, but few that are genuine like Mai Lien. She cannot be corrupted."

"You speak sound wisdom, my son. But right now my granddaughter is a curiosity to you. She is Vietnamese, an Asian, whose unusual beauty and different philosophy of life are unique to you. At present you find her refreshing and a comfort, so far from home and your own people. What will happen to your love for her when this uniqueness wears off and you must deal with the realities of your culture clashing with hers. We must be practical about these matters. Isn't it so?" Her Vietnamese flowed with the texture of warm honey.

"It is true, but my love for your granddaughter goes far below the surface of the practicalities of life. She has become a part of me. Her thoughts have become my thoughts, her feelings have become my feelings. My heart beats with hers. She has become my rice, and my strength would disappear without her, withering away like the banana plants which no longer receive water," he said, speaking from his heart, knowing that grandmother would easily detect any insincerity.

"Mai Lien is not without shortcomings. How would you deal with these," she asked, her eyes now searching his own.

"I have not been a patient man in the past. My training has required fast and accurate thinking. I have had to think critically and I recognize this as being a possible problem with Mai Lien who is more sensitive and patient than I. But being near her has given me understanding and I recognize that I cannot treat her as I treat my airplane, nor can I be as demanding. Mai Lien will love me forever. She will be the most faithful of wives. I will overlook many of her shortcomings because of what we share together. I will always remember our days here with you, the help she has given me and the peace she has brought into my life."

"My son. Mai Lien's love for you does not depend on how you treat her. Do you understand this?"

"I know this, but I don't understand it."

"I will explain. When my husband was killed by the VC many years ago, I was yet a young woman and could have easily found another man. But even though he had been a difficult man and treated me harshly at times, he was my husband, and I loved him dearly. A Vietnamese woman's husband is the most important thing in her life. More important than her own life. It was unthinkable for me to look for another husband, though it would have been the most practical thing to do in view of the basic comforts I may have gained."

"Do you miss him after all these years?" he asked.

"I still feel his warm, strong body lying beside me at night, his hand stroking my soft hair. His memory is as fresh as the smell of rice straw after harvest. Yes, I miss him, but my love for him has comforted me."

"I still don't really understand."

"No, I suppose not. It's in our blood, passed down from our ancestors. It is instinctive and natural for us to suffer our husbands. Mai Lien has this quality as strong as I have seen it in any of our women. But I believe her generation will be the last that will strongly retain the old traits. Even now I am beginning to see corruption and infidelity creeping into our women."

"I believe we are to blame. The Americans. The French. Contamination by the western world," he said sadly.

"Who is to say. It is the way of things."

The color of the sun changed from yellow to orange as it dropped closer to the tree line. The ducks and geese waddled to and fro, and the penned pigs rolled in the mud and squealed their delight. *Ba ngoai* talked on about Vietnam during the days when artillery and jet planes and curfew were unknown. When peace was upon the land and she was young and in love. She told him stories of family and traced Mai Lien's heritage back many generations to its origins in North Vietnam and Cochina. She told him of Mai Lien's history, her birth, poverty as a child, her parents, her education, her hopes and dreams. He committed it all to memory and made special note of the traditions, customs, beliefs, and principles that had been taught her.

Finally, *ba ngoai* rose to her feet and picked up her rice and basket.

"Remember all that I have told you," she said, looking at the orange ball now turning red, touching the tree line. "You will need it when your wife grows quiet and withdraws from you in her private place, and she sheds tears for the land of her birth and for her family and friends that she will never see again."

"You mean we have your blessing to marry?" he said, not daring to hope too much.

"Yes. My granddaughter will be a good wife to you. She will love you deeply and eternally. She will attend to your every need. You will find your refuge in her. Talk with her freely as you have, and listen to her wisdom as you have. She will benefit you with her hard work and devotion, and she will bear you strong sons." She stopped and turned away from the setting sun and looked at him. Her stoic eyes were wet with tears. "I will miss her," she said, "she has been my joy as she will be yours. Take care of her for she trusts you with her whole heart and life. She must depend on you in a land that will be strange to her. She will be afraid and make mistakes. This is when she will need you most. But she will never ask for your attention or help. She will suffer in silence, always wanting to please you, to be your good wife."

He reached his muscular arm around her small shoulders and tenderly dried her eyes with his handkerchief. "We will come back to see you many times," he said.

"I wish it could be so."

"But it will be," he said.

"No. When the Americans leave, it will be but a short time before the communists enslave us. One year, maybe two," she said prophetically.

He started to give her assurances, but he did not. He knew she was right. She had seen the communists consistently violate the people's faith and trust, and she had no illusions about the impotency of the South Vietnamese government. Besides, he felt that it was just a matter of time before the U.S. began looking for any reasonable face-saving excuse to get out.

Instead he asked, "Would you like to come to America and live with us?"

"That is generous of you to ask, my son. But I am old now and I have no desire to leave. The communists will not harm me. I am too old. They leave the old to themselves. It is the young they are interested in. The young they will put to work and seduce to their ideology. The old are useless to them. My family, my friends, are all here. My hope, however little remaining, is still

in Vietnam. There is nothing for me in America.
I will stay here."

His eyes burned. He turned away.

CHAPTER NINETEEN

Vic and Mai Lien were married in the U.S. embassy at Da Nang with Davis and Mai Lien's friend, Ngoc, acting as witnesses. As he had promised, Roger Dornbacher had Mai Lien's papers in order and she was free to accompany Vic back to the States. Vic recalled with some amusement, Vice Consul Dornbacher's parting words at the embassy.

"Sure, I had to pull some strings to get special permission for you and Mai Lien to get married. But it's the least I could do for you. We don't have heroes anymore. That's what's wrong with our country. No heroes. When I was a boy we had heroes. Not anymore. People back home don't give a damn about what you've done over here. But I do. You're a hero and I'm proud to give you preferential treatment. It was an honor to marry the two of you."

The ceremony had been brief, and although Vic was grateful for all that Dornbacher had done in cutting through the bureaucratic red tape, he still regarded the embassy ceremony as merely a formal exercise giving Mai Lien the necessary legal status for entering the U.S.

But the Vietnamese wedding ceremony was an entirely different matter. It had immense personal meaning for him. To him it was the culmination of all his efforts in Vietnam, the final expression of what he had learned and come to believe. Gathered around him this day were the people who meant the most to him, many of whom he would never see again, who he had learned to love with a capacity he had not realized he was capable of.

There was grandmother, the ageless *ba ngoai* who had been like a mother to him, worrying about his welfare and safety, teaching him the ways of old Vietnam, and advising him about Mai Lien. She had always been ready with conversation, stories, and food and drink for his comfort. Her ancient wisdom was boundless and he could listen and talk with her for hours. She had taken him in, a foreigner, as one of her own, and now with the marriage to her granddaughter, she regarded him as her blood son.

There were the relatives, the aunts, uncles, cousins, and *ba ngoai*'s sisters, all of whom had been kind to him, and like grandmother, considered him part of the family. They had approached him casually and with suspicion at first. But they quickly overcame this upon seeing his sincerity, and openly demonstrated their affection for him in the touching, smiling way that was so typically Vietnamese.

He regretted not ever knowing Mai Lien's immediate family in distant Saigon, but that was another story that he hadn't fully understood, and he decided to leave it be.

Friends from the village were also present, most of whom had their roots entwined with Mai Lien's, reaching back into history to generations of family association and intermarriage. They treated Vic with much dignity and respect, and had opened their humble homes and big hearts to him.

Then, of course, there were the pilots from his squadron. Davis, Pellegrini, Patterson, Colonel Johnson, and the others. Those like Moreno and Butler who had given their lives or had been captured after being shot down were with him in spirit, and Vic keenly felt their presence. He would forever be bonded to all these men by a force that had its origins in their confidence in each other. Daily they had faced extinction together, fighting from their supersonic chariots high above the earth in the playground of champions. In an unpopular and confused war where there was no meaning except in the individual engagement itself, they drew their hope from the loyalty they shared and from the pooling of their strength and courage.

The actual wedding ceremony was held by the beautiful meandering green river beside Mai Lien's home in the valley he had grown to love so much. Grandmother herself, in traditional Vietnamese custom, supervised the beautiful, intricate ritual. Relatives and friends gathered closely around the three of them as grandmother performed the wedding vows. It was a sensitive ceremony. The birds sang in the tamarind trees and the bamboo swayed over the river in the breeze. The women were dressed in their best *ao dais* and the children were all scrubbed and shiny. The young men eyed the pretty girls and grew envious of Vic. No guns boomed in the distance, no jets circled the sky.

Mai Lien's soft eyes looked downward in humble submission. Her little hands were pressed together below her breasts, elbows bent in reverent pose. Her face was expressionless except for the slightest hint of a smile from her lips. She listened to her grandmother recite the marriage vows.

Vic placed the traditional jade earrings on Mai Liens earlobes and encircled the gold chain around her neck. A diamond ring, a western invention, went on her delicate finger. She was dressed in a gleaming white *ao dai,* the symbol of purity adopted by Christian Vietnamese. Mai Lien was a "new" girl, and she had never known a man. Her beautiful black hair, which she normally let fall around her shoulders and cascade down her back, was now neatly rolled on top of her head and covered by the traditional wedding hat. She looked up at Vic through her enchanting Asian eyes while he finished placing the jewelry on her.

"Em se yeu anh mai mai," I will love you forever my husband, she said softly.

There was no doubt in his mind that it would be so. His sweet Vietnam.

CHAPTER TWENTY

Languid days drifted endlessly on waves of passionate bliss. The valley was stilled by the quiet sounds of bending bamboo and cooing doves. The burnished fields were ripe unto harvest and love lingered among the tamarinds. The living lotus was in flower—life was full for the two lovers. Time had coursed away on silent wings of air.

But bugles were again heard across the land. Rumors began growing of a strong offensive planned by the NVA and when Colonel Johnson called the wing together for a briefing it came as no surprise to the pilots the the big one had arrived.

"Men, we've been waiting a long time for this one. Washington has pulled out all the stops. Today you're going to fly cover for the biggest and most important raid of the war. 'Bullseye' is the target!"

Like a giant wave breaking on the shore, the room erupted in a roar. The men stood to their feet cheering, shouting to each other, and slapping each other on the back. "Bullseye," Hanoi. At last.

"It's about time," Pellegrini yelled to Patterson.

"Right. If they'd let us fight this war the right way we'd have been out of 'Nam' in two weeks," Patterson yelled back.

"Maybe they've finally seen the light back home," Davis added.

"Don't count on it. But let's get our licks in while we can," Vic put in.

The noise level dropped and the pilots returned to their seats eager to hear the details and get their instructions.

"The Migs will be up. You can count on it. Reccy flights have confirmed increased numbers of aircraft and activity at Kep and the other Mig bases," Johnson said. "Every F-105 in Vietnam and Thailand will be in on this one. The Migs will be waiting for them and we've got to get our Thuds in and out. There will be Migs for everyone today, and you know who's going to be leading them. He'll be up there, so watch for him. Be alert. Protect the strikers. Don't call a break until you're absolutely sure they're Migs. Remember, the air is going to be full of planes and it's going to get hairy. Wingmen, protect your leaders. Element leaders, stay with your flight leaders as long as you can. Backseaters, watch your six o'clock. There will be plenty of in close action today, within minimum missile range, so most of you will have the vulcan gun pods if you're not flying ships with guns already mounted. Also, we're going north loaded up mostly with Sidewinders this trip. What's the count Jerry?"

"Sixty ships, Colonel. Every F-4 available," Johnson's operations officer announced.

"Okay, post them."

The numbers for each squadron with pilots names were listed on the scheduling board. The squadron commander was leading the first flight, Vic the second, Davis on his wing. Pellegrini was Vic's element leader, Patterson flying his wing. Take-off times were posted next to the flights. The room was hot, the heavy air hanging motionless. Vic felt the sweat spreading over his body and he grew anxious to begin the mission. He listened to the weather officer giving out the usual information of cloud formations, altitudes, wind direction, visibility, azimuth, tides, temperature, and runways for take-off.

"Listen up now!" Johnson said. "Here's the attack profile."

He called off the Thud squadrons, when they would be going in, names and locations of the targets, and direction of their strikes. He reviewed the take-off times, rendezvous points with the fighter bombers and refueling tankers, and air-sea rescue ops. He assigned MIGCAP altitudes and went over intelligence reports on the heavy air defense system surrounding the North Vietnamese capital.

Vic could feel the tenseness of the other pilots. Everyone was jotting down notes, checking data, alert, sweating. He looked around the room. He knew some of these seats would be empty tomorrow. No one believed it would be his. A few men, the old timers, looked Vic's way and winked, confidence in their faces, determination.

Johnson went on with the briefing. Vic listened without concentrating, the important details already having been covered. He was at ease, not very excited, certainly not nervous. Yet expectant. It wasn't necessary to demonstrate his abilities any longer, no need to prove himself. A few more missions and he would have his hundred in. Then home. It would be all over and he could look back at Vietnam as something he would never have wanted to miss, but he would never want to do it over again. Time was only a memory to him now.

"Boys, they're going to be up there. It's going to be their best effort, but we're better." Johnson was building to the rally point now, instilling victory in his team. "I want kills! Bring me back kills. Get the strikers in and out safely. The Migs will be trying all their tricks to get through you to hit the bombers. Be tough. Get in close. Don't let them through. Keep off the radio unless it's absolutely necessary. Watch your fuel. Get out when you hit bingo. Don't hang around so long that it's too late. Some of you are going to get bounced on the egress and then you won't have enough fuel to get back. Remember that." Johnson waited for a few moments. Then with voice lowered and head down, he continued. "Some of you aren't coming back today. If you get hit, try and make it to the sea. Don't stretch it too long. Punch out right away if you can't make it." He paused again. "Much is riding on this mission so be aggressive. Good luck and Godspeed."

"Okay. Let's go!"

The men all stood as Johnson stepped down from the platform and walked past them to the door in the rear. On the way out he stopped to encourage a few of the men and to offer some last words of advice. He stopped in front of Vic.

"How do you feel, Vic?"

"I'm okay."

"Fine, son. I have faith in you. I want you to know that. I've always believed in you. You've had your difficulties over the past weeks but that's behind you. Right?"

"Yes sir."

"Good. Today's your day. Go get 'em!"

Most of the men followed the colonel out or milled around in pairs and in small groups, talking about the mission. Vic's flight was the second scheduled for take-off. He walked over to the locker room to dress. Something vital had emptied him. A mental void crept into his spirit and he became overwhelmed with weariness. He seemed so insensitive and alone now; yet not desolate, enveloped in a kind of echoing stillness. There was nothing more for him to be. He could no longer relate to those first days when his inspiration burned white-hot within his bosom. He seemed like a child then, unaware and unforgivably lost in his hope.

He would gradually leave them all now, like a man sleepwalking; riding his vision. being beckoned by the sky siren's music; through the towering white gates, going back again as he knew he must, to the origin of his illusion, to the lists above Hanoi where champions met, where he might have triumphed over his dreams.

The earth trembled and the Phantoms shuddered as their engines exploded into life, a cacophony of trumpeting erupting up and down the flight line, summoning to battle. One by one, the green and brown monsters crawled out of their caves to test the air again, following each other in a line, seething fire and hot ashes, bellies low to the ground, whining pitilessly.

He taxied into position and lined up, waiting for Davis to close on him. He tested his engines again, pushing the throttle forward and scanning his instruments. Escaping exhaust expanded the air behind him, distorting it into a transparent cloud.

The moment of truth again. The exhilaration that lesser men would never experience. The sense of strength and power was intoxicating. At this moment he was unconquerable. He and Davis looked across the space of runway between them, renewing their confidence in each other, silently binding themselves together. Drill nodded and Vic dropped his raised hand. In unison the two jets accelerated down the runway, throttles wide open, gallons of fuel being gulped thirstily. They broke ground together and climbed in poetry through wispy layers of clouds. Pellegrini and Patterson rose behind them, and the four hunters turned north in search of prey.

On toward the fields of battle they flew to engage the enemy on the high plateaus of endless air. North, always north, into the rising towers of bottomless cumulus that stood like tall gates marking their entry into North Vietnam. Through the gates they passed, climbing, climbing, higher and higher, penetrating the boundless limits where no man could breathe unaided and airfoils clawed for purchase. It was all so very familiar to him, yet so new, as if in a dream remembered from the past. The landmarks that guided him he knew as well as his own neighborhood back home. The villages, the rivers, the roads, all like playthings in a child's world far below. The South China Sea, the Gulf of Tonkin, Haiphong harbor, and Hanoi itself, today's target, would soon be gone from his experience, lingering in the back reaches of his mind to be recalled only when time permitted. The memories were already old. A feeling of growing separation was creeping over him. No longer did he feel a part of the war. He seemed more like an observer than a participant.

He had become detached. Gone was the awesome excitement and the balled up stomach. He was operating on instincts alone, blocking out any higher order of ratiocinations, allowing his subconscious to control his behavior. He was in automatic mode and he watched the drama unfolding before him as if for the first time.

He studied the coast of Vietnam below. Like a thin thread that lay loosely where someone had dropped it from high above, it stretched endlessly in two directions and disappeared into the earth itself. Even now it was slipping behind him, replaced by a sheet of glass, the sea of jade, sweeping ahead in a glistening arc. In the distance the world dropped away.

The war, the compulsion, the challenge. It was no longer important, only a memory. His thoughts were ahead, he was looking toward home. His war had ended. He was in the homestretch, coming down to the wire. A handful of missions left and he would be free, his tour over. Going home, putting it all behind him.

Strange how the newcomers behaved, wanting to hear the stories of the big battles, seeking advice, bristling with enthusiasm and hope, looking ahead to an adventure. He had been one of them once. And then they always asked about Tan, the mysterious way in which he would appear, the swiftness of attack, the intimidating black dragon markings. Who had seen him? Who was he, they always asked? Was he a Russian? Chinese maybe. Or was he North Vietnamese as most believed? Tan too was only a memory to him now. He had long ago given up his interest in meeting the communist champion. He would serve out his remaining time and go home.

"Strikers dead ahead," Davis' voice cut through his thoughts.

"I have them. Twelve o'clock and low," he said.

"Roger."

He gently pulled back on the stick.

"Striker leader, this is Tiger one with four Phantoms. We have you in sight. At your six o'clock and beginning MIGCAP."

"Roger, Tiger one. Proceeding to target, ETA fifteen minutes."

He twisted in his seat and looked back. About five miles behind and swinging over the Gulf was a second squadron of strikers lining up for their run. Above them and further out to sea a flight of F-4s circled on station waiting to escort them into the target. And miles ahead of him, beginning their attack in a few minutes, was Colonel Johnson and his strike force, first to hit Hanoi. For one hour the North Vietnamese capital would be bombed by the F-105 fighter-bombers.

The radio was quiet except for the usual talk. The Migs hadn't been sighted yet. The air was heavy with anticipation and the tension hung in the cockpits, screaming at the pilots, like at the beginning of a football game, waiting for the kickoff. Everyone was listening for a whistle, the first contact, the start of action, the release. The seconds ticked off. Still no calls. The first bombers should be over the target now, he thought. The seconds stretched into minutes. Where were the Migs? It was unbelievable. Maybe they weren't coming up. He could feel his palms sweating. All at once the air waves came apart with electrifying suddenness, Colonel Johnson's voice splitting the silence.

"Migs!"

"Where?"

"Ten o'clock, crossing to nine."

"How many?" someone asked.

" Six! They're starting in!"

"Drop tanks." It was Johnson.

"Four more at one o'clock."

"I have them!"

"Break, *now!*"

Then it was wild confusion over the radio. A ferocious fight was developing and it was evident that the Migs were attacking aggressively and in numbers. His eyes searched every patch of sky closely. He was calm, but alert. Red Crown called more Migs airborne. The air over Hanoi was fast becoming a circus. Additional Phantoms arrived on station.

He could see the smoke from the lead strike rising above the city ahead. The bombers below him wheeled into their turn, lining up for the attack. He weaved his flight over the Thunder-chiefs, watchfully, anticipating company. Three Mig 17s immediately appeared on his left. Then two more joined them, following close behind. He dropped his tanks. Like hungry wolves stalking their prey, the North Vietnamese menacingly tracked the U.S. aircraft, waiting for their opportunity. They weren't interested in him. They wanted the bombers. The communists flew parallel for a while studying the formation. Then the lead ships went high and the other two dropped under the bombers and started in.

"Let's take them! Pellegrini go low," he said, pulling back on the stick and hitting the afterburner.

He pulled his nose into the Migs and turned on his gun switches. The lead '17' started in, made a feint at the Thuds then broke away, realizing that Vic had too good a position on him. His wingman flashed in front of Vic and he got off a snap burst. The tracers arched out and he saw a few solid hits going into the fuselage. He pulled hard on the '17', cranking the F-4 around in the turn. the Mig pilot stupidly reversed and he swung in behind him in a diving turn. Vic selected HEAT and fired his first Sidewinder. But it didn't track, preferring to seek out the earth's radiant energy rather than the Mig's exhaust.

He had lost energy in the turn and fell behind the Mig. But he had wounded the Mig with his cannon and he saw vapor beginning to escape from underneath the airplane in a long thin trail.

He unloaded and swung out wide, picking up knots for another run on the Mig.

"Two bandits at two o'clock, crossing to one!" Drill called.

"Tell me when to break," he said, lusting in the action.

"Roger."

He started in on the wounded Mig again. In the back of his mind he kept thinking to get back to the strike force. He looked off to the right and could see the Thuds approaching the target area enveloped with smoke from the first strike. All five flights looked in good shape and they weren't under attack at the moment. Fortunately the Mig he was chasing was headed back toward Hanoi. Below him and going in the opposite direction, the lead Thud squadron was making its egress from the target. He looked over his shoulder. Far behind he could make out the third squadron of strikers preparing for their bomb run.

He turned his attention to the Mig in front of him. It had fallen further behind. He needed only a little more time. He inched the pipper forward. The Mig started a climbing turn to the right, giving a good display against the open sky. He changed his mind about using his gun and selected HEAT again. But his parameters weren't optimum, being within minimum Sidewinder range, and his second missile also missed.

"Vic, they're starting in."

He hated to let the Mig go.

"Okay, let's take it around."

They broke into the attacking Migs. The 17s didn't continue in, but pulled up again. He reversed, hoping that the Migs would return to the attack. But they streaked off without looking back. It would be a long and useless chase. He let them go. He looked back to see his wounded Mig fast disappearing from view, still streaming a wispy line of smoke. He'd probably get back to his field safely, Vic thought to himself.

The radio was filled with insistent and mixed calls, commanding attention to the wild action surrounding him. Colonel Johnson's flight was still in the area but getting low on fuel. His own tanks were above bingo but he kept checking just the same. He turned toward the bombers and began sweeping the skies, clearing the strikers. The triple A was heavy and SAMS were thick.

"I'm hit!" he heard a Thud pilot call.

He looked down and saw one of the ships dropping out of formation, on fire, hit by a SAM. The canopy blew away and pilot and seat shot out, twisting and rolling. The white parachute with orange panels blossomed. The man hung below, suspended, swinging from side to side like a clock pendulum. He rolled his ship and watched the man drift into a residential area then disappear among the rooftops. Suddenly, he heard Balinger's urgent voice from the back seat.

"Bogies, two o'clock!"
He craned to see.

"I don't have them," he said.

"High, moving to three."

"How many?" he asked.

"Six, seven, no . . . six."

"Do you see them, Davis?" he asked anxiously.

"No. I don't have them."

"They're gone now. I lost them," Balinger said.

He started a slow turn trying to locate the planes. His eyes crisscrossed the sky. Nothing. They had vanished. He turned back to the Thuds.

The strikers were going in now, each bomber diving on the target and dropping its load, then pulling away. They dashed for home in twos and fours and the ground trembled and shook behind them. Heavy puffs of smoke dotted the ground, swelling as they rose, finally mushrooming in a pall of gray and black that rapidly expanded into a thick cover, blocking visibility of the ground.

He continued his sweep, looking for a fight. The last of his fighter-bombers went in, unloaded, and departed. F-4s began leaving, low on fuel. He heard Johnson call bingo fuel and egress the area. He checked his own gauge. He was getting low.

"How's your fuel, Drill?" he asked his wingman.

"A few more minutes."

Time for one last sweep he thought, scanning the ether above him. He decided to check on Pellegrini and Patterson.

"Tiger one, Tiger three. Where are you?"

No reply.

"Tiger one, Tiger three," he called again.

"Tiger three," Pellegrini's voice came through the background talk.

"What is you position and fuel?" he asked.

"Southwest Bullseye. Joker fuel remaining."

"Roger."

Pellegrini would be turning for home soon. He looked at the thunderheads building in the south. How peaceful and calm, he thought, in the midst of the destruction below. Tranquility amongst chaos. He swung around the outskirts of Hanoi one more time and then started to turn south for home.

"I have four bogies at three o'clock! High," Davis called over the radio.

He turned his head. Four unidentified jets were cruising along with him. Could be Migs, no smoke. But too high to take.

"Shall we break?"

"No. We're low on fuel. Keep them in sight."

"Rog."

The bogies followed him, noiselessly hanging in the sky. He waited, watching. He wasn't sure whether or not to engage them if they turned out to be Migs. His fuel was dangerously low. They decided for him.

"Crossing to two o'clock now. They're rolling in!" Davis shouted.

He watched them start in. Four Mig 21s. Fast, sleek, bristling with ATOLs. The sun glistened off their silver skins. His mind raced. Decision time! They had the advantage. He was low on fuel, they had the speed and altitude. He could run or stay and fight. The decision had already been made.

"Break!" he cried.

They pulled into the attacking North Vietnamese, afterburners cooking. The enemy ships bored in to meet Vic and Drill head-on, then turned up abruptly, breaking off their attack. He cocked his head overhead and watched the shining bellies streak past his canopy, red stars flashing. He reversed his break, and swung around to pursue. He stared in cold comprehension as the four ships did something he had never seen before. Each Mig broke in a different direction. A fleur-de-lis to all four corners of the compass.

"Oh, oh!" he said to Davis, "We're tangling with four smoothies this trip, partner."

"Vic."

"Roger."

"Did you look them over when they went by?"

"No. Why?"

"The leader is sporting a pair of black dragons on his intake nacelle."

His mouth went dry, his tongue tasted like a piece of leather. His heart pounded loudly in his chest. A quiet shiver shot through his system and he felt chilled. The effect was quick, thorough, and passed through him without stopping. The initial impact over, his eyes became set in determination and his face tightened.

Tan! he said to himself. So destiny would not

ignore them. The two champions must meet. He should have known there was no other way. It was inevitable. So be it. He looked after the aircraft, trying to identify the dragon. What a time to encounter him, this low on fuel. He would carry the fight south, toward the sea, toward the tankers. He looked at his gauge once more. Fourteen hundred pounds! He settled in, mentally preparing himself for the engagement.

The Migs returned, rolling in on him and Davis, one at a time, synchronizing their attack with skill and precision. First one would start in and as soon as Vic would break into him a second would make a pass from behind. Sometimes they worked him in pairs, pecking at him, maneuvering for an advantage.

"ATOL!" Balinger cried. "Four o'clock."

Vic cranked around into the missile, the Mig broke, negating the ATOLs attack. He reversed, swinging around to follow the Mig.

"Eight o'clock, Vic!" Davis shouted.

"Reverse it!" he cried, turning into the new threat. The Mig climbed back up to re-position for another pass, lost in a cloud layer. He didn't follow.

After the first few passes he noticed that Tan was working his Migs in a well rehearsed pattern. To a pilot of lesser experience, the attacks would appear to develop at random and come from different points without any definite organization. But Vic had quickly determined that this was a well orchestrated performance, and that he was in a tight spot. It was apparent to Vic that Tan was using the same tactics on him as he had employed in downing thirteen previous U.S. aircraft, and if he and Davis were to get out of this alive, he was going to have to draw on all of his reserves.

"So this is how he does it," he said quietly to himself.

The g forces tugged at his head in the turn as he looked behind and overhead, the direction in which he had calculated that the next attack would come. A lone Mig appeared high at 8 o'clock and started in, confirming the pattern.

"Take it around to the left," he called to Davis.

Then as the Mig passed harmlessly behind him and climbed away, Vic called a hard right turn and went to afterburner. He unloaded. When the Phantom hit supersonic, he and Davis pitched up into a vertical, afterburners still boiling. He rolled ninety degrees in the vertical to give him visibility.

As he had expected, a Mig was off to his right searching for him. It was headed east about five hundred feet below. He came over the top inverted then rolled out on the same heading as the Mig. The pilot saw him and instantly broke into Vic without hesitation, placing the two of them on a collision course.

"Are you still with me, Davis?" He couldn't see his wingman.

"Roger."

The two jets rapidly closed on each other,

head-on. Vic was determined to force his opponent to break first. At the last moment the Mig pilot pulled straight up, standing the 21 on its tail, wanting Vic to pass under him. Vic quickly realized that the pilot intended to complete a one-hundred-eighty degree change of direction roll, coming out on his 6 o'clock. Instead, Vic pitched up with him, attempting to scissors the Mig. But he had too much speed when he went into the climb. The Mig pilot coolly counter-rolled. The black fire breathing dragons painted on the nose taunted him. Tan's black face mask, goggles, helmet, and white scarf were clearly visible as the two ships climbed canopy to canopy.

Vic realized he was in a precarious position. He was accelerating ahead of Tan, putting him out front when coming over the top, a place he didn't want to be with the much more maneuverable Mig. He dropped his flaps, cut his throttle and rolled. The Mig eased ahead of him and the two ships split apart. Back around they came, head-on once more. Up into the vertical again, and over the top, rolling canopy to canopy. Split, back around. Attack. Into the vertical. Roll out. Each pilot seeking the slightest advantage, stubbornly holding on. It became a battle of wills. The aircraft were no longer involved. It was a fight of human endurance, to see who could hold on the longest.

Tenaciously, Vic pressed his adversary, caught up in the passion of it all, reveling in the lust of battle. The coliseum was filled to capacity. The spectators were on their feet cheering as the two gladiators tore across the arena of sky, locked in mortal combat. He glanced at his fuel gauge, already knowing what he would see. The North Vietnamese ace was probably low too. The thought occurred to him that it was crazily possible that they could fight on, neither gaining an advantage, stubbornly refusing to give in, then both plummeting to earth, out of gas.

Suddenly, Tan rolled over and dove under Vic instead of climbing into the vertical again. Momentarily surprised, he hesitated. Then it came clear.

"He's had enough! He's making a break for home!" he shouted into his mask. Feeling cheated, he poured power to the Phantom and turned after Tan.

"Where are you, Drill?"

"Below you, on the right."

He looked down but couldn't see him. He pulled hard trying to cut Tan off as the Mig turned east, back to Hanoi.

"Do you . . . still have . . . me . . . Davis?" he said, the words breaking up as the 8 g turn forced the air from him.

"Rog . . . er . . . you're clear," Davis struggled, as he followed through the turn.

"Where's . . . Tan's . . . bud . . . dies?" he asked.

"I . . . don't . . . don't . . . see . . . them."

The Mig continued its wide turn. He was actually gaining on it, pulling inside in the tightening downward spiral. He could see that he had the advantage now, ever so slightly, but an advantage.

He no longer concerned himself with his draining fuel tanks. Someone else was flying his ship, an old hand, a calm veteran of many missions who had practiced and lived this moment since the beginning, patiently waiting for his time to arrive. The pressure suit squeezed at his tissues, wringing the moisture from his body in the high g turn. The altimeter spun crazily through 30,000 feet, 25,000, 20,000. The g forces hammered at him. He could hardly hold his head up. Faintly, he could see the Mig still out ahead of him, turning, turning. Around and around the earth spun, rushing up to meet them, 15,000 feet and down through 10,000. The Mig was only a blurred image. He gasped for breath, sucking deep from his mask. Suddenly, the Mig rolled out and plunged straight down.

There wasn't enough altitude. He was sure of it. For the briefest part of a second he tried to reason with the man flying his plane. But the man would have none of it. The stick went forward and he was instantly crashing through the sound barrier, a passenger on a roller coaster, watching the air speed indicator push through Mach 1. He wondered if he would make it. He grasped the stick with both hands and pulled, hard. It seemed frozen. But the F-4 slowly responded and giant arms enveloped him, crushing him into his seat, blackening his vision. He

291

pulled harder and the plane pitched through. His sight cleared and his head popped forward off the seat. He was screaming across the rocky spine of Mig Ridge, the dragonman right out in front of him!

The aircraft rocked wildly in the dense air. They were very low. At this speed and altitude there was no margin for error. A slight mistake and he would spread himself for a mile over the ugly gnarled hump. He was faintly aware of the jagged rocks flashing by—like stone crucifixes leaping out of their craggy holes at him. He fought to concentrate on Tan ahead. The glowing reticle bounced madly as he tried to bring the pipper onto the dragon ship. He checked his gun switches. Tan broke left. He fired a short burst. He thought he saw a few isolated hits around the tail. Lord, they were low.

Tan pitched up into the vertical, lit the Mig's afterburner and accelerated in a steady climb into the sun. Vic was hot behind, desperately trying to center the reticle. Passing through ten thousand feet and still climbing, he squeezed the trigger. Solid hits in the wing root! But the Mig held together. Tan completed the immelmann and immediately broke toward the ground again. Vic increased the g's to cut him off. The communist colonel deftly turned down into him, increasing Vic's angle of over-take. Vic pulled hard to prevent overshoot. Tan's nose was now low and Vic's too high. Vic pulled his nose down to continue the attack. Tan seeing Vic commit his nose low, quickly rolled 180 degrees through Vic's line of attack and reefed the smaller Mig around into him. The timing was perfect and Vic could not hold position with the dragonman, overshooting in front of the Mig. Tan skillfully continued the vertical rolling scissors around to Vic's 6 o'clock.

Metallic pings on the belly of the Phantom. Now along the side. Someone banging with a ball-peen hammer. The ship lurched sickeningly. The stick went dead in his hand. "Do you know Jesus, major?" The war beast twisted with involuntary muscular contractions, shaking violently, wresting sweet life away. Tan pumped more cannon shells into Vic, riveting him all along the fuselage from the canopy back to the stabilizer. The nauseating smell of vaporizing jet fuel escaping from ruptured tanks. Queasy panic in the gut. Revulsion at your own cowardice. Lieutenant, have you ever felt fear—I mean their fear? There's no kind like it. Feel their fear, lieutenant. The Migs out-turning you, pulling to the inside and slashing at you with their hot tracers and ATOLs. Listen, marine, and you can hear their frantic cries for help, for someone to get the pack off their trail. Turning, twisting and diving. Anything to break the grip.

"Drill! Get him off me—for God's sake help me!"

"You're burning, Vic! Get out, man—get out!"

Oh, Moreno. Was it like this? Butler—Richards. The still graveyards of Mig Ridge. The lonely escarpments. Have you ever bailed out over North Vietnam, Lieutenant? Would you have enough courage to survive as a prisoner of the communists? It takes courage, lieutenant.

"Get out, Vic — you're burning."

"Eagle three. There's a Phantom pilot in trouble. West side of the ridge," someone said.

"Do you see him?"

"Yeh. He's a sheet of flame."

"*Mayday! Mayday!*" It was Drill again. "Benedetti's on fire. Mig Ridge, tango-niner-four-one. Anyone in the area?"

"Roger — identify."

"Tiger one-zero-one."

"Give us a count."

"Anyone call RESCAP? We need a RESCAP."

"You got it."

"Who's hit?"

"Tiger one."

"This is Dettoit — we can cover for a few minutes."

"Three and four, cycle off the tankers."

"I've got a SAM heating up."

"We've got RESCUE — need a fix, Red Crown. Did you get good coordinates?"

"Vector . . . zero . . . zero."

"What's that?"

"Copy two at point eight."

Vic's ship fell off on its right wing. Smoke filled the cockpit. Tan pulled up alongside him, dragons clearly exposed on the Mig's nose. The two adversaries watched each other for a few seconds. Vic pushed up his helmet sun visor and gave Tan a weary salute. The dragonman returned the salute, rolled over the top of him in a split S and dove away for home.

I tried, Mai Lien. I gave it my best shot. But he was better. Oh, to become a champion—the sweet, heady fragrance of it all. Knowing that you're the best.

"Get out, Vic—you've had it!" Davis shouted.

The smoke grew denser. "Do you know Jesus, Major?"

"Get out, Vic! Get out! Jump!"

Black smoke roiled over the Phantom from nose to tail. The F-4 slowly rolled over on its back, exhausted.

"I'm going in," Vic calmly said into the radio. "Tell Mai Lien it wasn't as bad as I thought it would be. Tell her the struggle has ended."

Vic crashed on Mig Ridge. The explosion sent up a huge fireball among the tamarind trees. They were in bloom.

CHAPTER EPILOGUE

Ho Chi Minh City, Socialist Republic of Vietnam.
July 10, 1982.

Pretty little Hoang sat on the low hand carved teak stool and pulled the jade studded Chinese comb through her long black hair. The coconut oil made it shine like seal skin. She turned her beautiful sloe eyes toward the full length wall mirror next to her and watched the silky black strands cascade over her shoulders with each stroke of the comb, the ends settling on the floor around her bare feet.

She raised her trim doll-like body from the stool and placed the comb on the dresser next to the worn picture of a venerable Cochinese ancient dressed in ceremonial raiment. With loving eyes she looked at the old woman for a long time. It had been a while since she had last visited great-grandmother. She missed her familiar musky smell that brought back the secure feeling she remembered so well. Often when she was lonely and whimpering in bed, the old woman would part the mosquito netting and motion for her to come to the comfort of her arms.

"Hoang *oi. Di ngo khong?*" Hoang darling, can't you sleep? she would say. "*Lai day con,*" come here to me, child. And Hoang would jump from the poor wooden bed and rush to her *co ngoai*. Great-grandmother would then turn down the oil lamp and secure the mosquito net while Hoang snuggled under her arm, falling quickly asleep with *co ngoai's* pleasant scent lingering in her dreams.

Hoang affectionately ran her delicate fingers over the picture, being careful not to let her fingernails scratch the glossy finish. She remembered with tenderness how *co ngoai* now looked at her with great love in her old eyes and never failing to say when she visits her, "You have grown up to be a beautiful child."

She gently placed the photograph back in its honored place. I will go see my great-grandmother today, she thought to herself. I will bring her a basket of *xoai* and *cam*, her favorite fruit. She will need money too. And tobacco. But first

I must write a letter to my brother. He will be expecting to hear from me. It would not be right to make him wait.

She went to the little crude writing desk by the open door and took out her bamboo and flower etched stationery. She placed pen and ink beside the paper and sat down. The day's first rays of sunlight streamed in through the doorway warming her pretty Asian face. She sat quietly watching the crimson ball inch above the horizon while cooling morning breezes wafted loose threads of soft hair across her high cheek bones.

How wonderful it was to have a brother to share these gentle moments with. She glanced down at his open letter on the table. A secure feeling, one of hope, rushed through her.

Yes. Here was someone who cared, who wanted to understand. Someone she intuitively felt she could trust. Someone she wanted to know better. He was concerned about her and he made her want to share her feelings with him. She needed this badly — to tell someone how she felt — share her dreams with. Even though he was 12,000 miles away and she could never allow herself the hope of ever seeing him, she still wanted to be his friend, his good sister.

She picked up the pen and opened the well worn *U.S. Air Force Manual of Vietnamese and English Usage*. She began writing from her heart, envisioning him sitting in the chair next to

her:
   "Dear Vic Jr.,
      "Do you know Jesus?"

DYNAMIC NEW LEADERS IN MEN'S ADVENTURE!

THE MAGIC MAN #2:
THE GAMOV FACTOR   (1252, $2.50)
by David Bannerman

With Brezhnev terminally ill, the West needs an agent in place to control the outcome of the race to replace him. And there's no one better suited for the job than THE MAGIC MAN!

THE MAGIC MAN#3:
PIPELINE FROM HELL   (1327, $2.50)
by David Bannerman

THE MAGIC MAN discovers Moscow building a pipeline from a Siberian hell—with innocent men and women as slave labor. Only he can stop it . . . but only if he survives!

THE WARLORD   (1189, $3.50)
by Jason Frost

The world's gone mad with disruption. Isolated from help, the survivors face a state in which law is a memory and violence is the rule. Only one man is fit to lead the people, a man raised among the Indians and trained by the Marines. He is Erik Ravensmith, THE WARLORD—a deadly adversary and a hero of our times.

THE WARLORD #2: THE CUTTHROAT   (1308, $2.50)
by Jason Frost

Though death sails the Sea of Los Angeles, there is only one man who will fight to save what is left of California's ravaged paradise. His name is THE WARLORD—and he won't stop until the job is done!

THE WARLORD #3: BADLAND   (1437, $2.50)
by Jason Frost

His son has been kidnapped by his worst enemy and THE WARLORD must fight a pack of killers to free him. Getting close enough to grab the boy will be nearly impossible—but then so is living in this tortured world!

Available wherever paperbacks are sold, or order direct from the Publisher. Send cover price plus 50¢ per copy for mailing and handling to Zebra Books, 475 Park Avenue South, New York, N.Y. 10016. DO NOT SEND CASH.

More Adventure in
THEY CALL ME THE MERCENARY
by Axel Kilgore

#14: THE SIBERIAN ALTERNATIVE   (1194, $2.50)
When Frost wakes up straitjacketed in a ward deep inside the Soviet Union, he doesn't need two eyes to see they are going to plant
electrodes in his brain and turn him into a weapon for the KGB!

#15: THE AFGHANISTAN PENETRATION   (1223, $2.50)
Penetrating a tightly secured Soviet base in Afghanistan to rescue
an old Army buddy, Frost uncovers a Soviet weapon of frightening potential being readied for "testing" against Afghan freedom
fighters!

#16: CHINA BLOODHUNT   (1288, $2.50)
Frost doesn't know whom to trust as he works his way across
mainland China—with a Chicom secret agent. With China and
Russia moving closer to a shooting war, Hank has to keep America
out of it!

#17: BUCKINGHAM BLOWOUT   (1346, $2.50)
Left broken and bloody in a London alley, Frost doesn't remember
his own name, or that he's discovered a brutal terrorist plot. But
the terrorists haven't forgotten and are getting ready to write his
name for him—on a gravestone!

#18: EYE FOR EYE   (1429, $2.50)
After being buried alive under the rubble of a blown-up building,
Frost takes a well-deserved rest. But the KGB would rather he rest
in peace—and they kidnap his girlfriend to lure him out!

*Available wherever paperbacks are sold, or order direct from the
Publisher. Send cover price plus 50¢ per copy for mailing and
handling to Zebra Books, 475 Park Avenue South, New York,
N.Y. 10016. DO NOT SEND CASH.*